Hard Target

Hard Target

ELITE OPS—BOOK ONE

KAY THOMAS

AVONIMPULSE

An Imprint of HarperCollinsPublishers

Excerpt from *Personal Target* copyright © 2014 by Kay Thomas.

Excerpt from *Rescued by a Stranger* copyright © 2013 by Lizbeth Selvig.

Excerpt from *Chasing Morgan* copyright © 2013 by Jennifer Ryan.

Excerpt from *Throwing Heat* copyright © 2013 by Candice Wakoff.

Excerpt from *Private Research* copyright © 2013 by Sabrina Darby.

EPub Edition NOVEMBER 2013 ISBN: 9780062290847

Print Edition ISBN: 9780062290861

10 9 8 7 6 5

For Dr. Joe Stockwell—my college English professor,
first editor, and friend.
Thank you for being my inaugural fan.
And in memory of Aunt Skeeter a.k.a. "Pretty"—who
believed I could do this before I did.

Chapter One

Cancun, Mexico

"MEET ME UPSTAIRS. I want you and I'm taking you to bed."

Despite her pounding head, Anna Mercado smiled to stall for time and sipped her margarita. Delivering a not-so-subtle message, her estranged husband ran his fingertips lightly over the top of her thighs before adjusting the beach umbrella.

"We've already discussed this. I'm not sure that's a good idea," she said.

"No? I think it's one of the better ideas I've had all day." Max Mercado grinned, completely at ease with her seeming rejection. "You need more sunscreen or you're going to burn, babe." His accent made the declaration sound sexy as he climbed over his wood-and-canvas chair to grab the lotion from her bag.

She took another sip of the frozen drink and searched for what to say. Going upstairs with her handsome husband was a terrible idea. She looked past the pristine sand of the Ritz-Carlton's exclusive beach to the startling blue water of the Gulf and tried to remember how she'd been talked into this faux family vacation.

That was easy. Their very ill son had begged. She couldn't refuse Zach when he'd asked for so little in the past twelve months.

As much as she'd like to blame the wretched circumstances, Max's assumptions this morning were completely valid and entirely her fault. Yesterday she'd been looking for courage to face the future, so she'd let herself be talked into sharing a suite with him instead of insisting on her own room. She'd come dangerously close to sharing a bed with him last night as well.

But almost having sex had more to do with sharing two bottles of wine than talking—and absolutely nothing to do with courage. Lack of communication had long been an issue in their failing marriage. Lack of communication and Max's lack of exclusivity.

Compatibility in the bedroom had never been a problem for him . . . with anyone. If anything, it was just the opposite. Her husband liked to show every woman a good time in bed.

Today, she had the mother of all headaches and morning-after regrets over an evening that had led to "almost sex." She was not sleeping with him. She couldn't.

Even if that intimacy was . . . familiar. Safe. Easy. Comfortable. It wasn't love. Not anymore.

Despite what others thought, it didn't matter to her how wealthy Max was. As his wife she couldn't live with his infidelity. She took another sip of her frosty concoction and reached up to stay his hand as he went from rubbing sunscreen into her shoulders to massaging her neck.

Okay, so she liked his hands on her. And the man was beautiful. There was no denying it. With his Hispanic good looks and panty-melting charm he'd always been difficult to resist. Maybe this drink was starting to work as a hangover cure, or maybe she should just set it down on the side table immediately, because she was considering going upstairs with him.

"Zach's having a blast." She was still stalling. "I told him I would get him food from the beach grill when they open for lunch."

Their fourteen-year-old son was sand sculpting a great white shark with his cousins ten yards away, blissfully oblivious to his mother's dilemma.

"This could be his last shot at fun for a while. Once he checks into Children's Transplant Center . . ." All playfulness was gone from Max's tone.

"I know."

A year ago she'd never dreamed it would take so long for her son to get a new heart, or that his health would deteriorate to the point where they'd be forced to consider an LVAD heart pump to serve as the "bridge to transplantation." The countless meds they used and the pacemaker implanted six months earlier could no longer regulate his heart rhythm. Waiting had become a tangible enemy as time was running out.

That they were now waiting for someone else to die so their child could live was something she tried not to think about. The guilt would be overpowering. As it was, Anna jumped whenever the phone rang.

"Are you glad you're here?" Max's husky voice pulled her from the dismal thoughts. Seeing Zach so happy, she couldn't help but nod.

"Yes, I am. I didn't realize how much of a toll this has been taking. You're sure we can get there in time if the hospital calls?"

"With the company plane we can be at CTC in three hours. And we've got Julia to take care of him if any complications arise."

Anna glanced at the extremely competent and attractive private cardiac care nurse who'd flown into Cancun with them from Dallas. "I know, I just—"

"He's been on the wait list a year, Anna. They're not going to call this weekend. He's checking into the hospital Monday for the LVAD. God only knows how long that recovery will take."

"But—"

He was behind her and wouldn't let her interrupt. "I'm not asking if I can come back or if we can do the transplant procedure here in Mexico anymore. But we need to give him this time away from the strain and stress of it. Forty-eight hours is all. Let him enjoy his family. I need to give you both this time. Please, let me."

Anna squeezed her eyes shut. She wouldn't argue with him. Not anymore. It was too exhausting when he lost his temper.

Just for today, she wasn't going to look back and she wasn't going to look forward. She couldn't think of what the coming weeks held. The past year had been too hard, and the future was too scary to contemplate.

As much as she longed for something or someone to give her hope, she knew Max was not that man. But he was safe and he was all she had.

She nodded.

"So?" Her husband sat in the beach chair beside her. "Are you done beating yourself up about last night? It's okay, you know. We are still married. And I still want you. Come upstairs. Forget about all this for a while."

She blew out the breath she'd been holding and swung around to look at him through dark glasses. It was disconcerting that he was practically reading her mind. He wasn't usually able to do that.

"I can't. I need—"

"What Anna?" He interrupted as usual, but in the past he would have been irritated with this level of intimate conversation. Today he truly seemed interested in what she had to say. "What do you need?"

"Things that are not fair to ask of you if I'm not staying in this marriage."

"I understand. But he's my son, too. Did it occur to you that I might be scared and looking for a little comfort?"

His words shocked her to her toes because they mirrored her thoughts exactly.

Comfort sex.

She slid Chanel sunglasses down her nose to stare at him. "No, frankly that never occurred to me."

He stared into her eyes. "Lay the burden down, babe. Emilio will watch the boys and Julia is here, too."

The very capable Julia was under the huge shade tent shielding the boys from the blazing Mexican Riviera sun. Emilio, the tank-like Mercado bodyguard, was several yards away under another umbrella watching them all. His only concession to the beach setting was a knit shirt instead of a coat and tie.

Max's affluent family owned the largest tequila distillery in Mexico and took precautions everywhere these days, even inside an exclusive resort. Her husband was right. Anna wasn't really needed at the moment.

"I—" she hesitated but it had to be said. "You do understand I'm not staying."

He touched her face when she would have stopped there.

"I feel like I'm using you, Max."

He laughed, a deep rich sound that stirred something inside her from long ago. Those hypnotic brown eyes crinkled up at the corners as he brought her hand to his lips. "God yes, woman. Now come upstairs and use me some more."

She laughed with him then, every argument slipping away. "All right. But I have to get my head wrapped around all this. Plus I have to get Zach something to eat."

She took his hand and read the time on his expensive dive watch. "The grill opens in fifteen minutes. I'll be up right after," she said.

He grinned at her like a boy who is about to commit serious mischief and knows he won't be punished. Leaning over her body to kiss her, he caressed her shoulder and slid his palm down her arm into her bikini top to cop a very thorough feel. She gasped, but he was blocking everyone's view.

"The only thing I want you to wrap yourself around is *me*. I'll be in the suite. I've got a couple of calls to make." He kissed her again, making it crystal clear what he intended to do to her once she got upstairs. Then he was gone, waving to the boys and stopping to talk to Emilio.

She sat listening to the waves, surprised at how aroused she was. Maybe this was another mistake, but she didn't care. Her headache was fading and she was going for it.

She wasn't going to pretend he was offering courage or anything resembling hope. But what he could offer was pulse pounding, peel-the-paint-off-the-ceiling comfort sex. That was the only thing on the menu, and right now she'd take it, because the coming days were looking grim.

"TAKE ZACH FROM the party before the guests arrive. We won't dump her body until the designated time. It's all been arranged."

Anna stopped in the doorway of the Presidential suite, her husband's words abruptly penetrating her lust-fogged brain.

"No, I'm not worried. Haven't you heard? Mexico is the land of vicious drug cartels and random violence. My wife will be a sad statistic."

Was this a dream?

She felt the cold Italian marble beneath her bare feet and recognized Max's voice in the adjoining room, but she didn't wake up. The seductive words he had whispered moments earlier on the beach still resonated in her head.

The only thing I want you to wrap yourself around is me.

She'd come up immediately when Julia had volunteered to get Zach and the cousins' meals from the hotel's beach grill. But on the way to the room she'd been calling herself all kinds of a fool. She and Max were on the verge of officially separating even though they'd been living apart for several months. The counseling wasn't working. Having sex was a terrible idea. Even comfort sex.

Yet he'd been so attentive, so different on this trip. So anxious to please her, while keeping his temper completely in check. Last week she'd been considering which attorney to use in a divorce. Now she was just grateful she was standing here overhearing his phone conversation in the next room.

Her thoughts raced and her blood chilled, but her feet were glued to the imported floor. She stared across the opulent suite's living room to the open balcony doors. The heir to the Mercado Tequila fortune settled for nothing less than the finest, even when planning his family's demise.

An ocean breeze blew through the room, ruffling her hair like a playful lover. The Gulf of Mexico was just as blue as it had been ten minutes ago when Max kissed her on the sand, yet everything had changed. She was listening to her husband order their son's kidnapping and her murder.

Why? Did he want complete control over Zach's life?

"I'll meet you after. It'll probably be midnight or later. I'll be dealing with the fallout from their disappearances."

His laugh was low and rich, sounding the same as it had moments ago on the beach, but the words were cruel. "I've always been an excellent actor. Playing the grieving widower and desperate father won't be hard."

She'd been holding her breath and took a quiet gulp of air against the nausea that threatened. Perspiration was running down her back. Everything over the past twenty-four hours had been a lie, but she still didn't understand the reason.

"Yes, payment as we discussed. But you may have to keep him in seclusion until you hear from me. There won't be any margin for error." She heard impatience in his voice now.

Oh my god. What was he thinking?

Zach needed care and monitoring by qualified nurses almost round the clock. He had to go back to Dallas for the LVAD pump. She couldn't even process what would happen if the center called now with a donor.

She had to get Zach and herself out of here until she understood what the hell was going on. She knew she wasn't dreaming when she accepted the idea of getting on a plane without breaking into a cold sweat. Her fear of flying was completely swallowed up in her new fear of Max.

"I've got to go. Anna'll be here soon."

That shocked her out of her frozen reverie and she inched from the entryway, closing the door silently behind her.

Racing to the elevator, she threw herself inside and stabbed the lobby button. Zach should still be eating lunch at the beach with his cousins.

He didn't have the new phone that Max had just given him yesterday. She'd asked him to leave it in the room, concerned it would be ruined in all the sand and surf. At least she had the hospital pager in her beach bag. She didn't go anywhere without it in case the doctors of Children's Transplant Center called with word of a matching donor.

Where were their passports?

No!

She stopped walking beside the ladies' lounge in the lobby and wanted to scream when she realized their travel documents were in the suite's room safe.

Jesus . . . God. Help.

Tears were streaming down her cheeks as a maid pushing a cleaning cart opened the swinging door. "Are you alright, *señora*?"

"*Sí. Gracias.*" Anna nodded, smiling weakly before ducking into the restroom herself. She had to pull it together. Weeping while walking through a five-star hotel would draw more attention than she could afford.

Soothing music played a soft island rhythm. A wall fountain gurgled and overstuffed chairs beckoned—a tranquilizing retreat under any other circumstances.

Anna sank into one of the overstuffed chairs and felt her perspiration soak into the upholstery. She took a ragged breath. She had to have a plan.

Her whole life, she had always known her next step. Even when Zach got sick, and she felt as though she'd stepped into an abyss, the doctors had given her a course of action. Use meds, install a pacemaker, the LVAD if necessary, and wait for a heart. God, the only time she'd never had a plan had been when she'd met and married Max at nineteen in a whirlwind romance. She'd thrown caution—and her carefully considered roadmap for an education and career—to the wind to marry him, never dreaming what his enchanting exterior disguised. Her stomach roiled under the strain.

A plan.

The police? Not an option, even if they believed her wild story. With the corruption in the Mexican police force and the Mercado family wealth, she couldn't trust that they weren't already on the payroll.

Max wasn't taking Zach till later tonight, so she had a little time. But she was wearing a bikini with a sarong cover-up, plus she was barefoot with barely twenty dollars in cash. Everything—Zach's meds, her passport, Zach's passport, their clothes, plus all her credit cards—was in the suite with Max.

What was she going to do?

With startling clarity she knew, and the knowledge of what it entailed had her dashing for one of the stalls to empty the contents of her stomach. Kneeling on the cold hard tile, despair washed over her in relentless waves along with the nausea. After a few minutes, she rose on shaky knees to stagger to the sinks.

She was going to have to go back upstairs and have sex with her husband, putting on the performance of a lifetime and acting as if she hadn't just overheard him threatening to take Zach and dispose of her body like so much trash. She'd go to bed with him, pretending to be enjoying that "comfort sex" and when he got up to get showered and dressed, she'd grab her clothes along with Zach's and run.

Could she do it?

If she wanted to save herself and her son, she'd have to. But she had to have their passports, Zach's meds, and some cash before they could leave. They had to get out of Mexico this afternoon, before Max suspected she knew anything.

Chapter Two

Dallas, Texas

HE STARED IN disbelief at the damning words crawling across the bottom of the muted twenty-four hour news channel. *DEA Agent Leland Hollis testifies for the cartel in drug bust debacle at home of Ellis Colton. Colton sues government for six million dollars.*

Jesus. His picture on the screen was larger than the one of the president stepping onto Air Force One for the weekend. He didn't even turn up the volume, he'd heard enough earlier in the day. Trust the media to sensationalize the details and interpret them in the most shocking way possible

Shaking his head, Leland turned off the TV and headed for the hotel balcony with a bottle of single malt scotch and a glass. Rain had been falling for so long he assumed the patio chair cushion would be waterlogged when he sat, but a wet butt was a small price to pay. He wouldn't be wearing this suit again.

He longed to leave the hotel, but the thought of running into someone he knew was more than he could stand since the story had hit the newsstands along with the cable networks. Ellis Colton's attorney had insisted he stay at a hotel instead of at home, and given the nature of the case, Leland had been fine with that.

Being a DEA agent, there were plenty of Vega cartel members ready to take a shot at him, and several who knew exactly where he lived. One more reason to be grateful he was single. Leland would be going crazy right now if he had a family to protect in the midst of this insanity.

Still, tonight the walls of the Best Western were closing in, particularly after the life-changing decision he'd just made. Mentally, he'd left the agency when he'd made the phone call to the civil attorney weeks ago. But yesterday in the courtroom that determination had become etched in stone when he broke the 'blue wall of silence.' Finishing his testimony this afternoon had cinched it.

He plopped in the seat with a minor squish and propped his orthopedic boot cast on the glass-topped table, grateful to be outside. The pain in his ankle was knifing its way up his leg into his back. Three more weeks and he'd be out of the boot.

He contemplated taking a pain pill as the unopened bottle of Laphroaig 18 Year Old beckoned—a toss-up as to which was worse for his career. One was illegal, the other insidious. But in light of those headlines, it didn't matter anymore. He'd just quit his job, whether he'd wanted to or not.

The irony was that the only one who understood was Ford Johnson. After the fiasco that almost killed him, Johnson visited Leland in the hospital. Supposedly he had stopped by to check on his downed officer, but really the man had needed to talk. Ford had felt as much to blame as Leland for the disastrous bust.

Vicodin was in his dopp kit in the bathroom. His last bottle, although he had means to get more, and he was oh-so-tempted. It was easy with his contacts.

He'd like to tell himself he hadn't had much of a choice. But he'd always had a choice with the pills. He'd just chosen poorly once and had been paying ever since.

His feet vibrated from the bass thrumming in the room under his. He hadn't realized the speakers on the hotel televisions were that powerful. Taking a deep breath, he broke the seal on the bottle and poured the in-augural shot for his private pity party as the sliding glass door opened on the first floor patio below him. Dark music filled with despair and angst rocketed skyward, melting the balcony railings.

Wasn't that perfect?

Guitars shrieked with ear-splitting intensity and he wondered if he was going to have to call the management when he heard a woman's voice over the heavy metal. "Turn it down, honey. That's too loud."

"Mo-om!" Exasperation was clear in the one word as the patio door slammed shut, and a semi-peace ruled again with a slight lessening of the thrumming bass at his feet.

God bless America and mothers who would fuss about headbanger music played at thundering decibels.

The burner cell phone in his pocket jangled, surprising him. He recognized the incoming caller, the only person he would have picked up for. "How the hell did you get this number, Gavin?"

"You're not that hard to find. This is what I do." The CEO of Armored Extraction Guards and Investigative Security, or AEGIS, Gavin Bartholomew specialized in private security, risk management, and the recovery of people and assets in foreign countries.

"I know. You do it all. I shouldn't be surprised you found the number, but I just bought this thing yesterday. The only person who knows I own the phone is the checker at Walmart."

Gavin snorted. "Well I know now. *The National Enquirer* can't be far behind."

"I would laugh if I thought that wasn't true."

"Relax, Buddy, I lied. You weren't that easy to find, but why did I have to hear about this crap on CNN?"

Leland could hear the hurt in his former partner's voice. "I didn't want to bother you. You've had a lot going on. How's Kat?" Gavin's wife was one of Leland's favorite people. He stared at the glass of liquor but didn't pick it up.

"Feeling crappy. Nauseated. She's thrown up everything except her toenails today. She's finally resting now."

Stage IV breast cancer metastasized to the liver. Just

when you thought your own problems were insurmountable, someone else could remind you how much you'd rather not trade troubles with anyone.

"She saw you on the news before she fell asleep. Asked me to check on you," added Gavin. And that was so like Kat. To think of others even when she was . . . dying. It physically hurt to think about that.

"They warned us it would be this way, but I never thought . . . God, I fucking hate cancer." The fear in Gavin's voice made Leland's heart ache for both his friends.

They'd treated him like family, and he'd dropped off the face of the earth. Leland hadn't known what to say then, and he didn't know what to say now, but his friend refused to dwell on the horror that was coming. "Sooo. How are you? Gotta say, the news cameras did not get your best side."

Leland forced a levity into his voice that he didn't feel. "Screw you, Bartholomew. Every side is my good side."

Gavin's deep chuckle echoed over the line. "It's good to know you still have a rich fantasy life. What have you gotten yourself into?"

Leland didn't miss the unspoken subtext: *How did you end up testifying for the defense?* He had kept Gavin out of the loop on purpose because of everything going on with Kat, but if his friend had tracked him down—especially in the midst of his own personal crisis, he deserved an explanation.

"The cable news folks have covered all the basics, if not the finer points of the situation. A snitch sold a civilian CPA, Ellis Colton, as a Class One Columbian drug smuggler to my supervisor, Hank Preston."

"How did it go down?" asked Gavin.

Leland quit staring at the glass on the table and finally took a deep sip of the scotch. The salty vanilla taste and peat smoke were like coming home. He savored the feeling. It had been a long time since he'd allowed himself the luxury. Besides, this was hard to talk about.

"The DEA hit the Coltons' home with a commando SWAT team made up of local police and federal agents. They killed a sleeping toddler, critically wounded a second and severed Jan Colton's spine, putting her in a wheelchair for life. Except they had it all wrong."

Leland remembered the look of devastation on Ellis Colton's face. He took another sip and started to knock back the rest of the scotch but couldn't. Love made people so freaking vulnerable. He never wanted to be that unprotected. It took him a moment before he could keep talking.

"The criminal informant was lying about everything, and Hank Preston refused to accept that he was being played. Not one illegal substance was found in the CPA's house. Preston's snitch was Juan Santos. Remember that bastard?"

Gavin made unhappy sounds on the other end of the phone.

"Santos was paid over thirty grand for a fabrication and has since disappeared. It'd be comical if it wasn't so damn tragic." Leland could still hear the Colton babies screaming if he let himself focus on that night. He didn't even have to close his eyes anymore before prickles of sweat would break out on his upper lip.

"What happened during the raid?" asked Gavin.

"Ellis Colton had a gun and a permit to carry it. Something Preston would have known if he'd bothered to actually manage the case and order a background check. When SWAT broke down the front door, Colton thought someone was breaking into his house to rob him and fired back."

"How did you get shot?"

"A freshman SWAT member got caught up in contagious shooting. Bullets that got me and one of the babies were both from his gun. Guy was torn up about the kid. Not sure he'll ever come back from administrative leave." Leland wouldn't have been able to.

"And your career at DEA?" Gavin was forever the pragmatist, no matter how passionate the point of view.

"Toast. From the moment Preston ordered me to go on the raid. I should have gone up the chain of command and found someone who would listen to the facts. I didn't."

That was the piece giving him trouble. He hadn't been able to reach Ford Johnson. If he'd only done it differently . . . insisted on talking with Hank's boss, no matter what kind of high-level meetings the man was in or the shit storm it would have caused going over Preston's head.

"What are your plans?" asked Gavin.

"I just signed my DEA resignation letter."

"So, I'll finally be able to hire you away from my former employers. When do you want to come to work?"

Leland shook his head even though Gavin wasn't there to see it. "I don't know, man. I've got to take some time. Get this figured out. The boot comes off in three weeks."

Below him, the sliding glass door opened again and music roared, but only for a second before it was turned down.

"This place sucks, Mom. Why can't we stay at the Hilton? They don't have a pool here and there's only Disney and news on cable. I don't have my video games or my phone . . . I still don't understand why you didn't grab my stuff when you were packing. This completely blows." The voice was unmistakably that of a teenage male. It had cracked several times during the diatribe, so he guessed the boy to be no more than thirteen or fourteen.

Jesus. Leland had given his own momma hell at that age. But she'd given it right back, usually with scathing words or sometimes the back of her hand. He braced for what he feared might be coming.

"I've been telling you for three years, you could have a job with AEGIS whenever you wanted." Gavin's voice was in his ear, pulling him out of the teen drama downstairs.

Was working for an elite executive protection and risk management company what he really wanted? He stared at the almost empty glass. He was too young to retire and too old to go back to school. Still, he'd actually felt a weight lifting from his shoulders when he'd signed those official resignation papers earlier.

A woman's voice drifted up over his balcony. "Zach, I'm sorry you don't like the hotel. I know this is hard to understand, and I'm more sorry than I can say that your father's and my problems are spilling over onto you. We won't be here long. I'll try to figure out something about your gaming system. Just give me a little time."

God, didn't we all need that.

Leland let out the breath he hadn't realized he was holding. So she was one of those. A "Nice Mom." Leland had prayed for one as a young child. By the time he was twelve, he'd given up praying and accepted the bleak reality.

"Are you still there?" asked Gavin.

"Yeah. Let me think about it," replied Leland. "I need . . . a little time."

"What's there to think about exactly?" asked Gavin.

"So what do I do till then?" demanded Zach at the same time.

"How about we buy an in-room movie, or we could go to a theatre? That new superhero blockbuster we saw the previews for last month has just been released." Nice Mom was cool as a cucumber.

"Yeah?" The snarl in the boy's 'tude was checked a bit.

"Heck, we'll do both. Let's find a time for the nearest theatre and then if we're up for it, we'll order another show from the on-demand menu when we get back. It'll be a movie marathon. There's bound to be a cinema close by. We can grab a pizza afterward and bring it back with us."

Nice Mom was working it—hard. Zach didn't realize what a lucky young man he was.

"Just trying to get my head straight," mumbled Leland into the phone.

"Why couldn't I stay with Dad in Mexico for the weekend? I still don't get that. They were having a party and everything," the boy's voice wasn't quite as snarky now.

"I'm sorry. I know you're disappointed. I told you, the hospital called and insisted on more blood work before the surgery. I understand it's very frustrating. How about that pizza?" asked Nice Mom.

"Dunno. I'll have to think about it. I'll let you know." The door slid closed with a firm snap, and the shrieking guitars increased in volume, the bass echoing through his feet.

"I've got to think about it," echoed Leland.

"You do that, darling. I'll be right here." Nice Mom's words were whispered, but Leland could hear them, along with the bone-deep sigh, even from where he sat, although he doubted she realized he was above her. The music was probably too loud right outside the window. Furniture creaked on the floor beneath him as she settled into what he assumed was an equally damp seat.

"Leland? What's going on? Are you okay?"

"Sorry." Leland shut out what was happening downstairs, lowered his voice and focused on answering Gavin's question. "I'm fine. Nothing's going on. I'm just . . . working through this. Don't know how long it will take till I'm back to full-speed with my ankle after I get out of this boot. I appreciate the offer, but frankly, I don't know what I want."

There was a beat of silence. "Okay. I think I understand."

And the hell of it was, Gavin probably did. He had quit the DEA to start his dream company. The difference was Gavin Bartholomew had known exactly what he wanted to do when he resigned his government position. These days Leland's life felt so out of control, he had no clue.

"This is a weird place for me. I've always had a plan."

"Give yourself time. Let me know if I can help. You've got a job if you want it. And next time you're on TV, show 'em your good side."

Leland almost laughed. "Bite me. I'll be up to see Kat in a few days. We'll talk more."

"Sounds good. But ... don't wait too long on that visit."

The words were so matter-of-fact, Leland didn't catch the real meaning at first. It took a moment to sink in— Kat was closer to the end than he'd realized. *Damn.*

He hung up the phone with an aching soul, hurting for his friends. God, he was tired. He leaned back in his chair, staring at the bottle of single malt scotch again. He wanted to keep drinking until he felt pleasantly numb, or perhaps until he felt nothing at all.

The music under his feet kicked up another notch and the furniture below scraped across the concrete again, reminding him of his downstairs "neighbors." A teenage boy and a single mother who were obviously in the throes of a divorce. His well-honed "stay away" tendency kicked in and he started to rise, but before he moved off the seat, he heard the distinct sound of a cell phone keypad dialing.

Years of undercover wiretaps for the DEA gave him

no compunction about eavesdropping, even though some things he'd overheard on the job he'd prefer to scrub from memory. Still, he suspected this woman had no idea he was on the corner balcony directly overhead or how well the sound carried, even over the rain and the music. She obviously couldn't hear him over the thundering beat in the room behind her.

With his orthopedic boot there was no way he could be quiet if he walked inside. He stumped everywhere these days. So he sat with his bottle of scotch and unfinished drink, wondering why he cared one way or the other.

"Hi, Sweetie, I hate talking to your voicemail. We're here. It was crazy, but we got out on the last afternoon flight. Zach's angry, and I still haven't told him why we really left. I don't know if he'll believe me. Hell, I don't know if I'd believe me. Thanks for wiring the cash. I think I can access my own funds, but I'll have to be careful. Max froze our joint bank account."

Leland listened, mildly intrigued. This sounded like a soap opera. As a diversion it certainly beat the Disney channel, and at present he knew all the intimate details about what was on cable news.

"I don't know what I'm going to do about checking Zach into the hospital. Children's Transplant Center has security, but Max can still get to him there unless I'm with him every minute. Liz, I'm scared. And I really wish you lived closer to Dallas. Call me when you get this, okay? Love you."

What the hell?

Something definitely did not sound right, and it was more than just a woman ditching her husband. Did the guy hit her or the kid? Was her son ill? Over the years Leland had learned he could dismiss a lot of things, but people who hurt women or children were his personal kryptonite. Thanks to his own difficult childhood, he couldn't walk away.

The floor abruptly quit vibrating under his feet and the patio door below opened. "Mom? There's someone at the door to see you."

"Is it housekeeping?"

There was a non-committal answer from the boy.

"I ordered more towels. I had no idea you could use so many . . ."

Her voice was teasing, fading as she walked inside. But she didn't close the slider. He heard a murmur of voices. A man's low rumble, slowly rising then yelling.

"How did you find us?" The woman's voice was louder than he'd heard it all evening.

"Watch out!" The boy was yelling. "Mom!"

Leland heard shattering glass and a woman's piercing scream. "OH MY GOD! Stop!"

Chapter Three

MAX STOOD IN the doorway with murder in his eyes, holding a nine iron like a baseball bat. Anna's throat tightened, remembering his words overheard seven hours earlier: "We won't dump her body until the designated time . . ."

Surely he wouldn't kill her in front of their son?

Zach remained beside her even as she tried to pull him out of harm's way. Stunned, he appeared frozen in place, so she moved to step in front of him.

Max slapped her when she came forward. She cried out in surprise as much as pain. Her lip tore on his wedding band. She tasted blood.

"Why did you leave?" he demanded. "I can't stand it when you disrespect me like that." He gripped the golf club with both hands and started swinging like he was warming up in a batting cage.

Who was this man? They'd argued in the past, but

he'd never before touched her in anger. This was like someone else's nightmare.

She pushed Zach further behind her as the first strike took out their small carry-on bag. It was unzipped on top of the dining table. Clothes and toiletries flew through the air, and Zach seemed to recognize the wildness in his father's eyes and pulled Anna backward along with him into the room away from the swinging club.

"How did you find us?" she asked.

"You know me, babe. I've got lots of resources." He shoved her into the dining table and her elbow struck the edge of the wooden top, sending a lightning bolt of pain up her shoulder. Dazed, she fell back into the wall as Max attempted an uppercut with the nine iron.

Emilio watched dispassionately from the hallway. Weren't other hotel guests hearing anything? A dining chair smashed into the wainscoting inches from her face, and the framed mirror over her head started to fall.

"Mom! Watch out!" Zach rushed to her side, attempting to catch the frame. She threw her arm up to stop the mirror's descent, taking the full force of the toppling frame and blocking Zach at the same time. She couldn't help but scream again as the mirror slammed into her shoulders and shattered, splintering into thousands of tiny pieces.

One shard of glass tore through her sweater and cut her arm, but it didn't sting as blood welled up to soak her sleeve. She looked up at Zach, ashen-faced beside her. She'd lose it completely if she let herself think about what this was doing to his heart.

Her husband was going to kill her if he could. That was obvious. She straightened from the wall to face him. "What do you want, Max?"

"I want my son. And I want *you*, too. We need to go back to Mexico."

"I heard you on the phone in the hotel suite. You were planning to take Zach and dump my body."

"You misunderstood."

"The hell I did. And the fact that you just hit me, broke this mirror and you're holding that nine iron is all a misunderstanding as well?"

"Yes, it is. *You* misunderstood!" He pounded the club into the floor for emphasis.

"Zach is checking into the hospital Monday for the LVAD procedure, or did you forget that?"

"God dammit, don't you disrespect me. I'll have my son back in Mexico one way or the other," Max reared back to swing once more and a shot rang out. Shards of grout, glass and masonry flew into the air, some of it pelting Max's bare legs.

Anna screamed again and ducked as Max's swing went wild. He buried the club head through the sheetrock wall.

"Hey," shouted a stranger standing in the doorway. "Drop the golf club or the next bullet goes through your kneecap." He had a gun in Emilio's face and another pointed directly at Max's chest.

Max wheeled around in surprise, still gripping the club tightly, "Who the fuck are you? You shot me, you SOB. I'll kill you."

The stranger raised an eyebrow. "No, I didn't shoot you. That was the tile and glass ricocheting, but I can and I will if you don't drop that nine iron and step away from the woman."

Anna's relief overwhelmed her. Their savior was built like a professional bodybuilder with a deep voice and an accent only heard in the land of magnolia blossoms and the blues. His hands were rock steady on both weapons, and while his face wasn't classically handsome, it was trustworthy. His dark hair was short, and he was wearing one of those orthopedic walking boots that came up to the knee.

Acting saner than he had in the past two minutes, Max dropped the club.

"Emilio," Zach gasped, sidling up to Anna. The family bodyguard stood perfectly still with his hands clasped behind his head in the hotel hallway. "Why didn't you help . . ." Her son's voice trailed off when he figured out whose side Emilio was on.

The stranger motioned for the Mercado bodyguard to join the party, so that he would only need one gun to keep both Max and his employee under control. He then took what she guessed was Emilio's weapon and slid it behind his back into his waistband.

"Kid, call 911." The stranger ordered. "Now."

Zach scurried to the bedside table and picked up the phone, eyeing a paper sack at the door that Anna hadn't seen earlier. Its contents had been strewn across the carpet in Max's melee. Game cartridges, DVDs, an unopened iPad, and in the middle of the loot was Zach's handheld game console.

Max, you bastard, Anna thought. *If you'd really hurt me, Zach would have never gotten over letting you inside this hotel room.*

"It won't make any difference when you call the police. You know who I am?" sneered Max.

"Yeah. A low life scum who hits women. Nothing special."

"I'm Maximilian Mercado."

"No shit? The Tequila King?" The stranger studied him, assessing something. "You look taller on TV." Then he shrugged, clearly unimpressed. "I'm a scotch man myself."

She would have laughed if the situation weren't so dire. Max hated being dismissed as much as he hated being "disrespected." He was very proud of his company and his work.

But the stranger wasn't finished yet. "So I suppose that makes you an uptown scumbag who hits women and stars in his own silly commercials. You should know better. I would think a rich man like you had finer home training."

Max ignored the jab but she knew it burned. The Mercados traced their heritage back to aristocracy. Insulting Max's social etiquette in addition to the family business was sure to make him vengeful.

"Nothing's going to happen to me. I have friends in this town. Who the hell are you?" Max studied the cheap suit and tie that the stranger was wearing. "You're a rent-a-cop, aren't you? You know I can have you fired from this job. Evicted from your home." His voice was tinged with disgust.

The stranger remained silent and Max snorted derisively. "Or possibly arrested yourself for discharging your weapon."

The stranger continued to stare from deep green eyes. Finally he spoke in a drawl that made tortoises seem speedy.

"I don't think so, Mr. Mercado."

"It's my word against yours," argued Max.

A shuttered expression came over her rescuer's face as he nodded. "That's right."

And Max has no idea who this man is. I have no idea who he is. Dark eyebrows, high cheekbones, and a nose that had obviously been broken in the past gave him a dangerous look. The revolver he was pointing at Emilio and Max added to the impression.

The stranger glanced at Anna again with unreadable green eyes locked on the blood oozing from her mouth to her blouse. Something changed in his face, and he reached into his back pocket. Flipping open his wallet, he revealed a shiny badge with a big eagle at the top along with words inscribed in blue and gold that she couldn't quite make out from where she was standing.

"I'm DEA, Mr. Mercado. Now chill. You're about to be arrested for assault and threatening a federal officer."

To HELL WITH keeping a low profile and the letter of resignation he'd just signed. Leland wouldn't think about how his boss would hang him out to dry if this came back to bite him. Max Mercado was a psychopath and, famous or not, the man had just tried to bash Nice Mom's head in with a nine iron. He'd brought Gorilla Guy from the hallway to back him up in case there was any resistance.

"You're a federal agent?" Max's voice was barely audible.

"Right again," said Leland, walking Gorilla Guy toward the entryway while keeping his Ruger trained on Mercado. And you're screwed.

"She'll have to press charges," insisted Max. "She'll never do it." The "Tequila King" sneered at the woman he'd obviously knocked around before Leland got downstairs.

He had been too busy not getting shot or hit with a golf club himself earlier to notice but "she" was stunning. Max's wife had long blonde hair and striking blue eyes with a lush silhouette and legs that went on for days.

She wore shorts, a snug white t-shirt with a cardigan sweater and a wedding ring with a solitaire diamond the size of Texas. But the thing that caught Leland's attention over and above her jaw-dropping figure was the considerable amount of blood dripping from her bee-stung bottom lip and the gash in her right arm.

Surrounded by broken mirrored glass, a teenage boy hovered behind her. Apparently Max had been gearing up to beat the hell out of his trophy wife—and in front of his son, too. Leland sought to quash the red-hot anger that surged through him.

"You really need to brush up on your assault law before you go out with your nine iron, Mr. Mercado. She doesn't have to press charges. I witnessed the assault and you threatened me. I don't care how wealthy you are or how awesome some think your tequila is. You're spending the night in jail."

The elevator door *dinged* down the hall and two officers stepped out, pulling their weapons when they saw the gun in Leland's hand. They must have been in the lobby. This was going to get loud fast.

Leland calmly held up his ID and lowered his Ruger. "My name is Leland Hollis, I'm a DEA agent. This man was attacking that woman with a golf club and threatening me."

The officers hustled toward him and everyone started talking at once. Emilio a.k.a. Gorilla Guy tried to scoot to the fire escape but the police had their guns out, and more officers came up the fire escape at the opposite end of the hall almost immediately.

Apparently the hotel was one block from a police substation. Everyone moved into the room, and suddenly it sounded like a cocktail party. Despite her son's efforts with the towel, the woman's mouth and arm continued to bleed like mad. She was taking her sweater off now, and Leland suspected her pain was starting to override the adrenaline rush that had to have come earlier with the attack. The boy grasped her elbow, and the two were deep in conversation as chaos reigned around them.

"You okay?" she studied the boy as he wrapped another towel around her bleeding arm. But the kid wasn't making eye contact. Something was going on there.

Leland stared at them a moment more before scanning the room. By the doorway he spied electronic games scattered beside on overturned paper sack. *Nothing like a little bribery from Dad.* Leland's anger flared at Max, but he forced himself to focus and listen to the woman and her son while they spoke to the officers.

"I was in the room upstairs and heard people yelling. My name is Leland Hollis," he explained to the police and to her simultaneously as he showed his badge to the city's finest once again.

With the blood, broken mirror and golf club lying there, it was fairly obvious what had happened. Two of the four officers wasted no time in handcuffing Max and Emilio and leading them both away, ignoring their protests.

The woman looked like she was trying to get to the sofa across the room, and Leland took the opportunity to help her. Her son still clung to her other side and glass crunched under their feet.

"Where are they taking my Dad?" asked Zach.

"To the police station," said Leland.

The boy looked torn, unsure where his loyalties should lie. Leland appreciated the dilemma. This experience would mark the kid for the rest of his life. Crazy parents were difficult, no matter what the economics of the situation.

"Why do you have a gun?"

Smart kid. "I'm with the DEA."

"Why were you—"

"You okay? Feeling light-headed?" The woman interrupted her son's interrogation of Leland and pulled the boy down beside her on the love seat.

Leland was puzzled. Shouldn't they be asking if she was feeling light-headed?

Zach started to shake his head, but finally looked her straight in the eye and nodded. "I'm having a hard time catching my breath," he admitted.

This news seemed to really jack mom up.

She smiled brightly, but it didn't reach her eyes. "It's alright. It's just all this craziness. We need one of your white pills." She started to stand, but the room was filled with more officers replacing the two who'd just left. "They're on the bathroom counter." She looked helplessly at the crowd between them and the bathroom door.

One of the officers, unaware of the small drama playing out, took the opportunity to ask questions of Zach about what had just happened.

"Stop!" she snapped.

The officer stilled. "But ma'am, I need to talk to him."

Leland stepped in. "Not without his mother's permission. Why don't we take care of her arm first. You got a first aid kit?"

Officer Betts, according to his nametag, took in the blood and nodded. "Be right back. Looks like she might need stitches, but we've got supplies to fix her up till she gets to the hospital."

Leland turned to her again. "What do you want me to do?" His kept his voice calm amidst the pandemonium swirling around them.

She swallowed audibly. Clearly, she didn't trust that he could help her. "My son needs his medication . . . now. He has a heart condition with a pacemaker and this," she swung her uninjured arm to indicate the room, "is really exacerbating things."

Oookay. Being jacked up—totally justified. "Where's the medicine?"

"In my bag on the bathroom counter."

"I'll get it ... sit here." He put a hand on her shoulder and gently pushed her down into the sofa again. She started when he made contact with her collarbone. He wondered if that was a reaction to him or the husband who'd just tried to kill her.

Jeez. Where was Leland's "stay away" tendency now? Completely crushed under the "rescue her" tendency that kicked into high gear when he was around women who were in trouble. The problem was he couldn't always be there when the trouble was as unpredictable as it tended to be in his line of work. And his not being there could get someone dead.

Chapter Four

"I'LL HELP HIM get the medicine, Mom," said Zach.

"But—" Anna's stomach roiled. She didn't want Zach to walk away from her, even in this room of police officers. The stress of the entire day, the adrenaline rush and crash, and now nausea from all the blood seeping down her arm suddenly swamped her.

"I know what I'm supposed to do," he interrupted. "You taught me what to take if I was ever alone and needed my meds. Right now I need Atenolol. I can do it." Zach gave her a confident smile and disappeared into the bathroom with Leland clearing the way.

Alone on the sofa, her eyes burned from unshed tears while she waited. *I will not panic*, she thought, forcing herself to calm her breathing. Zach did know what to do. She'd taught him a lot of independence in the past year, despite his illness.

Her head felt like it was going to explode from trying

to figure out why Max would want to prevent Zach from checking into the hospital. Was having the police involved good news or bad, in terms of keeping her son safe? Could this kind of bizarre drama bump Zach from his place on the list?

Before she had time to dwell on that thought, Leland was walking toward her, stopping to speak with two other officers on the way.

"Where's Zach?" she asked.

"In the bathroom talking to one of the policemen. He got his own pill. Atenolol. It was white. That's correct, yes?" Leland settled on the sofa beside her, propping his orthopedic boot on the coffee table. "Zach says he's fine. He's sitting on the toilet lid, and they're talking the latest Transformers movie."

She wanted to believe him—that things could be this simple. But her life and Zach's illness never were. "Please, absolutely no questions about his dad. He can't be upset. This is extremely important. He's so ill. It would be a bad thing." She wanted to go and check on him herself, but Leland put a gentle hand on her arm.

"They understand. I've explained to the officer in charge, and he's telling the others about Zach's heart. They won't question him, but they would like to talk to you . . . in case there was something you needed to tell the police that you didn't want your boy to overhear?"

She turned to stare at him, hard. Could she tell him? He didn't flinch under the scrutiny, still she remained silent.

"I appreciate that you're scared, but you've got a real

mess here, and you have to trust someone. Would you feel more comfortable with social services?" he asked.

"No! Absolutely not." She surprised herself with the vehemence of her own response.

"Alright." He was looking at her like she was a frightened animal that he wasn't sure would bite or run.

"I'm sorry. I'm ... God, I'm overwhelmed. Can you give me a minute?"

He nodded as the officer came back with the first aid kit. "No problem. Let us look at this cut while you decide what you're going to do. You're still bleeding quite a bit."

She looked down only to see her blood all over the sofa. Bile rose in the back of her throat. The officer pulled supplies from the kit and went to get water while Leland started cleaning her arm.

This was crazy. She had to tell someone what was going on. Leland took her wrist as he wiped her fingers with sterile gauze. His hands were large and made hers look so small.

The visual distracted her enough to take her mind off the nausea and gather her thoughts. One: She needed help. Two: This guy seemed like he genuinely wanted to be it. And three: She had to start somewhere.

"My son, he needs a heart transplant, but there's no donor. He's AB negative and that's very rare. He's checking into CTC, Children's Transplant Center, tomorrow for a left ventricular assist device insertion. LVAD for short. The hospital is skittish about bad PR. This incident with Max worries me. I can't do anything that would jeopardize Zach's place on the transplant list."

"You think they'd bump him if his father were arrested for assault?"

"I don't know, but I can't take that chance. If they thought Zach wouldn't be safe coming home? Yes, they might bump his spot or make him wait for another heart while we straightened this out with the courts."

"It doesn't seem fair to punish your son for his father's behavior," said Leland.

"CTC doesn't operate like a democracy, and they aren't social services. They give the limited number of organs accessible to the patients with the very best chances for recovery."

"So they're pragmatists?" asked Leland.

She nodded. "The administrators at the center define the word. In my more reasonable moments, I know it makes sense. Where do you think a donor heart has more chance of success? With a child whose dad beats her mother every night or with a child in a stable home with loving supportive parents?"

Leland swallowed audibly before answering. "I can see that, but it's harsh, isn't it?" He tossed the bloody gauze on the coffee table and reached for more. "It sounds like being on probation," he added.

She held up her arm as he wrapped a sterile bandage around the injury. "That's a good analogy. As the patient, you know this going in, but there is no recourse if you're unhappy with CTC and their selection process . . . except to go somewhere else and start over with the waiting."

"That sounds extremely difficult."

"Understatement of the decade. We've been on the list

for over a year. I can't . . . I won't start over again. Zach is number one in line now, but he's out of time."

She touched her shorts pocket containing the pager as she spoke. "He's got a pacemaker and he's about to have a heart pump installed. That could buy him up to another year if we need it, but the surgery for the pump itself is brutal."

"So you and your husband have had an intense year?"

"Yes, but it got better when he moved out six months ago. At least I thought it did. Max couldn't handle the doctors or the day-to-day uncertainty. I found it easier to do this without him than dealing with his issues on top of everything else."

"Do you think you need a lawyer?" asked Leland.

"I don't know what I need. But you were right when you said it was a mess."

The officer returned with the water and asked if she would feel up to giving her statement. She didn't want to. She had no idea what she was going to say "officially" to the police, and the walls of the room were closing in.

"Can you hold off on the statement until we get her arm taken care of?" Leland asked, seeming to pick up on her distress.

The officer nodded and gathered the used gauze before he backed off.

Leland's fingers were especially gentle as he continued to clean the blood away, heedless of his dress shirt and slacks. "I'm sorry but there's no way to avoid the ER. Stitches are inevitable here."

"I tried to catch the mirror as it fell. That was foolish,

I know, but Zach was standing beside me. I was scared it was going to fall on him."

"Makes sense. They'll get you to the hospital and stitched up as soon as this is over."

As soon as this is over?

As far as she was concerned, this was just beginning. Before it had only been the LVAD and transplant, worries that were huge enough in themselves, but now it was Max trying to take Zach and kill her. While this man had listened and empathized with her concerns over Zach's place on the transplant list, explaining the events of the past seven hours to Leland Hollis would sound fantastic. It was a lot to ask of someone, to believe such an outrageous story.

A sense of hopelessness overwhelmed her along with a fresh wave of nausea. "Can you excuse me a minute?" She stood and eased past the officers to walk toward the bathroom.

Feeling light-headed and dizzy, her mind raced as her emotions swirled. She was halfway across the room when her vision went dark around the edges. She tried to sit but missed the bed as the room began to spin and the floor rose up to meet her.

Leland rushed toward her and her last coherent thought was: *He moves awfully fast for a guy in a boot cast.*

LELAND WATCHED ANNA Mercado sinking to the ground, hoping he could catch her before she hit the

floor. The damned boot slowed him down. He almost
made it, but tripped at the last minute. They landed
together in a heap. Breaking her fall with his body, he
settled with a *humff* on his back—his arms full of soft,
curvy woman.

The breath was knocked out of him, but he didn't
mind this type of assault. Anna Mercado wasn't exactly a
burden, and his body was going on autopilot in response
to having a woman lying on top of him for the first time
in longer than he cared to remember. He took a deep
breath.

God she smelled good. Her skin felt like silk under his
fingertips as he ran his hand down her arm in an attempt
to lift her off his chest.

"Hey, you okay?" he asked for the second time, gently
rolling her from his body to the carpeted hallway floor.
Her eyelids didn't flutter, and he felt the first stirrings of
alarm overriding his arousal. She wasn't coming to and
her face was chalk white. One of the officers called for an
ambulance as her kid started to panic.

"Mom? Mom? Mom, wake up!" Zach slid to the floor
beside them.

Leland was concerned on two levels. Anna was in a
dead faint, and her kid's lips had gone from healthy pink
to pale blue in fifteen seconds. He checked her breathing.
Jesus, she'd explained the heart situation. Now he was
worried both of them would need CPR.

Her hair smelled like lemons. A completely inappropriate and out-of-context thought, but right there with
him just the same.

"What's wrong with her?" Zach demanded with a shaking voice.

"I don't know. Has she been sick?" he asked.

The boy shook his head. "Not that I know of."

Her breathing was shallow, but steady, as Leland checked her pulse. Her fingers were long and slim with medium-length nails painted fire-engine red.

Zach stared down at her and his eyes filled. "She's been really stressed out lately with all my heart stuff, but nothing like this has ever happened before. What do you think is wrong?"

Leland shook his head. He had no idea, but keeping Zach calm was paramount while they waited on the EMTs. "Get me a wet wash cloth from the bathroom." The boy leaped up, obviously longing for some way to help.

"What's wrong with her?" Zach asked again, scurrying back seconds later with the dripping cloth.

Sirens sounded in the distance.

"I don't know, but they'll figure out what's going on." Leland nodded toward the door and the increasing noise.

Anna's eyes fluttered open as the paramedics came in. By the time they had her on the gurney she was awake, if not fully coherent.

The EMTs were questioning Leland, and he didn't have much information for them beyond the obvious. He didn't want to be sucked into this any further than he already was. Zach was trying to answer some of their questions, too, but even between the two of them, they didn't know much.

"We need to get her to the hospital, to see what the

problem is." The first EMT said. They started rolling the gurney out of the apartment.

Anna was now fully awake and agitated. "I don't need to go to the hospital. I'm fine. Just a little dehydrated. I got dizzy."

"I'm afraid they're going to insist," said Leland. "You were out for several minutes, plus with that cut. They need to stitch you up."

"But what about Zach? I can't leave him here alone."

The boy was there beside her—leaning down, wild concern in his eyes.

"Mom, are you okay? You scared me when you wouldn't wake up."

She put her hand up to his face. "Honey, I'm fine. Really. They're just going to fix my hand." She turned her face to Leland's. The question of her son's well-being still in her eyes.

He didn't hesitate, despite his earlier resistance to becoming any more involved. "It's okay," said Leland. "I'll take care of him."

"But I don't know you," she said, oceans of uncertainty in her eyes. "Who are you?"

The unspoken question was clear. Anna knew his name. What she meant was, who would offer to do such a thing for a stranger?

He answered the only way he could. "I'm someone you can trust."

Chapter Five

WHERE IN HELL were they?

Sitting at Carlita's bedside, Tomas Rivera wondered for the thousandth time if God had it in for him because of his past sins, or if all of life was just a crap shoot—the good and bad dying randomly, no matter what their paths in life. He didn't have time to contemplate the implications because, at the moment, everything was going to the devil.

He'd had a good, workable plan. He always had a plan. A perfect candidate. Willing to give everything up for a price.

That price had been steep, but to save Carlita, Tomas would have paid anything. Had already paid in fact. A good portion of the funds being provided upfront "in good faith."

Yet somehow the fool had managed to get himself killed in a drive-by shooting. That one of Tomas' men had most likely pulled the trigger was the height of irony. One day, when this was over and Carlita was well, he might appreciate the dark humor in that—but not today. Because as of this moment, there was no recovering what Carlita needed. He was fucking tired of people doing stupid shit.

His phone vibrated and he stood to walk into the hallway so he wouldn't disturb his wife's nap. She had such trouble sleeping these days.

He listened for thirty seconds before interrupting. "Take care of the problem now." Tomas's blood pressure spiked as he gripped the phone even tighter.

"But sir, this is a major US city. It will be challenging to obtain the . . . ah . . . product without detection."

Once upon a time Tomas would have been empathetic to the man's plight, but today he didn't give a damn. "I'm sure you'll come up with a solution."

"I don't know how we'll—"

Tomas cut him off. "I don't want to hear excuses. Find them and don't call me until you have the 'product' in hand." He heard the deadly coldness in his voice and knew the other man could as well. Good, there would be no time lost in the message getting out to others.

"Yes, sir."

Tomas hung up and turned off the ringer, fully confident his orders would be carried out to the letter. He considered Rivera lieutenants to be disposable, and they often were, if they didn't do precisely as he asked.

The orders he'd just given were painful but necessary. He was deceiving an associate in a horrible way. Most likely there would be a scandal when the truth came out.

But no one would wonder when it was over. And those that knew him wouldn't be surprised when they heard. Tomas Rivera did what needed to be done, no matter the cost to him or to anyone else.

He'd been proving that since he'd changed sides twenty years ago. From decorated Mexican soldier to feared cartel operator in three short-but-violent years. You didn't fuck with Tomas Rivera.

He was nineteen when he joined his country's Special Forces program and twenty-one when he left to join the cartel he'd been pursuing. It had been a conscious decision, not that there had been much choice. The one upside was he'd kept his younger brothers and sisters out of the ugliness that surrounded growing up poor in cartel country—clawing his way to the top of the hierarchy and surprising everyone with his ingenuity, business acumen, and ruthlessness.

This opulent bedroom with its Aubusson rug, silver accessories and designer draperies was as stark a contrast to his upbringing as it was to the hospital bed and machines whirring and gurgling in the relative silence. He had no idea what the equipment was doing beyond recording each heartbeat and breath of the woman he loved. Measuring how many more moments she had on this earth before the disease ravaged her completely.

Tomas wasn't a wise man in terms of academic learning, but there were two things he did know with certainty. One, he'd married far above his original station in life and two, his wife would be dead in less than a week if they didn't secure a new candidate.

Why Carlita Vega had chosen to love him instead of the others begging for her hand humbled him in a way that would have surprised his enemies and friends alike. Last month it had been twenty years since the sister of his best friend, Ernesto Vega, walked down the aisle to him as a blushing bride. What should have been the start of a dynasty became the ultimate rivalry, ending with Tomas breaking away from the Vega family to start his own business.

Leaving the Vegas had been bitter, messy and the greatest challenge of his life up till now. Sadly, he and Carlita had no children of their own. While other men in his position might have taken mistresses and had bastard sons to bring into the business, Tomas had only Carlita as his family. His own brothers and sisters were no longer a part of his life, even though he'd delivered them from the devastating poverty of their childhood. But Carlita was all he'd ever wanted or needed. She was more than enough.

His reputation as a ruthless drug lord would have been irrevocably damaged if others knew what he was willing to sacrifice for her. Ironically, no sacrifice from him was necessary or could be even remotely helpful at this time. His heinous reputation, earned in the jungles of Columbia and Mexico, could do nothing to help in her struggle. Someone else would have to save the life of the woman he loved.

Carlita opened her eyes and moved the covers at the same time. "There you are," he smiled through the pain welling up at the sight of her perilously thin body. "I wondered how long you would rest."

"Am I at home?" She tried to peer around the room. "I'm so hot . . . so thirsty."

He nodded as he brought a glass of water to her cracked lips. She was always thirsty now.

She roused a bit more. "This feels like a dream. Every time I wake up, something has changed.

"Don't worry, we just moved you back here to make you more comfortable."

She smiled and reached for his other hand.

"It's lovely to be home. Thank you. I much prefer to die here."

"No! Don't say such things. You're not going to die."

"Oh, Tomas, we both know the truth. It's too late. No one will swoop in at the last minute."

"But what if they did?"

Her eyes took on a new light. "What are you saying?"

"We have a candidate."

"But someone has to . . . to die for that to be possible."

Ah, and there was the rub. Though Tomas Rivera would gladly die for his wife, his death would serve no purpose.

"What if, Carlita?"

"I think it would be a miracle."

His wife was a devout woman. Tomas had no intention of telling her that if his plan worked it would be no miracle but the blackest of sins. Even for him. He who had committed such atrocities in his time.

"Hope for a miracle, my darling."

Carlita's eyes drifted closed.

"Always," she sighed, slipping back to sleep.

Chapter Six

ANNA HAD ASKED, "*Who are you?*"

That was the question of the hour. Leland wasn't certain himself, and he couldn't believe he'd just volunteered himself as her son's keeper. As soon as he'd said the words, he wished them back. But then Anna closed her eyes, seemingly at peace for the first time since he'd met her, and he didn't have the heart to say no.

Zach walked with him to the parking lot and they watched Anna being loaded into the ambulance.

"Where are they taking her?" asked Zach.

"To Presbyterian," answered one of the EMTs.

"Can I ride with her?" Zach asked.

"Sorry, no one under 18 in the ambulance unless they're the patient."

Zach looked at Leland with longing in his eyes. "I understand you don't know me at all but, please, can you take me?"

Leland could refuse as well, but that would be cruel after everything that had just happened. "Okay, but let's get the hotel to move you to another room first." He stuck out his hand. "We weren't properly introduced earlier. I'm Leland Hollis."

Zach shook his hand and his head at the same time. His eyes held an obvious protest about not following right behind the ambulance.

"I understand your concern, Zach, but they won't let you see her as soon as she gets to the hospital anyway, and you don't want to bring her back to this mess, do you?"

There was a long pause. Leland stared the boy down, and the kid straightened his shoulders.

"No. 'Course not."

"Alright then. It'll only take us a few minutes. We'll move y'all's stuff to my room for now and get the management to come up with a new room or have yours cleaned before we get back."

"Yeah, 'kay. That's a good idea. We don't have much stuff. Just a carry-on bag with a change of clothes and our passports. I think my mom's purse is still in the bathroom though."

"Right, with your medicine. Let's gather everything and call the front desk from my room."

They gathered the luggage, Anna's purse and the grocery bag of games and electronics Max Mercado had brought with him. Zach walked up the stairs with Leland stumping behind. He'd left his own door wide open, and the boy wandered inside.

"I gotta grab something." Leland's ankle hurt like hell

from his earlier sprint down the stairs, and he popped three Vicodin from his dopp kit. After dumping his unfinished glass of scotch down the drain, he locked his patio door and grabbed a shoulder holster and jacket. He wasn't going to just tuck his Ruger GP100 into his waistband at the hospital. This had all the hallmarks of being more serious than he'd first suspected.

Zach picked up an unopened game from the paper bag he'd brought upstairs and walked to the trash can, preparing to drop it in. "I can't believe I let my dad inside for this." He shook his head. "I wanted this game so badly last week. I begged for it, but I wouldn't have traded my mother for it."

"She knows that."

The boy didn't answer.

"So tell me about this game," said Leland, unsure of how to proceed.

Zach tossed the case to him. *Millennium Terminator II.* "Bad guys come back through time trying to change things up so that they can fix their fortunes in the next century.

Leland hadn't heard of it, but that meant nothing. "Sounds tight."

"Maybe. I've heard the graphics aren't everything they were expected to be."

Leland picked up the 3D handheld gaming console. "Are you a big gamer?"

The boy shrugged.

"What do you like to play?" asked Leland.

"RPGs mostly. Role-playing single-shooter games are my favorite."

"I used to game a little myself but not anymore. I don't know much about the current market."

"The graphics are everything now. I think Phoenix Circle is the best company, but there's a pretty big debate about it in the gaming world. The better technology still comes out of Japan." Zach's eyes lit up as he spoke about something he obviously loved.

"Interesting. You sound like you know a lot about this."

"I read about it online. I can show you this new game . . . if my mom—" Suddenly his face was serious and the light that had been there a moment before was gone.

"That'd be great," Leland enthused even as he realized he was extending the time he'd be spending with the kid. He picked up the house phone and dialed the front desk as Zach continued staring at the sack.

"I'm not so sure. None of this seems very important anymore." The boy picked up the bag of pricy electronics and put it in the garbage can.

Leland ignored the theatrical action until after he'd talked with the front desk about a new room and hung up the phone. "Your mother is gonna be okay. Let's head up to the hospital to see her."

On the way out the door Leland pulled the bag from the trash and set it on the coffee table. This was shaping up to be a long evening, and electronic entertainment might be in order no matter what Zach was feeling at present.

The boy stared out the window on the drive downtown, not talking. As they merged onto Central Expressway, Leland realized this was probably not a good thing. "So how long have you and your mom been at the hotel?" he asked.

"Just checked in this afternoon."

"Where did you come from?"

Zach wasn't making eye contact. Instead, he was staring at the intricate leather bracelet on his own wrist, snapping and unsnapping the clasp. "Cancun," he mumbled.

"Are you from there?"

"No."

So the boy was now giving him as little information as possible. Leland didn't want to treat this like a police interrogation, but Zach wasn't making it easy.

"Was this a vacation?" he asked.

"Sort of."

"Where you from?"

"Here."

"How do you like Dallas?"

"Sucks."

Oookay. One and two word answers. Not so good. Leland had no idea what he was doing. No clue what teenagers thought or felt. The kid had been "Chatty Kathy" for a few moments when they were talking about video games, now he wouldn't talk at all.

Maybe this was normal. Leland wasn't Dr. Phil, but there was this elephant in the middle of the living room, so to speak. Hell, he might as well go for it.

"So that thing with your father. Has this been going

on for a while?" They were on an exit ramp and just pulling to a stoplight.

At first Leland wasn't sure the boy had even heard him, then Zach looked away from the window to stare into his eyes. The pain there was palatable, intense. Zach shook his head.

"I'd never seen my dad like that before, but now I'm wondering if maybe it's been going on for a long time. They used to argue before he moved out. I'd hear him yelling, but I didn't think—" His eyes filled and his face grew red. "All this time I've been blaming her. I didn't want to believe that my Dad . . . I still can't believe what he almost—" he shook his head again as tears ran down his cheeks. "Why can't we go back to how we were before?"

A car behind them honked. The light was green. Saved by an impatient driver, Leland felt a ridiculous amount of relief over not having to delve into that question right now.

"I don't know, Zach. But it's going to be okay." Leland gave him a quick nod, then drove, still at a complete loss.

"How is that possible?" the boy asked, but turned away when Leland might have answered.

What he would have said, Leland had no idea.

His home life had been "difficult" at best. Although he knew his father, Leland's parents had never been married and his mom had been nothing like Anna Mercado. He'd grown up on the wrong side of the tracks and would probably have ended up in juvey or the state penitentiary but for joining the ROTC in high school.

He'd been looking for a way out, a place to belong. And

he'd found it in the rigorous military student-training program. With his significantly above-average IQ he'd earned a full college scholarship offered through ROTC. Anxious to leave his childhood home behind, he'd joined the Army when he graduated from Sam Houston State University and never looked back. After two tours overseas, he'd joined the DEA.

Zach Mercado was from a completely different place—a privileged background, a good home, a good mom, every advantage. Except for a dad who was a lunatic, willing to hurt the boy's mother in front of him, and a failing heart.

Zach was staring out the side window again.

"We're almost there," said Leland, about to turn into the hospital parking area.

"How is she going to forgive me?"

Zach's question brought him up short. "Forgive you? For what?" Leland pulled into a parking place.

"I let my dad into the hotel room."

Leland clenched his jaw.

"I let him in and he . . . he could have killed her. I can't believe I did that for a damn video game. What kind of person am I?"

Because Leland had been asking himself that same question for the past several weeks, he understood the depth of Zach's pain. Guilt could be a wretched thing. May Max Mercado roast in hell one day. The man had done a horrible injustice to his own child.

Zach was crying in earnest, but somehow, despite his inexperience, Leland knew this wasn't the time to coddle him. It was time to speak frankly.

"You're a good son who loves his mother. You made a mistake. I doubt this is your first, and it sure as hell won't be your last. Tell her you're sorry and ask her to forgive you. She will. She loves you more than she loves herself."

Zach looked at him, tears wet on his face. "How do you know that? You don't know her."

"You're just going to have to trust me on this."

THEY PARKED IN the ER entrance at Presbyterian and hustled into the hospital. It took a few minutes to explain who they were and to locate Anna's exam room.

"Hello," Leland knocked on the door but Zach burst in and threw his arms around her neck. "Mom!"

Anna was in a hospital gown and a nurse was leaning over her, examining the cut on her arm.

Anna hugged her son with one hand.

"No doctor yet," Anna reported. "Just lots of nurses, taking blood and such. More important things are happening here tonight than me."

The nurse looked up from her work apologetically. "There's been a big pile up on LBJ. We've gotten five trauma cases in the past half hour."

"No worries. I'm fine," said Anna.

"The doctor will be here as soon as he can to take a look at that arm," the nurse promised before slipping out the door.

Zach gripped Anna's fingers, silent but anxious. Leland understood the boy's concern. The kid was wondering if his mother would forgive him.

"Thank you so much for bringing Zach," she said. "I don't know what I would have done if you hadn't been there."

"It's no problem," said Leland, anxious himself to leave the two alone so they could talk.

"Oh, but I think it was. I appreciate your saying that though." She squeezed Zach's hand. "We're a mess and I know it."

"Mom." The boy sat in the chair beside the bed, never letting go of her hand.

"Honey, it's gonna be okay. I've been lying here thinking. Mr. Hollis came along at just the right time, and I'm very grateful."

"I'm so sorry." Zach bent his head, no longer able to look her in the eye.

"You're sorry? You've nothing to be sorry for, darling."

"I let him in." The boy was crying now and Leland felt like he was eavesdropping again, distinctly more uncomfortable than he'd been on the hotel patio an hour ago.

"He's your father, Zach. Of course you would let him inside."

"But Mom, I think I knew something was wrong. I should have been suspicious that he was using the games and iPad to convince me to let him in."

Leland inched silently toward the door, seconds from a clean get-away. He could feel the concern and care in the room even though he'd never experienced that acceptance with his own parents. Zach was going to be okay. His mother loved him. She didn't hate him for betraying her or letting his dad in their hotel room. The doctor was going to sew up Anna's arm. Max Mercado was going to jail. They were going to have a happily ever after . . . well, sort of.

"Wait, please," Anna called to Leland. "I really don't know how to thank you."

"You have already, I'll just be going." His back was to the door when the doctor breezed in, barely knocking.

"Hello, Mrs. Mercado. I'm Dr. Travis. I have your preliminary blood work. Mr. Mercado?" He shook Leland's hand but didn't give him a chance to answer or correct the mistaken assumption. "And your son?" He nodded to Zach.

He dove in without giving anyone a chance to answer. "I have a few questions. The first one is for you, Mrs. Mercado. Is there any chance you could be pregnant?"

Chapter Seven

ALL THE NOISE around her faded away. Anna started to shake her head, then stopped and closed her eyes. *Oh sweet Lord.* There hadn't been a snowball's chance in hell until this morning when she'd had sex with her soon to be ex-husband. "Only if God is out to get me," she murmured.

"Does that mean it's a possibly?'" Dr. Travis asked.

Extremely aware that her son was in the room and listening intently, along with Leland Hollis, who she really didn't know at all, she closed her eyes and nodded. "It's an extremely unlikely possibility but, yes, it's possible."

Anna imagined she could hear the blood coursing through her veins. An explanation was necessary, if not for the doctor, at least for her son and this stranger who'd become the next best thing to their guardian angel tonight.

"I haven't used birth control in years. My son was born only after multiple in vitro treatments. My husband

and I had no luck conceiving again. I assumed there was no need for preventative measures."

She focused on Zach sitting in the chair beside her. Speechless and mortified, his hand had gone slack in hers. That was just as well. She had no clue what to say. The doctor nodded and prattled on.

"I agree pregnancy is highly unlikely. I'll order a little more blood work and a urinalysis to figure out what caused your fainting spell. I'm thinking dehydration. But we'll add a couple more tests just in case. If you were pregnant, how far along would you be?"

She swallowed audibly. "One day."

Without a word Zach got up and stalked from the room, slamming the door behind him.

Dr. Travis seemed oblivious to the emotional land mine that had just detonated. "That's too early for us to tell."

"Do you want me to go after him?" Leland asked her.

She turned to look at him, completely unsure of what she'd find, surprised he was still in the room. Every man she knew would have made a beeline for the exit by this point. But no, he was standing at the door, staring at her. Not exactly as if she'd sprouted horns, but she was about to touch her forehead to make sure when he finally spoke.

"I'm going to wait outside to give you some privacy while you talk with the doctor. I'll be glad to find Zach and take you home when you're ready."

She nodded, uncertain of what she could say to make this all not sound so . . . awful.

Dr. Travis turned to him. "You're welcome to stay, Mr. Mercado. We're just going to sew up her arm."

Leland pinned the man with a frosty glare. "I'm not Mr. Mercado. I'm a neighbor who brought Zach here to the hospital."

"Ah," said the doctor, belatedly realizing he'd treaded into areas she didn't want to visit in front of her son and a neighbor. "I'm sorry, my mistake. I assumed."

"No problem," said Leland, his voice clipped. "I'll go find Zach."

She stared at him a moment, again at a loss for words. He'd had a perfect opportunity to bail on her and he hadn't, or at least not yet. "Thank you. I don't know how long I'll be."

"Don't worry. I'll be here when you're done." His tone toward her was considerably warmer than the one he'd used with the doctor. He closed the door softly as he left.

Anna took another glance at Dr. Travis and decided to lay her cards on the table. "I had sex with my estranged husband this morning. This evening he tried to kill me. That's how I got the cut on my arm. I'd rather have a lobotomy than a baby."

Obviously this ER doctor had heard everything but that particular story. His eyes widened and his bedside manner finally appeared. "I understand. Let's see what we can do to put your mind at ease about . . . things." He marked something on her chart. "And I'll take a look at that arm now as well."

THINKING HIS ANKLE was marginally better thanks to the painkiller, Leland was drinking bad coffee and ignoring a Jerry Springer episode on the lounge TV when Zach showed up in the waiting area. The boy sat across from him and put his head in his hands, looking like a kid who has just been told the truth about Santa Claus.

Leland knew when he took a seat here instead of heading to the parking lot that he was making a conscious decision to get involved. He still wasn't sure why he wasn't in his Jeep headed back to the hotel. He blamed the Vicodin he'd taken earlier for his lethargy. He'd had the chance to leave when he'd walked out of that exam room, yet he hadn't exited the building.

Something about Anna Mercado and her son resonated within him. He'd fought it, but this was becoming a losing battle. He'd recognized the expression in Zach's eyes when the doctor had asked his bombshell question.

"A baby?" Zach mumbled. "I can't freakin' believe this. Things are so complicated right now with their separation. How come she'd do that?"

Leland read the boy's face and recognized the wordless last question: Aren't I enough to love?

He stared at his feet and took a deep breath. *Jesus.* He was in so far over his head he was drowning, and there were no life ropes to be had.

He didn't possess the skill set or proper parental experience to deal with this, not to mention his own issues with similar baggage. What experience he did have made him more of a terrible warning than a shining example, but no one else was available, so he had to try something. For starters Zach's mother was nothing like his. He'd seen enough already to know the kid had a leg up on life with someone who cared as much as Anna did.

"Zach, you need to chill. The doctor thinks it's highly unlikely your mom is pregnant. That's just a question they have to ask every woman before they do certain tests. Besides she wouldn't love you any less, even if she did have a baby. So get that through your head. She'd do anything for you. Hell, she has from what I've seen."

The boy was silent and Leland filled the uncomfortable void with words. "Sometimes people get caught up in a situation and don't . . ."

He stopped. What did he say now? *"Your mom and dad did the deed, but it was just sex. She had no intention of getting knocked up?"*

Christ, he did not know what he was doing. So he was going to quit before he said something completely inappropriate to this boy, even if he had to shove his own shoe in his mouth. They sat in an awkward silence but apparently Zach wasn't ready to stop wrestling with the issue.

"I know she's been sad and lonely while I've been sick. They split up, so it kind of makes sense. I hated that they were getting a divorce. But that was before I knew what was really going on, that he would hurt her." Zach shook his head. "I still can't believe it."

"I imagine it's been difficult for her since your diagnosis. Sounds like she has been doing a lot on her own. Not everyone's mom loves them like that. So you think you could give yours a break?"

Zach was quiet, either unwilling or unable to engage.

Leland had no idea if the boy had heard anything he'd

said. For now, he was relieved the conversation was over but unsure if he'd helped the situation or hurt it. This was so not his kind of gig. As soon as he got Anna and Zach settled back in at the hotel, he was done.

Relieved that he'd come up with a workable exit strategy, he leaned back in his seat and pretended to watch the domestic train wreck on Springer. *How does one guy get three women pregnant while in prison?*

He was on his third cup of bad coffee and puzzling that biological conundrum when the nurse from earlier approached him. "Mrs. Mercado is ready to check out now. She was wondering if you were still here."

"Of course. I'll drive the car around to the entrance."

"We'll bring her out."

Zach looked up, unsure of where to go. Leland knew exactly how he felt. "Want to see if she needs anything? I can meet you with the car."

"Yeah, okay." And Zach was gone.

Whatever Leland had gotten himself into was about to begin, but it wasn't going to last long. He wasn't the boy's dad or the woman's husband. His neck itched just thinking about the unresolved mess that lay ahead for Anna and her son.

He had no obligation here, and that was a good thing. He had enough of his own drama to deal with, and this mess with the Mercados was something that could make Jerry Springer look tame. Grateful he wasn't going to be part of it for longer than it took to get everyone back to the hotel, he cranked his Jeep and headed for the ER entrance.

Chapter Eight

ANNA SAT WITH her back to the passenger door, facing Leland and Zach. It was so late, they'd decided to wait till morning to go to the police station and file her official statement. Beyond that no one was talking much. There was an uncomfortable stillness, and she didn't know how to break it.

She wasn't sure if Zach was angry, in shock, or in denial. This was confusing her on half a dozen levels, so it had to be blowing the boy's socks off. And Leland? She had no clue what he was thinking beyond getting back to the hotel and vaporizing.

They finished the drive in deathlike silence. She could practically hear crickets chirping. When they got to the Best Western, Zach helped her out of the car, despite his solemnity. Together they headed to the front desk only to be greeted by a very long line of folks coming off a tour bus in front of the hotel.

"I'm pretty sure they were going to put you in a new room, but things may have changed while we were at the ER," said Leland.

She nodded. "Blood and glass is probably a bit much for the night cleaning crew."

"I can go and get our things from Leland's room while y'all wait in the line," Zach offered.

"I can bring the luggage down," said Leland.

"No, it's just the one suitcase and my mom's purse. I'll do it," insisted Zach, obviously eager to not be hanging around his mother.

"Okay," nodded Leland, too tired to argue. "Here's the keycard."

Zach made a beeline for the stairs. Anna watched the fire exit door for a long time after her son pulled it shut behind him.

She dreaded turning to face Leland. She couldn't imagine what he was thinking—of her, the situation, or the mess he'd gotten himself into by befriending her. The kindest thing she could do to repay him would be to send him on his way.

Prepared to do just that, she took a deep breath. "I don't know how to thank you. You saved me."

"It's no problem. Like I said—"

She turned, interrupting him. "Don't. I can't imagine what you're thinking of this entire soap opera you've witnessed tonight."

They stood soundlessly until they were next in line. The night clerk was working alone, and his eyes lit up in recognition as Leland spoke to him.

"Ah, Mr. Hollis. Could you please have a seat in the lobby while I get these arrangements finalized?" The man nodded at Anna, taking in the bandage on her arm. "I understand you've been in the ER. Our computers are acting up. I don't want you to have to stand while you wait."

Leland nodded his thanks and guided Anna to the conversation area in front of a faux fireplace.

She took a deep breath before beginning. "I should be mortified about all this, and on one level I am. On the other hand, I'm so grateful you were there. I don't know what I would have done without your help. So I can't be sorry. As for the questions the doctor was asking—"

"That's none of my business."

"You're right, it's not your business. But I'd like to explain because . . . well, I'm not sure why exactly. They say confession is good for the soul, don't they?" She felt her smile tremble and hoped her expression wasn't as shaky-looking as she felt.

For some reason it was important to her that he hear this. Since she didn't expect to lay eyes on him again after tonight, her story felt anonymous. Like talking to the person beside you on an airplane and telling them things your best friend doesn't know.

He watched her with unnerving intensity, his eyes holding a green fire that should have been intimidating. She appreciated that he wasn't saying anything. This admission would be impossible with interruptions. She needed to speak the words quickly to get it over with. The problem was, she wasn't sure where to start. Diving in seemed the best option.

She took a deep breath before speaking. "First of all, I'm not pregnant."

When Leland's face didn't change with that declaration, she kept going. "After Zach was born, Max wanted another baby and initially I wanted to give him one. But after twelve years of fertility specialists . . ." Her voice trailed off as Leland's eyebrows rose.

"I know, it's a long time," she said, reading the questions so clearly in his puzzled expression. "Along the way, our marriage disintegrated. Max wasn't abusive, he just . . . disappeared."

"Had he ever hit you before tonight?"

"No. He yelled a lot, a whole lot, leading up to when he moved out a few months ago. But until today I'd never thought he'd try to hurt me. When he got his own place, our relationship got better. His leaving took the pressure off. I'm pretty sure he was seeing someone else. He'd had affairs even before Zach's diagnosis, but once he moved out it was 'good riddance.' By that time I didn't care. It was such a relief to have him gone."

Something about that seemed to bother Leland, but he didn't comment. Instead, he asked another question. "Why was he was searching for you here exactly?"

She huddled into the sofa before she said anything else. "I never explained. It sounds so unreal, and given the fantastical events of the evening, I wasn't sure how much more you would believe.

His piercing gaze never wavered. "I'm still here and

I'm listening." Both statements could be taken to mean he could leave or stop listening at any moment, but this was as good an invitation as she was going to get.

"Zach, Max and I were all together in Cancun, Mexico this morning. It was meant to be a treat for Zach before the surgery. The reason we're here in this hotel is that I overheard Max planning to stage a kidnapping where they took Zach away from the resort and killed me. From what Max was saying on the phone, I think the plan was to make it look like a cartel kidnapping.

"I didn't stop to think, I just did what I had to do. We couldn't leave without our passports, so—" She swallowed hard. "I went to bed with Max as if I'd overheard nothing. After . . . when he went to shower, I took Zach and got to the airport with our travel documents, Zach's meds, and a change of clothes." She tried to keep the agony out of her voice but Leland's discerning gaze made it clear she hadn't been successful.

"That must have been incredibly . . . disturbing," he said.

She barked a harsh laugh that she didn't expect Leland to understand. Having Max's hands on her after what she'd overheard him planning had been horrifying. What she'd imagined rape must be like. Except she'd had to act as if she was in ecstasy, when in reality she'd been so repulsed she was worried about throwing up again.

When Max had been inside her, she'd focused on her plan to escape. She'd made lists in her head of what she'd pack, the order in which she'd collect everything. She'd focused on getting to the airport. Her fear of flying had seemed the least of her worries. As soon as the bathroom door closed behind him, she'd been out of the bed like a shot.

She stared at Leland and nodded. "Yes, it was difficult." Her voice didn't even break on the words.

"You haven't been to the police yet?" His question was more of a statement.

She took another deep breath, anxious to move on. "No, for the reasons we talked about earlier with the transplant. Max is very influential here. I can't risk anything happening with Zach's place on the list. My plan is to get Zach into the hospital tomorrow, then deal with his father's issues."

Leland made a non-committal "hmm" sound.

"We'd fought about where to do the treatment a while back. Max wanted to do it in Mexico because organs are more readily available there. I didn't want to because I think the doctors and care are better here. Max swore he'd given up on that plan, but given tonight's events I'm not so sure he ever did. Why would he want Zach back in Mexico now? Right before his LVAD operation?" The thought of her son being in a Mexican hospital for such a complicated operation was more frightening than her being in bed with Max this morning.

She stopped, no longer wanting to reveal details of her life and failed marriage to Leland who sat intently watching her. He'd been nodding from time to time as she spoke, but now he was silent.

Her heart rate punched up and her hands were sweating. Why had she ever thought she needed to explain all this? He had to be planning how fast he could leave after he got her and Zach into a new room.

She watched for a reaction as he leaned back in his chair, breaking eye contact to study the television that was playing a late edition of the news. "That's quite a story," he finally said.

"Do you believe me?" she asked.

"Does it matter?" His question wasn't accusing, but it rankled as he studied her face again with that unchanging fervor.

The shock of the question sank in, but she didn't have time to pull it apart before he continued. "For the record, I do believe you. But I'm not the important one here. Zach is. He needs to know as much as you can tell him, for starters that you're not pregnant and as much of the truth about you and your husband's separation and what you overheard in Cancun as you can share. He's very concerned."

Leland was right. She knew he was, but his words still irritated her. "What do I tell him? His father, despite his many faults, loves him. How do I tell Zach that Max wants me dead? I won't be able to take those words back once I say them." She felt lost, and part of her wanted nothing more than for someone to tell her what to do. Another part of her wanted to stand on her own and to be left the hell alone.

Leland gave her a calculating look. *He's not sure how much to say*, she thought.

"Zach's old enough to recognize your marriage is falling apart. He told me as much tonight. Lying about that will only give the information more power than it has. So talk to him. You don't have to go into detail about everything to tell Zach that you love him and would do anything for him." He leaned forward, putting both feet firmly on the floor. "What's the harm in your son knowing that?"

His words surprised her. She tilted her head to look at him and wondered exactly what Leland did as a DEA agent. "You ever think about going into family therapy?"

He laughed—a booming, hearty sound—so rich, deep, and unexpected that it resonated inside her. She actually felt the echoes bouncing around in her chest.

"No, ma'am. I've never thought about that kind of job change before."

"So what is it you do exactly?" she pressed.

"Nothing you want to hear about tonight. We'll talk about me next time." He smiled and she noted the lines of exhaustion around his eyes.

The hotel clerk walked over with her new card keys. Their room would be on the second floor, next door to Leland's.

"I wonder where our personal bell hop is?" he asked.

The calm that had been slowly unfurling inside her chest fled. "He should be back by now." She looked around, intent on not overreacting after the drama-filled day she'd had.

"It's alright. He's probably playing a video game. Let's go up. We'll check on him and get you moved," said Leland.

The elevator door *dinged*, but Zach wasn't there. Leland opened the fire exit door before stepping into the elevator car. The stairwell was empty as well.

The first lick of real fear shimmied up her spine. What had Max said? *He'd have his son back one way or the other.*

Watching the numbers tick by on the elevator, Anna's cool demeanor fled and her head was awash in "what ifs." They stepped off the elevator, and she hurried down the corridor beside Leland, scared to death of what she'd find.

"I'm sure he's just kicking back up here in my room for a moment. It's been a tense evening," he offered.

She didn't believe that and wondered if Leland really did either. At the end of the hall, it was obvious something was wrong before they got to the room. Leland's door was wide open but hanging askew on the wooden frame. Bile rose in the back of her throat as she rushed past him, stumbling into the trashed room.

Her eyes darted around the space. She couldn't breathe. Video games and the iPad from Max's package were again scattered over the floor along with Zach's iPhone and the clothing from their carry-on. A broken chair lay on its side. This was déjà vu.

She stared at the chaos, her mind refusing to accept what her eyes were taking in. Her emotions caught up when she spied a wet smear of blood marring the white Formica dining table. Beside the stain lay a folded sheet of paper with her name boldly printed in block letters.

She felt herself come apart as her breath caught in her

lungs. Pushing past Leland, she stopped in the middle of the room. Her knees buckled and she sank to the floor. Squeezing her eyes shut did little to block the rising horror.

Nothing could hide the truth.

"Oh my god, they've taken Zach."

Chapter Nine

LELAND STUDIED THE room. It was easier than watching Anna try to beat back overwhelming fear and panic. Her arms were crossed around her middle as she silently rocked forward and backward on her knees. He didn't touch her as she fought to pull it together. That would have been another mistake to pile on top of the boatload of major errors he'd made this evening.

He didn't want to believe the painfully obvious himself. The boy had been taken and had put up a hell of a fight on the way out.

How long had he been gone? Ten minutes? Five minutes? Thirty seconds? Who had taken him?

Max Mercado as the culprit seemed a stretch given his current location—cooling his heels in jail. But hearing Anna's story, the Tequila King appeared to be the prime candidate. Max was richer than God and had powerful connections.

It would have been comforting to think Mercado had the boy if it wasn't for that blood on the table. The man wasn't likely to harm his own son. Yet Mercado had vowed that he'd have the boy one way or the other. Did that mean dead or alive?

Leland moved forward and leaned down to examine the note. A smudged patch of blood marred the white surface of what appeared to be ordinary copy paper. He carefully lifted the folded note using a pen. It was probably too much to hope for fingerprints, but you never knew.

The message was written in blue ink and block letters—direct and to the point.

We have the boy. If you want to see him again, bring $750,000 to the Cantina El Flamenco in Baxtla, Estado de Veracruz-Llave before 7 PM Saturday evening. No police or the boy dies.

Jesus. Saturday was tomorrow. He glanced at his watch. Seven PM was only a little over eighteen hours from now. Baxtla was in the middle of freaking nowhere, at least 140 miles from Mexico City and smack in the middle of cartel territory.

Was this really Max Mercado's doing? It would have to have been set up before the man was arrested. There was no way Anna's husband could have arranged it otherwise. But why do it at all?

Max doted on his son. Since the boy was ill and needed a heart transplant, taking him seemed a sure way to kill him. Kidnapping made no sense, but the idea of its being an unhappy coincidence made Leland's neck itchy. So far, Max had been too involved for this not to be connected as well.

"Anna?" He knelt down to help her up. She was still rocking back and forth on the floor, but at his address she stopped moving, even though she kept her eyes tightly closed. He took her hand and eased her to her feet. Her fingers were freezing. He didn't know what to do. He'd never thought of himself as being good at comforting people, so he simply held her hand.

Obviously this was killing her. But Leland couldn't think about that. He needed to focus on who to call for help in getting Zach back. Part of that process was figuring out what exactly this had to do with the Mercados.

Did they owe money to the wrong people? Had Max reneged on some kind of deal, or had he orchestrated all of this? Why hadn't Leland considered that Max might send someone else? Had the Vicodin he took before leaving the hotel chilled him out to the point of idiocy? What had he been thinking to let Zach come up here alone?

There was another reason the boy might have been taken, but he didn't want to tell Anna about that possibility either.

Could Zach's kidnapping be related to his cartel testimony at the Vega trial? The boy *was* taken from Leland's own room. It was terribly suspicious. He needed to tell her, but to do it now, when she was in such distress seemed cruel.

Still, what if this was his fault?

God, a part of Leland wanted out and away from all this. He wasn't willing or able to take on another life and death situation. He'd thought he was done with that, leaving that life and obligation behind when he'd signed the DEA resignation letter just a few hours ago.

Another part of him wanted to do whatever it took to find Zach. Having stopped Max's rampage earlier, Leland felt responsible for the boy's and his mother's safety, regardless of whether this had to do with his own cartel testimony or with Max's possible shady business connections.

But Leland had failed the last time he got so deeply involved. He'd made mistakes, bad judgment calls. People had died as a result.

Clinging to his hand, Anna stood beside him and read the note. Silent tears streamed down her face. He knew when she'd finished reading because she let go of his fingers and turned without a word, hurrying to the bathroom.

He could hear her vomiting into the toilet and waited until he heard the commode flush and water running in the sink before he walked into the bathroom.

She was rinsing her mouth, her face a splotchy red color and her nose running. She didn't "cry pretty" like some women. That was vaguely reassuring.

Before his eyes she pulled herself back together. It was astonishing to see that kind of strength and control. That she was even functioning after the shock of this on top of the day she'd had was remarkable.

She sniffled once more and wiped her face with a towel

before speaking. "This is surreal. I've always known kidnapping was a possibility in Mexico. But here in Dallas? Why would they come after us here? They had no way of knowing where we even were unless . . ."

"Unless what?" he asked.

She pulled in a deep breath. "It keeps coming back to Max, doesn't it? Could he have set this up when he was searching for us?"

She stared at the letter, then back at him.

"It would have been tough but not impossible," he said.

"Where is Baxtla exactly?" she asked.

"In the mountains. It's a tight timeline."

She nodded. "How did they find us?"

"The whole world knew Max was here a couple of hours ago. Do you know of anyone who wants to hurt your family?"

"Here in the US, no. In Mexico, everyone's scared of the cartels. It's why we have personal security."

That was true enough. To be wealthy and live in Mexico at the present time was to be a target.

She shuddered. "Last year the accountant for some friends of ours was kidnapped. The couple owned several factories in Monterrey. Local authorities were no help. Five hours after they discovered the kidnapping, the accountant was dead. My friends packed overnight bags and left the country for good in a private plane."

She worried her lower lip as she spoke. "They left everything. Their home, their livelihood, their lives. They'll never go back."

"That was a wise course of action," said Leland. "Kidnappings are as common in Mexico as breaking and entering in the US. It's become a business. The accountant will be taken for his knowledge of the owner's finances. After the financial information is accessed, the owner or another family member is also taken and the kidnappers are able to ask for a ransom, down to the penny, that can be liquidated from the company's assets. The police are no longer trusted because in many cases they're in on it. Kidnapping is the quickest way to raise cash."

She was staring straight ahead when she answered. "It's why we moved back to the US."

"Were there any specific threats against your husband or family at the time of your move?

"Not that I know of."

"What about right now?" he asked.

"I have no idea. After this afternoon, I don't know Max anymore. I don't know anything anymore." He heard the defeat in her tone and studied her, unsure of how much to share or of how much she could handle.

He kept coming back to the fact that the boy was taken from *his* hotel room. Leland was a DEA agent who had testified in a huge case involving cartel evidence. There were more than a few people who wouldn't mind causing him or those associated with him harm.

Maybe this wasn't about the Mercados at all. Maybe it was about Leland and his issue with the Vegas. Maybe Zach had just gotten in the way.

Still, that all seemed a huge coincidence based on what

had happened earlier with Max. Besides, the ransom note was addressed specifically to Anna. The Vegas knew enough about Leland to know he didn't have a spare $750,000 lying around.

Try as he might to convince himself otherwise, it didn't matter who was responsible for Zach's kidnapping in considering whether or not to help Anna get her boy back. Now it was all about *how* to get him back. Leland's rescue tendency was taking over, despite his initial concerns about getting involved. And his neck was still itching.

"What do we do now?" asked Anna.

"Can you get the money?" He spoke at the same time. It was a blunt query, but they were past niceties.

"I don't know. I think Max froze our joint bank accounts. I couldn't use my card this afternoon at the ATM, but I didn't try face-to-face at a bank. It could have just been my debit card affected. If I can get to our accounts, I can get the cash."

He glanced at his watch. "It's after ten PM."

"Our bank has extended phone hours since they're main office is located on the west coast. I'll go online first, then call." Her voice was scarcely a whisper as she stared at the blood on the table.

He could tell by her tone that she was thinking too much. He picked up his laptop along with her oversized handbag and hustled her out. "We're going to your new room. I have an idea."

She didn't protest but moved with him next door. He wanted to leave his room as undisturbed as possible until he could look things over. The area might need to be processed for evidence at some point.

Plus, he had to get her away from that blood on the table before it really sunk in how much she'd lost. She was holding things together now, but he suspected that was only because she wasn't processing—as evidenced when she automatically handed over her card key when asked.

She sat on the edge of the bed in her new room as he passed her his laptop. Her cold fingers brushed against his. Without something to keep her mind occupied, she was going to be a mess.

"Let's see what you can find out," he encouraged.

As long as he could keep her focused, she'd be all right. But once they ran out of forward momentum he could see her cratering fast. She hadn't broken down for more than a few moments, and under the circumstances he didn't suppose there was any typical reaction for having your child kidnapped. In the same situation, personally he'd settle for numbness.

He looked at her head bent over the computer. She was worrying her bruised bottom lip again as she typed in the website and password. He'd seen her tentatively dab at it with her tongue twice already, and he got a punch to the gut watching her. Naturally his body decided now was the time to notice. For a split second he imagined his mouth on her lips and a few other places he had no business going. He turned his back in the hope of stopping the wayward thoughts, but that wasn't terribly effective.

She pulled out her cell phone and made a call. Moments later she had news. "I can't get into our joint savings or checking accounts, but I can access our home equity line of credit."

She shrugged. "Max set it up right after we got married. I'm still listed as a co-owner of the house, so I can withdraw funds, too. I bet he was online and in a hurry when he shut everything down from Cancun. You can't close access to this line of credit from a computer. He must have forgotten about the home equity account. The maximum I can withdraw is $800,000."

Leland took a moment to process that. $800,000 in a home equity line of credit? That was a far cry from the paltry reserve in his starter home.

"How do you get to the money?" he asked.

"It's like a checking account. I can transfer the cash anywhere I want. It's just a matter of telling them how much equity I'd like to move. I set up a personal checking account exclusively in my name when Max and I separated. Her fingers flew over the keys and she talked to the banker a few moments longer before ending the call.

Her voice was strong as she ended the call. "Okay, I've transferred the $800,000 to my individual account."

Stunned by the amount of money they were discussing and not too proud to admit it, he stared a moment before answering. "Really?"

Seemingly unaffected, she nodded and kept typing. Suddenly she stopped and looked at him. "I know, it's kind of scary, huh?"

Leland shook his head. "It solves the ransom funding issue, so I think it's awesome. When can we pick up the cash?" he asked.

"In the morning." She worried that lip again and his throat went dry.

Unable to speak as his body tightened a notch, he nodded. He had to get over this—whatever it was—now. Why of all times was his libido waking tonight and with such a vengeance? He needed to figure out the next step but wasn't sure he had one.

While he might feel out of his depth on the kidnapping, he knew one person who wouldn't be. Gavin was going to hear from him sooner than either of them had expected. Hopefully his friend could make sense of this and get Leland out of the middle of it.

MOMENTS AGO, WALKING down the hotel hallway to her "new" room, the sounds had been muffled and Anna had felt as if she were wading through molasses. She kept telling herself this wasn't real. It couldn't be.

Maybe if she told herself that lie enough, everything would be okay.

After making the account transfers, Leland encouraged her to take a shower and brought her suitcase from his room. Getting cleaned up seemed as good an idea as any.

Her new room was handicap accessible with a shower wand that could be moved up and down. She turned the water as hot as she could stand and let it pound on her lower back. It was more difficult than she bargained for to keep her injured arm dry even with the handheld shower.

Steam rose around her face, making breathing a

challenge as well. She didn't realize tears were streaming down her cheeks until she turned off the tap. Frustration and fear had won, making her cry even harder.
She pressed a towel against her mouth, desperate to pull
herself together and not scream aloud.

Zach was gone. She had no idea if the people who had
him knew how to care for him. He must be so frightened,
and that was the last thing his beleaguered heart needed.

They'd threatened to kill him if she didn't cooperate.
Max had attacked her with a golf club and threatened to
kill her. Had that all happened just today?

This morning she'd been on a beach in Cancun, sip-
ping a margarita and considering the impropriety of
having sex with her estranged husband. Tonight she was
in a hotel room in Dallas trusting a stranger to get her
son back from kidnappers. It all sounded like the plot of
a bad Lifetime Television movie.

She had to pull herself together. She was no good to
Zach like this, but try as she might, the tears wouldn't stop.

She wrapped the towel around herself and slathered
on hotel body lotion in an effort to do something normal.
The cream smelled like peaches. She shook her head in
despair. Zach loved peaches.

She threw the bottle in the trash with a bit more force
than necessary and brushed her teeth, slipping into the
silky black sleep pants and matching lace camisole Leland
had retrieved from the other room. She wished for a robe
and took care to put a bra on underneath the cami. The
look without it was too sexy. She'd bought these pajamas
for the trip to Mexico, her little rebellion.

She hadn't planned to be sharing a room with Max but imagined she'd see him at some point or other wearing the slinky loungewear. More of a *look what you're missing* gesture, the joke was certainly on her, and her pettiness was coming back to bite her now.

She only had one change of clothes left. The bloodstains on her shorts and shirt from today were extensive but, hoping for the best, she tried soaking them in cold water anyway. Brushing her hair, she caught a glimpse of herself in the mirror.

Her nose was swollen, and her face was covered with bright red splotches. Tears continued to stream silently down her cheeks. She looked like hell, but that was the least of her worries.

God, she couldn't do this. She wasn't strong enough. She was at the end of her proverbial rope. The fraying knot she'd been hanging on to for the past sixteen hours had unraveled this afternoon, and she was now in free-fall.

Who was Leland Hollis and why was he staying to help her? It made no sense. Nonetheless, she was trusting a man she hadn't known four hours ago to keep her from hitting rock bottom—to save her and Zach.

Was this insanity? Leland had suddenly become her lifeline, and the man could be gone when she walked out of this bathroom.

She wouldn't blame him for that. Why should he stay? Everything he'd encountered so far involving her had been trouble.

But he'd said he was going to help. She clung to that hope and, at the same time, she hated being so vulnerable.

Would she ever be able to stop crying?

The room was quiet when she finally eased the door open. Was he still here, or had he come to his senses and left?

She heard the low rumble of his voice and let out the breath she hadn't realized she was holding. The patio door was open. He was sitting on one of the cushioned chairs outside with his booted foot propped up, talking on the phone.

Good. She didn't want him to see her weeping like this. A trivial, insignificant worry in the midst of all this, but there it was. She no longer cared what it said about her to think such a thing. Her pride was now part of the past. Nothing mattered but Zach.

She couldn't quite make out what Leland was saying but decided it didn't matter. She was physically and emotionally wiped, wanting nothing more than oblivion to take her away as she lay on the bed and curled under the covers. In the stillness, his low Southern voice flowed over her like a quiet stream, soft but distinct.

"Point taken. But honestly, I'm not in the middle. I'm trying to back out as fast as I can."

She held her breath, all thoughts of not caring about what he said forgotten.

"No. I have no idea if she's telling the truth, but she's not faking her son's disappearance."

She lay perfectly still during a long pause, her mind racing with the possibilities of what those words meant.

"I realize she's trouble. So I'll be careful and quick, in and out. I appreciate the help and the . . . advice."

What did he mean? She'd thought it couldn't get worse. Did he really believe she was lying about this? What if he decided to leave? She had to convince him to stay and help her.

She despised the feelings of weakness that continued to swamp her, but she couldn't do this on her own. Her pride at being self-sufficient was no longer an issue. She needed Leland Hollis to get Zach back, and she'd do whatever she had to do to convince him to stay.

She couldn't consider what that made her. Zach's safety trumped everything.

She heard him end the call and braced herself. She'd already been through this once today with Max. *Was it just this morning?*

Her stomach didn't even twist this time at the thought of what she was about to do.

Chapter Ten

"DOES TROUBLE JUST FOLLOW you around?" Gavin's voice was tinged with disbelief and something else Leland couldn't name. But he didn't mind. This was a true clusterfuck. He leaned back in the still damp patio chair, explaining what had been going on since he and Gavin had spoken a couple of hours before.

"You need a freaking keeper, Hollis."

Leland nodded his head in miserable agreement with the assessment.

"Would you explain again how this woman's son ended up in your hotel room? And I'm not just busting your ass, it's important."

Leland walked through the story again, relieved he'd gotten Anna out of his room and into this new one. His reasoning had been two-fold. One, to get her away from the blood on the dining table that was likely her son's and two, to keep from imagining her in his own king-size bed.

As ill-timed as that last idea was, he was still struggling to keep images of her bee stung lips and where he'd like her to put them out of his head while he talked to Gavin. At the moment she was in the shower and he was doing his damnedest not to imagine her there with the water splashing over her lush body.

"I'd like to get the ransom note analyzed," Leland said, pulling himself back from the shower fantasy. "I doubt there will be anything there but you never know."

"My people can take care of that. Bring it with you when you come to the office. I agree there probably aren't any prints, but we need to make sure. Give it to Nick Donovan. He can do it through our channels. No one will know."

Gavin gave Leland phone numbers and directions to AEGIS's security offices. "You sure you don't want to come in now?"

Leland considered it as he glanced at his watch. It was almost midnight.

"No. The damage has been done. They've taken her son. What else can they do? Tonight she just needs some rest. We'll be there first thing in the morning." He took a ragged breath. "I shouldn't have let that kid out of my sight."

"Why? Are you psychic? The crazy father was in jail. None of the Vegas knew you were there. There was no reason to think the boy was in danger. Is guilt the reason you're jumping into this with both feet?"

"I'm not jum—" Leland was doing his best not to jump in.

Gavin *humpfed*, interrupting an ill-advised rant. "This is not your fault, but you're diving into it headfirst. Do you feel responsible for the woman because you saved her earlier or because you think you should have been able to predict the kidnapping like some carnival fortune teller?"

Leland took a beat and drew another deep breath. He didn't want to answer that. Didn't want to even acknowledge the idea, although Gavin was only half right. If this had nothing to do with him, Leland was free to walk away once he dropped Anna with Gavin's people. He wouldn't have to be involved anymore.

And why was that so appealing?

Because he was scared to be involved, to care too much. Caring made you vulnerable. The memory of Ellis Colton's devastated face swam before Leland's eyes.

He wanted to fix this mess because he hadn't done the right thing by Colton's family. The hell of it was, Leland could spend his whole life atoning for that screw-up and never make up for it.

The bathroom door opened with a slight creak, but he didn't look over his shoulder.

Gavin kept talking. "I'm not getting all preachy, but I am worried for you. This afternoon you had no idea what you were going to do tomorrow, and now you're in the middle of a kidnap rescue."

"Point taken." Leland lowered his voice. "But honestly, I'm not in the middle. I'm trying to back out as fast as I can."

"Could have fooled me. Just remember that woman is damn lucky you were there. She'd be in the hospital—or worse—right now if you hadn't been. Do you really think she's telling the truth?"

"No. I have no idea if she's telling the truth, but she's not faking her son's disappearance." *No one's that good an actor.*

"Of course." There was a pause, and he heard Gavin take an audible breath in the silence. Leland pictured his friend on the other end of the phone, pacing as he spoke. "Man, I'm not saying don't feel, but don't let it cloud your judgment. It could get you dead."

Leland almost smiled. "I realize she's trouble. So I'll be careful and quick, in and out. I appreciate the help and the . . . advice."

"The advice is worth what you paid for it. Besides I'm counting on your coming to work for me when this is all over."

Leland laughed softly.

"Take care of yourself and call my people if you need anything before then. Nick's good, a former SEAL. You can trust him."

"Will do. Kiss Kat for me." Leland hung up and sat for a moment before moving back inside.

His ankle hurt like a bitch. Running down those stairs earlier had not helped. He'd sell his soul for a couple of Vicodin, but that would slow down his response time and seemed like a terrible idea with everything going on. He walked in and closed the patio door behind him.

Anna was curled in a fetal position, one very bare shoulder peeking out from under the covers. He could tell from her breathing she wasn't asleep. Her body shuddered occasionally as she lay there.

She'd been crying. He figured she'd had the time to really think about all that had happened today when she stopped to shower and now the full implications were hitting her.

He was at a loss as to what to do or say. Patting her shoulder seemed insufficient and just plain wrong as there was so much skin showing. Yet he couldn't stand by knowing she was hurting and do nothing. He walked into the bathroom to get her a damp washcloth and caught a glimpse of himself in the mirror.

I'm about to screw up. About to get way more involved than I ever intended.

He sat on the side of the bed and slid the Ruger out of his shoulder holster, placing it on the bedside table. Leaning forward, he dabbed at her cheek with the damp towel. She turned over to stare into his face with a pain-filled expression.

Her eyes were wet. She still wasn't a pretty crier, but it didn't matter. Something in her gaze caught hold of him. He swiped at her temple with the cloth and before he realized it was probably not appropriate, he'd reached out to brush a lock of hair from her forehead.

What the hell am I doing?

She reached up to touch his wrist. Surely she was going to bat his fingers away, but her devastated gaze slowly changed to something else as she put her other hand on his shoulder.

Whoa. This doesn't seem right.

She pulled him down to her and settled that mouth he'd been trying to banish from his imagination against his lips. He immediately stopped thinking about right or wrong. And when she slid her tongue past his and pressed her body firmly against his chest, his mind completely disconnected.

It had been a helluva long time since he'd been laid. His job and the subsequent craziness of his lifestyle had conspired recently to ruin his social life. That was the only thing that could explain why he so readily slid his arms around Anna, bringing her closer still. All he could feel was her warm, bare skin. Even the scent of the cheap hotel soap was erotic on this woman.

She was kissing him, but he knew she couldn't mean it. This behavior had to be a coping mechanism for her grief. And that was pretty much his last coherent thought as the blood rushed away from his brain.

Unfortunately, his body didn't recognize the sensation of her chest molding against his as a form of pain management and responded in a way that left no doubt as to whether or not he was attracted to her.

She ran her hand down his back and across his ass as he tried to remember why he cared that she'd been intimate with her husband only hours ago. If he wanted to help her find Zach, this was exactly the wrong thing for him to be doing.

He told himself she was fragile. She was hurting. Then she whispered one word in his ear. "Please."

After that his body didn't care about her vulnerability anymore. His dick had no conscience, but *he* should. He knew he should.

He started to pull away and she murmured, "Help me."

He froze as she kissed him again, taking it deeper this time with a kind of desperation that he knew had absolutely nothing to do with him and everything to do with finding her son. Still, when she tugged his bottom lip into her mouth and pressed herself against his erection, his objections melted like ice cubes on a hot July sidewalk. All he could concentrate on was how good she felt underneath him and how good he was going to make them both feel, if he could just get his mind to turn off and not wonder how they were both going to react when the fireworks were over.

He swept his tongue against her lips and pulled back to look in her eyes. "Are you sure about this?" he asked.

She didn't reply. Her eyes were closed as she raked her fingernails lightly up his back again.

"Anna, I don't think . . ."

He touched her chin, and she stopped, opening her eyes to stare straight at him. "Don't think. Just make love to me."

His body tightened and he held her gaze as she started unbuttoning his shirt. His hands were on either side of her head as he continued to study her face. Her eyes were no longer filled with grief, but rather a look that he mistook for longing until she got his shirt all the way untucked.

Ripping the final buttons off in her haste, she tugged on her bottom lip again with her teeth. If he hadn't been staring into her face he would have missed it. The small cut from earlier started bleeding again as her hands went to his belt. And like a bucket of ice water over his head, that stopped him cold.

"Hang on," he kissed her injured mouth softly, trying to take her aggressive frenzy down a notch.

But she was done with patience and done with talking. She reached up and pulled her camisole off, revealing a black lacy bra that made Leland's throat go dry. Her breasts pushed at the top of the cups. He longed to run a finger across the slope of her chest, but he sat back on one knee instead and balanced his booted foot on the ground—straddling her and looking his fill at her fantasy-inducing figure before he put a stop to this insanity.

She shuddered under his gaze and he almost ignored the niggling doubts. It would be so easy to reach forward, undo the bra clasp, and finish what they'd started. He knew in his gut it was wrong. Her gaze was unmistakable now that he recognized it. It wasn't lustful passion he was seeing reflected in her eyes, it was . . . resignation.

Running his palms over the tops of her fingers, he pressed the backs of her hands down into the mattress to hold her still. She was gorgeous, lush, and giving a pretty good impression that she wanted to be screwed.

But the expression on her face was a fairly obvious clue that it wasn't because she *wanted* him. She *needed* him to help her get Zach back. This was payment for his services to be rendered at a later date.

From her actions earlier he knew she'd do anything to get her son back. Just like she'd done with Max earlier today. She'd been backed into a corner then, and she must feel backed into a corner now. That unpleasant thought took hold, and the knowledge should have cooled his passion right away, but his blood was still pumping south and his body hadn't caught up to his brain yet.

This was how she would make sure Leland stayed with her to get the job done. The devil on his shoulder shouted that he could ignore her ulterior motive. Take what she was offering and not concern himself with *why* she was offering. Hell, she was expecting him to fuck her. She'd practically begged him to.

He could probably even make her forget about her wretched circumstances for a little while. But he knew she'd regret lowering herself to this afterward, and on top of everything else the woman was facing he couldn't let her deal with that kind of self-loathing, too. Particularly as he was still trying to figure out how to leave her with Gavin's people tomorrow and let them handle it. Having sex with her under those circumstances would make him an incredible asshole.

"Anna." He tamped down the bitterness in his tone, frustrated with himself on several levels and disappointed that she thought sleeping with him was necessary to secure his help. "There's nothing I want more at this moment than to make love to you."

He pressed himself into her so there could be no doubt about that statement and heard only regret in his own voice. Obviously she heard it too. Her expression transformed from grim determination to extreme embarrassment.

"But I can't. I'll hold you and stay up with you all

night, but I won't let you use sex as some kind of bargaining tool. If I did, I wouldn't be able to help you later. You'd be regretting what's happened here and distance yourself from me. If we're going to get Zach back, I need all of you on my side."

He knew he was right in stopping this insanity when the first thing she said was, "You'll stay and . . . help me?"

He nodded. *We.* He'd said it. *If we're going to get Zach back.*

Her blue eyes filled, but she didn't deny his earlier accusation as she worried that lower lip that had worked on him so earlier. He swallowed his chagrin.

After all that had happened tonight, he couldn't believe that she thought so little of him. But, of course, she didn't really know him. She didn't realize how her low and apparently correct opinion of him burned.

He'd like to think she was completely off-base. But realizing what he'd been thinking moments earlier about leaving her with Gavin's people, she had cause to be concerned. This had been about her trying to secure his help. Sex would have bound him to her. Would have obligated him to help her. To not leave until she'd gotten Zach back.

If she only knew. The promise of sex wasn't what had convinced him to help. The reality that she'd been willing to do anything to save her son had been what flipped him. She'd been willing to have sex with a virtual stranger.

She was desperate to save her boy. He could forgive her that. He took one last long look and kissed her forehead before raising himself up off her.

His actions would have been a noble thing if he hadn't

just caught himself in a huge lie. He didn't want her to rely on him, to need him.

He didn't want anyone doing that.

He didn't want Zach's kidnapping to have anything to do with him because part of him still longed to walk away as soon as he deposited her with AEGIS. But that wasn't happening now, he was here for the duration. Even so, the knowledge didn't stop the wanting.

The only solution was to disconnect his emotion from the situation. And that didn't make him noble, it made him a pragmatist.

Still, he hadn't been lying to her when he'd said making love to her like this would ensure that he'd be no help as she tried to find her son. As it stood, once he got up from the bed she'd be pushing him so far away, he was going to need a bus ticket to get back to where they were now. But he couldn't help that. They'd deal with the consequences of the failed seduction later.

"I'm sorry," she said, crossing her hands over her chest. He stood, hiding a grimace of pain from his ankle, and turned his back to let her rearrange her clothing. He buttoned his own shirt as best he could, leaving it untucked since the front was hopelessly wrinkled anyway.

"I was wrong to throw myself at you."

He shook his head, and stood up, stumbling a bit over his boot. "There's nothing to apologize for. Grief and fear are overpowering emotions."

She stared at him, profound sadness filling those deep blue eyes.

It wasn't that I didn't enjoy it. But he didn't say that out loud. He didn't say anything that he really wanted to: what had been in his heart before he sat down at her bedside.

I was going to stay and help you regardless. I wasn't leaving. You didn't have to do this.

No. Saying that would only make her feel worse and he'd said enough already. It was probably best to leave her alone and get himself another shirt from the room next door.

Despite his many misgivings, he was staying. And she would most likely think he was a son of a bitch before this was all over, once she figured out Zach's kidnapping could have been because of Leland's involvement with the cartels.

Still, he was sticking. They'd go to the AEGIS office and he would help until the boy was back with his mother or they'd found Zach's body. Whether or not he'd survive the latter after his experience with the Coltons scared the hell out of him, but he was sticking anyway.

"I'll be back in a few minutes," he said, pulling the door closed behind him.

Leland walked next door cussing himself six ways to Sunday. Had there been a way he could have stopped things from going so far?

Maybe. If someone had poured ice water down his pants.

But he wasn't a saint by any stretch of the imagination, and sex hadn't been on his agenda in longer than he cared to contemplate. He'd stopped things with Anna as soon as he was able, but that didn't prevent him from feeling crappy about the circumstances.

He opened his room, planning to grab his clothes and take them next door. Not knowing the situation, he couldn't leave Anna alone for long. The door swung open and he stopped at the threshold. The room was dark and he'd left a light on. The hair on the back of his neck rose as he reached for his gun. His fingers touched an empty holster.

Shit. His Ruger wasn't there. It was still sitting on Anna's bedside table next door. He been so distracted by the derailed sex, he'd forgotten to pick it up before he left.

Hell, his dick might just be the death of him.

He swung back into the hallway flattening his back on the wall beside the doorframe.

What was he going to do now?

Chapter Eleven

LELAND STOOD WITH his back against the wall, considering his options. Someone had been in his room since he'd moved Anna next door. They could still be there.

He wasn't sure *who* this whole kidnapping thing was about. Him or the Mercados? But at this point what else could the kidnappers possibly want?

A chair creaked in the gloom behind him, and he caught the familiar whiff of distinctive cigar smoke. Letting out the breath he'd been holding, he peered around the corner to see a cheroot's glowing tip in the darkness.

"Hosea Alvarez, what the hell are you doing here?" Leland flipped on the light and shut the door behind him as he stumped into the room, relieved and pissed at the same time.

"Is that any way to greet your best informant?" The voice was heavily accented and cocky. Just like Hosea.

"I repeat. What are you doing here?" demanded Leland.

"Just checking on my amigo and stopping by to give a little friendly advice on a mutual acquaintance."

"How did you find me?" asked Leland.

With his ear to the underbelly of crime in the city, Hosea was a gun-for-hire for those on the shady side of legal activity in Dallas. He'd previously worked for the Vegas, but after a stint at Huntsville he'd found less lethal and more legal ways of making money. Leland suspected the man knew where the bodies were buried for more than the Vega cartel.

He had been one of Leland's best informants for the past five years. While they weren't exactly friends, he certainly trusted Hosea more than his other sources.

"After the events of the evening, your location is not exactly uncommon knowledge. A little bird told me where to find you. I gotta say: As a safe house, this place sucks." Hosea shook the ash from his cigar into the empty scotch glass from earlier.

Leland ignored his purposeful jab and focused on the important information in Hosea's commentary. "Ernesto Vega's people?"

"Surprisingly, no. It wasn't anyone connected with Ernesto. At least, not any longer. Besides, now that they've seen how your testimony went at trial, I don't believe the Vegas are inclined to harm you. In fact, Ernesto wanted me to offer you a job. He thought you might be looking for one after today. I don't think he was completely joking."

"Right." Leland snorted. No way he'd believe that.

Ernesto Vega would just as soon ice Leland as look at him. He'd cost the cartel too much in lost product. Ernesto's brother Cesar had threatened to kill Leland's extended family the last time he'd busted a shipment.

Leland had gotten that comforting tidbit directly from a Vega lieutenant in custody. Just another reason to be grateful he was single. "Not sure I buy that, Hosea."

"Believe it. The man is truly grateful for what you did."

Hearing that made Leland sick to his stomach. "I wasn't testifying for the Vega cartel."

"I know but it turned out that way and they don't forget those they owe. Ernesto has this thing about pay back, the good and the bad."

"Cut this bullshit. Who told you where to find me?"

"Someone who does not necessarily have yours or Ernesto Vega's best interests at heart."

"They'll have to get in line to be on that list."

Hosea smiled. "Regardless, I thought you should know. This man is no one's friend."

"Who we talking about?" asked Leland.

"Juan Santos."

Leland froze. "What the hell?"

"One of your favorite people, no?"

Leland snickered sarcastically to hide the white-hot fury welling up inside him at the mention of the snitch whose faulty information had destroyed so many innocent lives. "Oh yeah. Juan's a great guy." He let the sarcasm go at that.

Hosea Alvarez was an informant, just like Santos had been. Except Hosea's information had always been good and had never lead to a fiasco like the Colton raid. Leland wasn't going to air the DEA's dirty laundry with him. Even though the man probably knew more about Santos's involvement with the Colton disaster than he should.

"Is Santos still working with Tomas Rivera?"

"Last I heard, but who knows anything about Santos for certain. The man is certifiable. I saw him earlier this evening."

Leland listened without interruption, focused on hiding the tension in his face.

"Your name came up," Hosea continued. "You're famous, you know. Being on FOX and all that shit."

Leland rolled his eyes.

"Santos told me where you were." Hosea's tone changed. "That concerned me, so I decided to check on you myself."

"Why would Santos care to know my location? It doesn't make sense."

Leland wasn't working the Rivera cartel. There was no reason for Tomas Rivera or his informant to be interested in him. Leland's own dubious cable-news fame aside, multiple other DEA agents were assigned to the Rivera cartel.

"Can't tell you that. Rivera has taken over most of the territory in Eastern Mexico and is in the process of moving his operation across the country and further into South America. Maybe your work on the Vegas pulled you into some of Rivera's areas and you didn't realize it."

Hosea took a long drag on his cigar, and Leland waited him out. Taking a seat on the edge of the bed, he took the weight off his ankle.

The excruciating irony here was that Tomas Rivera and many of his men were once members of the Mexican Special Forces, tasked with taking out the Vega cartel. The US had even trained Rivera's brigade in techniques to aide in the "war on drugs." But that was all from the distant past.

Before Tomas decided it was more profitable to sell drugs for the Vegas than to stop the spread of cartel violence, with their superior training and brutal tactics—Tomas's men, along with Ernesto and Cesar Vega—quickly became the most feared cartel in Mexico until they had their own falling out and parted ways.

"Do you know why the Riveras and the Vegas quit working together?" asked Leland.

Hosea usually had the scoop on everyone, but this time he shrugged. "The details have always been pretty sketchy to me. Maybe some kind of family thing? You do know that Tomas is married to Ernesto and Cesar Vega's sister, right?" said Alvarez.

Leland felt his eyes widen in surprise. "What? No, I didn't realize that."

Hosea nodded, happy to be telling what he knew. "Yep. Carlita Vega married Tomas Rivera, must be over twenty years ago. I was barely more than a kid myself and had just started working for the Vegas."

How did Leland not know this? He'd been working the Vegas for five years. The length of time Tomas had been married sort of explained it. A completely different group of agents was investigating back then, but still. A family connection like that would certainly have been noteworthy.

"This was way before Tomas left the Vegas," continued Hosea. "Hell, Tomas and Ernesto were closer than Ernesto and his own brother Cesar for a long time."

"Any idea what happened?"

Leland had known Tomas was married but didn't know the wife was Vega's sister and he was sure no one currently at the DEA had ever heard a whisper of it either. Why the hell hadn't that information been in the case notes?

What else did he not know?

His informant shrugged again. "I was in Huntsville when whatever happened to break up that alliance went down. All I know is that the families don't work together now—not ever."

Leland's laugh was mirthless. "Well, whatever the reason, it's a good thing for the DEA."

Alvarez nodded with a bleak smile. "If the Riveras and Vegas ever join forces again they'll be all but impossible to stop."

Leland shuddered inside. God knew it was hard enough now to keep the cartels in check with the two families working separately. He stared at the smoke curling from Alvarez's cigar. The hotel management was going to have a fit over that, but he wasn't about to complain.

"Word has it Tomas was behind that Mexican journalist's murder last month," offered Hosea.

Leland raised an eyebrow. The journalist in question and his wife had been tortured, disemboweled and hung from a bridge in the middle of Boca del Río last month, all because of a story written about the Rivera cartel. Leland wouldn't be surprised to hear that Juan Santos had been part of that grisly scene.

Hosea continued to study him through the cigar haze, but Leland didn't want to share the dismal thoughts running through his mind. "I still can't understand what Santos or any of the Riveras would want with me," he said. Up till now, Tomas Rivera and Juan Santos had been someone else's headache.

"Hell, I don't think it matters whether you understand the why of it or not. According to what I heard, Tomas Rivera's got a serious hard-on for you. I'd watch my back if I were you." With that Hosea stubbed out his cigar and stood to leave.

It was a little late for "watching his back" where Zach was concerned. Did any of this have to do with the boy's disappearance, or was Santos's interest all a separate issue having to do with Leland and his work with the DEA?

Kidnapping the boy simply because Leland's recent testimony had inadvertently benefitted Tomas Rivera's enemy, Ernesto Vega, seemed a stretch as a motive, even in the über-vindictive world of cartels.

Nothing made sense, unless . . . "Do Rivera or Santos have any dealings with Max Mercado of Mercado Tequila?" Leland asked, still aching to confirm that he himself wasn't the cause of all this misery for Zach and Anna.

Hosea tilted his head. "The Tequila King? Don't know. Rivera has his fingers in a lot of different pies these days, all in the name of diversification. Santos works for whoever pays him the most."

"Mercado's boy disappeared tonight from this hotel room. I want to find out if the kidnapping is related to me or to Max Mercado."

Hosea homed in on the blood on the Formica table-top. "Kidnapped?"

Leland nodded and something changed in Hosea's eyes. Less lethal employment wasn't the only reason he'd quit working directly for the cartels. Leland suspected the man had problems with their methods as well.

"I'll poke around. If I find out anything, I'll let you know. Certainly puts Santos in a different light though, doesn't it?" Hosea headed for the door.

Leland stood up. "Keep the boy's disappearance to yourself."

Hosea stopped in front of him. "What boy?"

Leland pulled his wallet from his back pocket. Information always cost money, even when the gift horse showed up of his own accord. Remarkably Hosea shook his head.

"I like working with you, Leland. You've always shot me straight. Consider this my good deed for the day. Be careful, my friend, and get the hell out of this hotel."

Chapter Twelve

WHEN THE DOOR opened, Anna wasn't sure if she'd been asleep for fifteen minutes or five hours. She bolted upright in bed to see Leland carrying a computer backpack and a garment bag over his shoulder. His shirt was unbuttoned, a different one than he'd been wearing earlier.

"We've got to get out of here," he said. "It's not safe." His soft accent contradicted the urgency of his words and actions as he went straight to the bedside table and retrieved his gun.

She squeezed her eyes shut before answering, hoping she was dreaming. When she opened them again, he was studying her. Embarrassment from their earlier encounter washed over her even as his emerald-eyed gaze sent a bolt of awareness straight to her lower belly, the tightening sensation shocking her as much as his words.

The stark fear and the zap of lust warred inside her, the fear barely winning out. Yes, this was real. She'd been so focused on making Leland feel obligated to help her with Zach, she'd ignored the attraction that now threatened to engulf her.

"What else can these people possibly do? They have Zach. They can't expect to get their money if I'm out of the picture."

She heard the acrimony in her tone and recognized it for what it was. Chagrin over everything that had happened earlier, fear of the situation and her dependence on him—all poor reasons to take her uncertainty out on the man trying to help her.

"The people I'm worried about have nothing to do with the kidnapping." He didn't look at her as he moved to the window and stared past the curtains into the night.

"What do you mean?"

"This has to do with me, Anna. Some very bad people know I'm here. It has nothing to do with Zach's disappearance, but we have to get out of here now." He turned to face her again.

"How do you know this?" She stood on autopilot, slipping her feet into her shoes.

"An informant of mine just showed up next door. I'm DEA, remember? He came to warn me."

"What did he say?"

"I don't have time to explain it all now. Once we're safe I'll tell you. Let's just get it together and get out of here."

She opened the lid of her suitcase. What did this mean? Something was niggling at the back of her mind, but she couldn't tease it out. Fear was creeping in, overriding all rational thought.

"We won't check out," he said. "We'll just leave through the back exit."

"Where are we going? I have to get the cash tomorrow."

"I know." He stared at his phone, obviously reading a text. He tapped a few lines on it before replying. "It's a safe place, I promise. But let's take your car. It's less likely anyone knows what you're driving."

That made sense. If anyone was just cruising the parking lot looking for him, they'd assume he was still here if his car was. She handed him keys and retrieved her toiletry bag from the bathroom to stuff in her suitcase.

"Wait. Why do I need to leave? If I'm not the one the bad people are after, seems I might be safer on my own."

He looked up from his phone. "Do you really believe you can get your son back by yourself?"

She heard his barely controlled patience in the question. For the first time since she'd met him, she heard irritation directed toward her. It bothered her.

Still, she would be foolish to go with him if he were the source of her peril. Part of her cringed at the thought of being left by herself in this situation, but the self-preservation part argued it might be better to strike out alone. Being as far from Leland as possible could be the better way to go, for her and for Zach.

She wanted to say this diplomatically, as kindly as she could. But there wasn't really a good way to put it, so she just blurted it out. "I don't know, but it seems I might be safer without yo—" Glass at the window broke with a soft *psfft* sound.

"Get down!" Leland shouted as he rushed toward her, fast even with his boot. "That's coming from the parking lot."

Two more shots broke through the window and smacked the wall by the door, *thwunk thwunk*, right where her head had been seconds before.

She hit the floor beside her half-packed suitcase, adrenaline kicking in and the argument to stay on her own forgotten. With shaking hands she tucked her clothes and toiletry case into the carry-on bag and zipped it closed, focusing on the zipper-pull to keep herself from completely panicking.

Her heart was beating so fast, surely it would pound out of her chest. Leland shoved her feet first between the bed and the wall next to the bathroom. "Get back there," he commanded. He drew his revolver and crawled to the window to peer out of the curtains again.

She poked her head around the bed to watch and pulled her suitcase toward her. The bag had just become her security blanket. He didn't stay at the window long but hurried to the door, listening before he cautiously opened it and slid his arm out into the hallway. He stuck his head out, then came back to her.

"There's no one out there yet. Let's go before they get up here." He picked up his bag and slung it over his shoulder along with his backpack, leaving his hands free.

She nodded, no choice left but to believe him and follow. His reaction to her failed seduction earlier allowed her to trust him like she wouldn't have otherwise.

Despite her misgivings, apparently he really did want to help her, no strings attached. God knew it would be easier to leave her behind.

She climbed to her feet, grabbing her suitcase and purse to race behind him out the door in her pajamas and black flip-flops. Her life might be complete chaos, but by God, she'd have clean underwear.

It was unnaturally quiet. She sped behind him to the fire exit. The carpeted floor swallowed up their footsteps.

Leland's gait was uneven in his boot, but it didn't seem to slow him down. When he hit the crash bar at the end of the hallway, she heard the elevator door *ping* behind them and froze in her tracks. Suddenly she couldn't move.

Leland didn't hesitate or look back to see who was coming off the lift. He grabbed her free hand and pulled her through the doorway down the steps, only stopping when they cleared the stairwell at the side of the building. He peered around the edge of the cinderblock wall.

One man stood beside a Mercedes under the hotel portico. The passenger door was open, but there was no luggage. They didn't appear to be checking in.

"Where is your car?" he whispered.

"Over there. A blue Camry," she pointed behind them in the opposite direction from the Mercedes.

He studied the man a moment longer before tugging on her hand, and together they raced across the parking lot on the other side of the hotel. Even with his boot, he was moving faster than she was. Her breathing was ragged, and despite the earlier rain she could feel the left-over heat of the day seeping up from the asphalt.

It was the end of November, and yet the wildly variable Dallas temperature had hit eighty degrees this afternoon. She focused on exhaling and inhaling. If she thought about how scared she was, she'd freeze up again like she'd done in the hallway upstairs.

Perspiration coated her face and slid between her breasts, a combination of fear and sticky humidity. She expected a bullet between her shoulder blades at any second. Despite the earlier showers, the air still smelled like rain.

Her car's keyless entry kept Leland from having to fumble with digging out the keys from his pocket. They reached the sedan at the same time. He tossed his things in the back seat. She pulled her bag into her lap and sat in the passenger seat, quietly closing the door.

Contrary to what she would have done, he started the car and crept from the parking lot at the opposite end of the hotel. The man with the Mercedes couldn't even hear them from under the portico. When Leland pulled onto the street, he sped up but never gunned the engine.

Several blocks from the hotel her heart slowed to the point where she could finally speak without gasping for air. "Will that man follow us?" she asked.

He shrugged. "I don't think so. He had a partner. They may not know we're gone yet."

"How do you know?"

"I don't, Anna. I'm just guessing from what I saw."

She knew she was frustrating him, but she couldn't stop her questions. "I'm not doubting your tactics, but you promised you'd answer all my questions when we were away. When we were safe." He stopped at a red light.

"You're right. I did." He took a deep breath and turned to face her. "What else do you want to know?"

"How did you know they were coming?"

"The informant I told you about showed up in my room next to yours. Right after we . . ." He trailed off.

She felt the blush creeping over her face and was grateful for the darkened car.

"Why did they shoot at you?"

"That's an excellent question. With these men, I have no idea."

"Where are we going now?"

"To friends of a friend."

"More informants?" she asked.

He laughed in genuine amusement. "Not hardly."

"Will we be safe? Shouldn't I just let you drop me off somewhere else, and you can deal with your 'issue' on your own?"

His gaze pierced her. "Do you really want that, Anna? Do you think you'll be able to manage on your own? You have a lot on your plate." His voice was uncharacteristically cool.

Anger pricked along her backbone and her face felt hot for another reason entirely. She hated being reminded that she was in such a vulnerable position. "I don't know, but the thought of your 'friend's friends' scare me."

"They're ex-DEA and Special Forces in the security business. You'll be safe."

"How do you know?" she insisted.

He smiled. She could see his lips curving in the light of the dash and knew what he was going to say in that deep Southern drawl before he said it.

"You're just going to have to trust me."

Chapter Thirteen

ANNA WAS SILENT as Leland drove the rest of the way to Gavin's office in West Plano. Leland assumed she was still thinking over whether she would be better off on her own. That was craziness, but he hoped she'd be coming to that conclusion herself.

He wasn't surprised to find the AEGIS office situated in what would be considered a private aviation community. Gavin had told Leland about his unique office situation a while back. Walnut Creek Residential Airpark looked like any other gated North Dallas community, except where there would normally be garages and driveways, there were also hangars and taxiways.

Nick Donovan was standing beside the neighborhood's security kiosk when they arrived at the gate and introduced himself to both Leland and Anna with a firm handshake. Dressed in cargo shorts and a tight black t-shirt with short hair casually mussed, the former SEAL

looked like a walking advertisement for *GQ* magazine—
even at this ungodly hour.

"Did you have any problem finding the place?" he
asked Leland.

"No, Gavin sent me directions."

"Good."

The guard slid open his drive-through window and
handed Donovan an electronic tablet, promptly shutting the window again without comment. A recent
blockbuster was playing on the television screen situated
alongside the security camera feeds from the subdivision.
Nick was about to electronically sign the visitor's logbook
when Leland interrupted him.

"I don't know what we're dealing with here, so I'd
rather not have a record of mine or Anna's presence, even
in a guard's digital logbook."

Nick didn't raise an eyebrow. He simply nodded and
typed into the register, then chatted with the guard when
he opened the window to retrieve the tablet. The guard
never looked at Leland or Anna, obviously anxious to get
back to his movie.

"Welcome to Walnut Creek, Mr. and Mrs. Smith,"
said Donovan.

Leland chuckled. "Went to a lot of trouble there I see."

"Easier to remember," said Nick, completely at ease.
"Mind giving me a ride? I jogged down here after I got
Gavin's text."

"Climb in," offered Leland.

Nick shut the door to the back seat of the sedan and
directed them down the street through the subdivision.

Each house sat on an acre of property, with garages and one-plane hangars beside the residences. Short taxiways led directly from each home's hangar to a 3500-foot private runway.

"Appreciate your meeting us. Did you have to drive far tonight?" asked Leland.

"No, I currently live here at the AEGIS office."

Leland glanced at Nick in the rearview mirror. "How does that work?"

"Having the main office in the airpark is more convenient than being in a typical Dallas high rise or even a warehouse. The AEGIS teams are able to fly in and out with more discretion and less interference from the FAA since we're over twenty-four miles from a municipal airport, and we aren't required to have a tower. It's the perfect location."

Nick directed them to the back of the subdivision.

The house was a little unique in that it was built on stilts over the hangar and a three-car garage, all at the undeveloped end of a cul-de-sac surrounded by trees.

"Makes a lot more sense now," said Leland.

Nick nodded and pulled a remote from his pocket. The garage door opened.

"Given the sensitive nature of our business and surveillance equipment, this isn't a building that can be left unmanned on a predictable schedule or subjected to a leasing office and cleaning crews," said Nick.

"Is it hard to stay covert in this kind of neighborhood?" asked Leland.

Nick shrugged. "The population consists mainly of

executives who fly back and forth to work each day or re-
tired individuals who just like to fly. The residents assume
I travel for a living. They've finally stopped trying to include me in the homeowner's association or to set me up
on blind dates and have just left me alone." He got out of
the back seat and headed to the door.

Anna didn't move. She'd been silent since Nick introduced himself. Leland suspected she was still stew-
ing over their earlier discussion about the ambush being
his fault and having nothing to do with Max Mercado or
Zach's disappearance.

He'd been right not to tell her of the possible connection, and that was a generous way to look at what he'd
done. He'd told her what he hoped was true. The ambush
at the hotel had nothing to do with Zach's kidnapping or
the cartels.

Basically, he'd lied.

But he didn't yet understand the possible cartel connection himself, and she would still be peppering him
with questions in that hotel room if he hadn't said what
he had and gotten her the hell out of there. When he did
finally own up to this, she was never going to trust him
again.

But keeping her safe trumped being truthful.

And leaving her to fend for herself was out of the
question. He wanted to be sympathetic, but the idea of
her on her own was insane. He had no patience for that.
"We'll be safe here," he offered.

She nodded. "I suppose so, for now."

Nick was at the back door, a bit of impatience in his

stance as well. Leland couldn't blame him. They had gotten the man out of bed at two AM.

"Let's go." Leland tugged the keys from the ignition.

Anna slid out of the car, pulling her bag along with her. She didn't speak to either of them as she walked around Nick and made her way indoors.

"Friendly much?" murmured Nick under his breath. Which was totally unfair.

Leland felt the need to defend her. "She's had a helluva a rough evening. Give her a break."

She needed time to rest and wrap her head around everything that was happening at warp speed, not some *GQ* jackass getting his panties in a wad because she didn't fall all over him.

"Gavin said you were in a bind," said Nick.

"The man has a flair for understatement."

Donovan tilted his head. "Indeed."

"Let's just say that it's been a long night. Here's the note." Leland had slipped it into a plastic dry-cleaning bag from the hotel. "I doubt you'll find anything, but—"

"You never know till we try," finished Nick.

Anna stood silently in the entry, her exhaustion and the day itself evidently catching up with her. Leland empathized. His ankle throbbed like a bitch. Jogging down the fire exit stairwell twice tonight and then racing across the asphalt had not been good to him. He needed Vicodin now, but after the catastrophe at the hotel he was concerned about it affecting his judgment.

"Gavin told me a little," continued Donovan. "I imagine you're both wiped. I've only got one guest room outfitted with a bed. Everything else is office space, but you're welcome to it. I know you've got to get to the bank before we fly out tomorrow. We'll shoot for an early afternoon departure and talk details in the morning. Okay?"

"Sounds like a plan." Leland felt Anna tense beside him as Donovan led them toward the stairs and the guest room.

"I'll sleep on a sofa, Anna. You can have the bed."

She nodded. Leland mulled over her silence. This was all moving so fast. He wasn't sure if she was shutting down, allowing the shock to overtake her, or if she was still rethinking staying with him. Whatever it was, she needed to lie down before she collapsed.

"Sorry, no sofas. Loveseat okay?" asked Nick on the way through the living area with nary a sofa in sight.

Love seats that would be at least two feet too short to sleep on comfortably were the only available seating. Inwardly, Leland groaned. He needed to get his ankle elevated or he'd be paying for it tomorrow.

"I'll make do," he muttered.

Nick showed them to the guest room and left them to figure out sleeping arrangements themselves. A queen mattress covered with a fluffy comforter and several pillows beckoned. Anna stared at the bed but was seemingly rooted to the spot.

"You need to rest," he said.

"You do, too," she argued. "You can't possibly sleep on a love seat. You're limping already. I can't imagine what trying to stretch out on one of those mini-sofas down the hall would do to you."

He was surprised she'd noticed or cared, but he was grateful. The pain was ratcheting up to the point where even his back was screaming. Being so off balance in the boot had done that.

"Besides, I'm too scared to close my eyes," she added.

"You're safe here."

"But my son's not. I'm frightened of what I'll see if I fall asleep. Zach crying, hurting, getting sicker without me there to take care of him."

He didn't have an answer for that, so he pulled back the covers. "Get into bed, Anna." He cupped her shoulders in his hands and gently pushed her to a sitting position.

"I can't do this anymore," she mumbled under her breath.

"You're not alone. We're going to have a team of people helping get Zach back. Now lie down." *I'm here.*

She crawled under the covers, looking defenseless and broken as she lay there staring up at him.

"Will you stay with me for a while?" she asked. "Not like before," she hurried to add. "I just . . . I don't think I'll be able to get to sleep by myself."

From the way her expression changed, he could tell that had cost her to ask. Her face went from vulnerable to closed in an instant. There were all kinds of reasons it was a bad idea for him to stay, but he wasn't about to argue. He didn't want to.

He longed to hold her like he'd promised he would earlier, if she asked. He tried to tell himself he was only doing this because he needed to lie flat and get his ankle elevated, not because he wanted to feel her in his arms again.

He grabbed a couple of anti-inflammatories from his backpack and swallowed them dry, staring at the Vicodin bottle for a moment before shaking out three tablets instead of the four he wanted. He hated relying in any way on this medicine, but he was hurting so much he'd never sleep tonight without it. He wasn't addicted . . . yet. But he was getting dependent. He wondered again how it was affecting his discernment.

Still, they were safe here. He could afford to take the painkiller and allow the drug's narcotic lethargy to seep over him. This might be the last time he could let his guard down for a while.

He went to the other side of the bed and took off the heavy orthopedic boot before climbing on top of the comforter and grabbing a couple of pillows to prop up his entire leg. Once he got situated, he turned his head to look at Anna.

"Come here." He took her hand and pulled her closer, threading his fingers through hers.

She curled into his side like it was the most natural thing in the world. The warmth of her body soaked into him from hip to knee, even through the down comforter. She took a shuddering breath as he put his arm around her.

"It's gonna be okay," he said.

"How?"

"I don't know yet. But we will find Zach. You just have to take it one step at a time."

"You sound so sure."

"This guy, Nick, and his people. They're good, trained by the best man I know."

He felt her nod, then yawn beside him. She snuggled in closer and he lay perfectly still, listening to her breathing become deeper. His body responded to having a woman pressed against his side, and the pain medication hit his system.

It wasn't long before he drifted off himself.

Chapter Fourteen

FIVE HOURS LATER Leland woke with his arm possessively slung around Anna's waist. He'd turned on his side during the night but somehow kept his ankle propped up on the pillow. Thankfully she was still fast asleep.

Light filtered in through the curtains and dappled the bedspread. Anna's hair spread across his chest. Her head was tucked under his chin. In the lazy warmth of the covers, he took a deep breath and concentrated on how she felt in his arms: the impossibly soft skin, the flowery scent of her shampoo.

An unfamiliar feeling of contentment stole over him. He tilted his head down to take another breath and couldn't help but notice the curve of her breasts in the lacey black top.

Was this what it would be like to wake up with someone every day? To have that sense of belonging to another? The appeal of the idea surprised him. What was it about this woman? She was a mess, but he was undeniably attracted to her.

His palm still rested against her bare stomach where her camisole had ridden up in the night. His groin tightened at the thought of what else could be appealing in waking up with a warm woman in his arms. The next moment he was untangling his legs from the covers and chiding himself for indulging in fantasies that didn't belong here.

He felt only slightly guilty for regretting what hadn't happened. Happily avoiding what would have been an awkward non-morning-after experience if she'd woken in his arms just now, he watched Anna sleep a few moments longer. Her mouth was bruised, her bottom lip swollen from the punch she'd gotten yesterday at Max's hands.

Leland's stomach lurched. He wouldn't be able to do what he had to if he dwelled on that thought. He pried himself out of bed and fastened himself back into his boot.

Sitting on Nick's deck, he called the cop who'd arrested Max Mercado yesterday and asked a favor. Afterward he grabbed a shower in the other bathroom down the hall so as not to wake Anna, changing into clean jeans and a knit polo shirt.

His back and ankle were achy, but it was nothing like the eye-crossing pain of last night. He took four anti-inflammatories and decided to forgo the Vicodin completely.

When Leland stepped into the kitchen, Nick was on the phone and wearing gym clothes. Waving Leland to the coffee pot, Nick hung up and spun around on a bar-stool.

"Morning. You look like you're on your way some-where."

Leland took a mug from the cabinet. "I'm going down-town. I need to talk to the husband, Max Mercado, while he's still a guest of the county jail."

"Husband?" Nick took a swallow of his own coffee. "The man must be fairly broad-minded."

Estranged husband. Leland smiled nonchalantly. "From what I can tell, no, not so much. He's a real piece of work. But I need to know if he had anything to do with their boy's disappearance."

"Well, you were right about the note. It's completely clean except for the blood. That part's a little unusual. It's AB negative."

Leland poured himself some coffee and nodded. "That would be Zach. His blood type is very rare from what I understand."

"So what's your plan?"

"See Mercado. Figure out what he knows about this."

"Think you can get to the jail in time?" asked Nick. "This guy can post his own bond, can't he?"

"Oh yeah, he can definitely afford it, but he hasn't been booked yet." Leland took a big sip of the rich brew. "Busy night downtown. The arresting officer is losing some paperwork for a few hours so they can hold him a little longer. I've got some questions for The Tequila King."

Starting with did Max know about his son's kidnap-ping? Anyone could lie over the phone, but in person it would be hard to fake the shock of hearing about your own child's abduction.

"I won't be long. I know we've got to get to the bank before flying out. If Anna wakes up, tell her I'll be back before noon and we'll go pick up the ransom money."

"That may make us tight on time getting out of here," said Nick, refilling his own cup.

Leland watched in amazement as the man put four heaping scoops of sugar in his coffee but no milk. "Have her call ahead and give the bank a heads up about what she wants beforehand. They can get started on getting the cash together for her. That would save us some time."

"Will do. I spoke to Gavin again this morning and he said to put myself at your disposal. If you want, I can take her to pick up the money." Nick stirred his sweet coffee brew while Leland considered the offer.

For about ten seconds. He refused to name the possessive feelings that Anna hanging with *GQ* Nick brought up inside him. He didn't want to think about how her skin felt under his palm or how her hair had smelled against his chest this morning either. But he did anyway.

"Why don't I go with you both when I get back? I'd feel better if we had two people watching Anna and the cash." And that was the truth, albeit not all of it, given the situation last night with the cartel's men.

"$750,000 is a lot of money. How do you want to carry it? Backpack or duffel?" asked Nick.

"I imagine you're the expert on ransom delivery. You decide."

Nick nodded.

"How was Kat when you spoke with Gavin?" asked Leland.

"Resting. Marissa Hudson, Gavin's business partner, has seen them more than I have lately. She'll be in later this morning. Marissa thinks Kat's getting closer to the end."

"I got that impression last night when I spoke with Gavin as well." Leland took another sip and drained his coffee cup. "Cancer sucks."

"Yes, it does."

There was a long silence.

"How'd you end up working with AEGIS? Gavin said you were a SEAL?"

Nick's dark laugh belied the smile that didn't quite reach his eyes. "I knew Gavin when he was DEA. We worked together."

Leland raised an eyebrow, hoping for some kind of explanation. A SEAL working with the DEA?

Nick shrugged. "It was a delicate situation."

Gavin had said Nick was a former SEAL, though he'd never mentioned working with Nick before he left DEA. Several things dawned on Leland at once and the entire situation suddenly made a lot more sense. He also quit asking questions.

When would a Navy SEAL and the DEA do business together? When the SEAL was a spook.

Gavin would never have mentioned that Nick, the former SEAL, was also part of the CIA's National Clandestine Service. No guessing which letters in the alphabet soup of covert groups he worked for within the NCS, because it all boiled down to one thing.

Nick was Black Ops, or he had been until recently.

LELAND TOOK ANNA'S car and made it to the jail in thirty-five minutes. The officer from last night had done a huge favor for Leland and cleared the way for him to see Mercado in an interview room with no recorders or cameras. Max would have jumped up when Leland walked in but for the handcuffs holding him to his seat. The Tequila King looked a little worse for wear after spending the night in jail. The Lew Sterrett Justice Center had a reputation as being one of the worst county jails in the country and that was quite a claim to fame.

"What are you doing here?" demanded Max. "I thought I was going to see my lawyer."

"You'll see him eventually. I have a couple of questions while you wait."

"Fuck you."

"Not on your best day, Max. I don't swing that way. But where you're going, there are plenty of guys who do."

Max's face turned red with anger, but his attitude hadn't budged since Leland met him the evening before. "I'm not answering anything without my lawyer," he insisted.

"Okay. Then why don't you just listen?"

"I'm not going to prison for what happened yesterday. You know it and I know it."

"That's true, asshat. Assault won't necessarily land

you in prison, although kidnapping will." Leland sat down at the interview table.

"What are you talking about?" asked Max.

"Your son was kidnapped last night from the hotel where your wife was staying."

"No! Zach? Kidnapped?" Max tried to stand but the handcuffs held him down, the smugness immediately replaced by a wild look in his eyes. "Where's Anna?"

"She's safe."

"She wasn't taken?" asked Max.

The phrasing of that question struck Leland as odd. "Did you have anything to do with this?" he asked.

Max looked down before meeting Leland's gaze. "Of course not. With his meds, his heart? That would kill him."

"Yes, it could," agreed Leland. "Do you know anything about it?"

"No, I swear to God." Max's cuffs clanked together against the metal chair. "What do the kidnappers want?"

Leland leaned back and stared at him. He wasn't sure if Max was lying or not, but the man certainly wasn't telling the whole truth. That was for damn sure. Still, Max hadn't faked his shock at Zach's kidnapping. If he had, the man deserved an Academy Award.

"They want cash," Leland said. "Delivered by your wife to a specific cantina in Baxtla, Estado de Veracruz-Llave. That's the dead center of cartel country. An unusual request, no? One might think they didn't want her to survive the trip."

Max shook his head. "I have no idea what's going on."

"Hmm. I think it's unusual because yesterday you seemed determined to get your wife and son to Mexico."

"No! This is not my doing."

Leland still couldn't figure out if the man was lying. Most perps swore up and down that they were innocent, even when they were guilty as sin. He wondered if he should have brought Anna with him to watch through the glass. She might have been able to tell if her husband was being truthful or not.

Still, Leland didn't regret leaving her sleeping. She needed rest. If she was going to deliver the money in Mexico, the coming days would be brutal.

"Okay, Max, a couple more questions and I'll let you get back to your bridge game. Do you have any dealings with the Vega or Rivera cartels in Mexico?"

"What do you mean?" Max wouldn't meet his stare.

"It's a simple question. Do you now or have you in the past ever had dealings with either of those cartels. Perhaps for your business?"

Max gazed at the glass wall behind Leland with something akin to fear in his eyes.

"No one's there, Max. It's just you and me."

"I don't know anything about the cartels. I swear it." Max still wouldn't look him in the eye.

Leland studied the man, certain he'd just heard another bald-faced lie, but whether or not Max's involvement with the cartels was related to the kidnapping or something else entirely, he had no idea.

If you ran a legitimate business in Mexico as large as Mercado's, there was no doubt you'd have to deal with the cartels from time to time. Shipping routes, protection money—there would absolutely be some overlap.

Leland desperately wanted to hear something that indicated Max was responsible for Zach's disappearance and the shots fired into his hotel room. So far, he hadn't.

After Hosea's warning, Leland was fairly convinced the ambush was because of his own job with the DEA. Believing he might also be responsible for Zach's kidnapping hurt. It felt too much like Ellis Colton's family, someone getting hurt because he'd failed.

Leland still wasn't sure if a cartel had anything to do with last night's events, but all of it together made him extremely uncomfortable. He did not believe in coincidences, and this was just too much.

It seemed more likely that Max would have had something to do with the shots fired into the hotel room, but there was no way to connect the dots there either.

Max interrupted his thoughts. "Will Anna take the money to Mexico?"

"Yes. She doesn't really have a choice, does she?"

A look of profound relief washed over Max. "Where is the cash coming from?"

Leland stared at him. "Where do you think?"

"My accounts." Max nodded. "Good. That is the right thing."

Leland had expected him to object, but the man surprised him. "Who's going with her? She cannot go by herself."

Leland didn't answer.

Max scrutinized him a moment before understanding

dawned in his eyes. He nodded again. "Yes, you should do it. She'll be safe with you."

"You think so?" asked Leland. This was important. If Max hadn't ordered the shooting last night, he would still think Leland was a safe person to take care of Anna.

"I don't like you," continued Max. "But I'm not a fool. Baxtla is in the middle of nowhere. That makes it an extremely dangerous place in Mexico. If she is going to get Zach out, Anna needs someone who can protect her and the ransom money."

Leland contemplated Max's face but didn't speak.

"You will go with her, yes? I'd send Emilio, but she would never trust him after yesterday."

Of course, she wouldn't. "I'll go with her." There was no reason to tell Max he'd already made the decision.

"You take care of her," Max said. "She won't allow me to any longer."

The spurt of sympathy Leland felt for the man was surprising. Max was an ass, but his son was ill and missing. As bizarre as it was for him to be asking Leland to go with Anna, the situation didn't feel as odd as it should have.

A father would do anything to protect his child.

Leland's question was, *Just how far would Max go?* Would he stage his own son's kidnapping? There had to be a special place in hell for a man who would do that.

Chapter Fifteen

ANNA WOKE UP at 9:45, surprised that she'd slept so long. The bed was empty, but that did not surprise her. She sat on the edge of the mattress for a moment, wishing desperately that the past twenty-four hours had been a bad dream. Yesterday morning her biggest worry had been how to convince Max that sleeping together was a mistake.

Today's priority? Getting the money for Zach's kidnappers and figuring out how to get to the Veracruz district of Mexico.

Where was Leland? He hadn't left a note, not that she'd expect one. They weren't lovers. They were . . .

Who knew?

It didn't matter what they were or for what reason he was helping her find Zach. For now, all she needed to know was that Leland was on her side.

She stood and walked into the bathroom. Today they

were going to get the $750,000 from the bank and fly to Mexico. Surreal as that sounded, this was her life.

She stared in the mirror, hardly seeing her reflection. Her thoughts were laser-focused on Zach. Where was he? Was he sick? Was he scared?

Her eyes filled. Those kinds of questions would overwhelm her if she let them. She had to focus on doing the next thing, getting herself together for the day—a shower, clothes.

She turned on the water and took off the yoga pants she'd slept in as the shower temperature warmed up. She'd wash her hair, get dressed, and change the bandage on her arm. She wasn't sure what came after that.

Eating breakfast? Coffee? One thing at a time.

She pulled on a colorful gauzy skirt and tank top, the last clean clothes in her bag. The bright colors didn't cheer her as she'd hoped. Still, if she didn't look too far down the road, she wouldn't freak out. Like climbing a tall tree, one shouldn't peer down from the dizzying height. As long as she didn't venture too far ahead in her thought process, she could do this.

Twenty minutes later she was pouring a cup of coffee in Nick Donovan's kitchen and hunting something to eat. He walked in wearing gym shorts, a t-shirt with a sweat stain down the front, and a towel around his neck.

A tall, trim woman with auburn hair was with him. Wearing black workout gear, she carried herself like a runway model. Her tank top was damp as well.

"Good morning," Nick said. "Anna, meet Marissa Hudson. This is my boss."

"Hello. It's good to meet you." Anna felt herself switching to autopilot.

The woman reached out to take her hand in a firm smooth grip. "You, too. Call me Risa."

"Want some coffee?" Anna held up her mug.

Nick shook his head.

"No thanks, I'll start with water." Risa's voice had a Texas flair with a Kathleen Turner hoarseness that men usually found sexy. Her green eyes missed nothing as they looked Anna up and down, but her gaze wasn't un-friendly. Together she and Nick looked like something out of a fitness magazine.

"I'll take some water, too." Nick headed for the refrig-erator.

With his jet-black hair and chiseled features, the man could be Max's brother. Anna hadn't noticed so much last night, but she found the similarities disconcerting today. Long-limbed and cut under his tight t-shirt, from what Anna could see, the most obvious thing that set Nick apart from her husband were his electric blue eyes.

"Did y'all go for a run?" she asked.

"No. We've got a speed bag and a heavy bag down in the hangar."

She nodded, not knowing exactly what either were but assuming they had something to do with boxing. She re-treated to a safe topic. "Where's Leland?"

"He had to run an errand," said Nick. "He asked me to tell you that he'll be here before noon and we'll go to the bank, then to get the money."

She nodded.

"He suggested you might want to call and give them a heads up that you want that much cash."

"Where do you bank?" asked Risa.

"Texas Mutual."

Risa smiled. "There's a branch near here. We've used it before for clients. I know one of the managers. Can I call for you?"

"Um . . . sure." Anna didn't want to think about Risa's knowing someone who would give them three-quarters of a million dollars in cash and not ask questions.

"Do you know where Leland went?" Anna asked.

"I think I need to let him tell you."

She tamped down the spurt of frustration that blossomed when Nick said that. She hated that she was in a situation where she needed to be *handled,* so she turned to the woman. "Marissa. Risa, thank you for letting us crash here."

Marissa nodded. "Any friend of Gavin's is welcome."

Anna didn't point out that Gavin didn't know her from Adam's housecat. Again, she owed Leland. Marissa left her in the kitchen with Nick, and Anna was again struck by how much the man looked like Max.

"Risa and I have some work to do to get ready for the trip. There's a television in the den and a few DVDs, but I'm not sure there's anything there you'd like. I'm mostly an action-adventure or documentary guy."

Anna smiled. "I'll be fine. Are you both going to Mexico with us?"

He nodded. "Risa and I are flying you and Leland down."

Someone else to help. Relief washed over her in waves. Leland had done that, and she hadn't even asked. "Thank you. Thank Risa as well . . . I don't know what else to say."

"This is what we do, Anna. So, no worries. I've got to go now and sort some things out."

"Of course. I've got a phone call to make. Can I sit on the deck while I do that?"

"Certainly."

Anna pulled out her cell, chagrined to see the number of missed calls, all from the same number.

She almost wished Nick had said *no*, she couldn't use her phone. Her sister was going to have a seizure when Anna told her what had happened. She grabbed her coffee and wandered out to the deck, puzzling over how to explain this without freaking Liz out completely.

Her sister picked up on the second ring. "Where have you been? I tried calling all last night after I got your message, and this morning, too." Liz's voice was filled with concern.

"I'm sorry. Things have gotten crazy."

"Have you heard from Max? He called here yesterday afternoon trying to find you. He sounded so angry. I was worried when I couldn't reach you."

In as unemotional terms as possible Anna described what had happened since they'd spoken yesterday morning when Anna was trying to get out of Cancun.

"Zach's gone?" Liz was furious and horrified at the same time. Anna wanted to tell her it was going to work out, that they were going to get him back. But the words seemed too trite for what was happening.

"How can I help? Do you want me to come? You need your family."

Anna smiled into the phone. Liz was the oldest and had always been "the fixer" in Anna's family. "No. Don't come, not yet. I have someone helping me."

"Who?" A perfectly valid question, but in this moment, it felt so negative.

Explaining would be dicey. *I met a man yesterday who's traveling to Mexico with me to pay the ransom.*

Okay, that sounded insane. Liz would think she was crazy and wouldn't shy away from saying so. The thought of an argument was more than Anna could stand, but lying wasn't an option.

"A man. He's law enforcement and has . . ." she wasn't sure what to call Nick and Marissa, ". . . connections. They're helping me."

"Who is he? I thought you said you couldn't go to the police. Oh, honey, are you sure you aren't going from the frying pan into the fire?"

She could be. Those were all legitimate questions but ones Anna couldn't explore here and now. "It's going to be okay. He's not police, so it's alright. This is the only option I have to get Zach back, so I'm taking it. I can't do this alone."

Her sister was warming up to argue, and Anna knew she couldn't handle that in her current state of mind. "I have to go. I'll keep you posted."

Her sister was sputtering over the line, but then she surprised her. "I don't like this, but I love you, Anna. And I trust you most of the time, except when you're holding a box of Lady Clairol hair color in your hand."

Anna laughed. She had helped dye Liz's hair once when they were in high school. It hadn't quite turned out the shade of red they were hoping for. "You're never going to let me live that down are you?"

"You keep yourself alive through this, and I'll stop, I promise." Liz's words sounded thick. Anna knew her sister well enough to recognize the tears in her voice.

"It'll be okay, Liz. You're going to have plenty of time to keep giving me hell about it."

"You make sure of that, you hear?"

"It's a deal."

THIRTY MINUTES LATER Leland stopped inside the house to watch Anna on the deck. He'd already touched base with Nick and Marissa. Everyone was on track to leave as soon as they returned from the bank and changed into appropriate clothing for their trek into Mexico.

Anna's eyes were closed as she leaned her head back in the sun. She looked more at ease than she had since they'd met. He hated to disturb her. This was likely the last moment she'd have to relax before they got Zach back.

He was thinking positive. They were going to find her boy.

"Good morning," he said, sliding open the patio door.

Her eyes popped open, and long blonde hair swept forward across her face when she jumped to her feet. He was sorry to see her moment of repose end.

"Hello. Where've you been?" she asked, pushing her hair back.

"I went to see Max."

"That's not what I expected to hear."

"I needed to see his face when I talked to him."

"What did he say?" asked Anna.

"He claims not to know anything about Zach, and . . . he asked me to go with you to Mexico." Leland hadn't been sure he was going to tell her that part, but he needed to know what it meant.

She looked puzzled. "Max asked you?"

"Is that surprising?"

"Yes, the Max I know would never have asked you for something like that. Particularly after the confrontation you two had. I—" she stopped.

"What?"

"I don't know whether it proves Max had nothing to do with this or proves he did. Asking for help is so out of character for him. The loss of face, he has a real thing about that."

"I wondered the same thing. But could concern for his son make him act in an unusual way?" Leland asked. She was looking overwhelmed. He wished they didn't have to talk about this now, wished she could get a break from it all.

"I don't know what to think. Does it matter? Either way I'm going to Mexico." Her voice sounded defeated and her posture was slumped. Her bangs were in her eyes again, but she made no move to push them out of the way this time.

"True. Either way you're going. But, Anna," he reached out even as he knew he shouldn't and brushed the hair from her face himself. "You're not going alone. Understand?"

She nodded but didn't look convinced.

"Risa talked to her people at the bank. Are you ready to go pick up the cash?"

She stood. "As ready as I'll ever be."

Chapter Sixteen

THREE HOURS LATER Anna took a deep breath and gripped the armrest as the bantam-sized plane took off. God, she hated flying. The smaller the plane, the worse her discomfort. Max loved to fly, and when they were together, he'd dragged her all over. She'd loved the places they'd seen, but had hated getting to them.

Yesterday, she and Zach had flown commercial with relative ease. There'd been so many other things to worry about, her phobia hadn't been an issue. Today, all she could focus on was how miniscule the aircraft felt.

"You okay?" Leland asked.

She shook her head. "Not a good flier."

"Is it the size of the plane or the weather?" asked Marissa over the roar of the engine.

"Neither, it's being in the air, period. Usually I take something so I can relax, but—"

"You don't have anything with you," finished Leland.

Her anti-anxiety medication hadn't been in the bag she'd grabbed from the hotel suite yesterday morning. It had been on the bathroom counter, where Max was showering.

She gave Leland a tight nod as Nick spoke over his shoulder. "It's about a three-hour flight."

"I'll be okay." She smiled, knowing that was a lie, but what else could she do? She was so tired of feeling weak and ineffectual in all this.

"Would music or a movie help?" asked Leland, digging into his backpack and holding out an iPad mini.

"I'll try anything."

He handed her the tablet and some headphones. "Not sure what you like. I've got fairly eclectic taste. Feel free to explore and see if there's anything that would work."

She stared at the mini tablet in her hands and was mortified when her eyes filled, remembering Zach and his electronics.

Leland's voice was quiet in her ear. "I'm sorry. I just realized that might not be the best distraction."

Her blue eyes widened, and she reached out to touch the back of his hand. "No, I'll be fine. I'm being too emotional."

She'd meant for it to be a reassuring touch, to let him know that she was okay. But he surprised her when he flipped his hand over and pulled her fingers against his, threading their hands together.

"Don't worry about it." He squeezed her palm. "Just hang on. We'll be on the ground sooner than you think."

His voice was warm and reassuring. She donned the

earbuds and pulled up his iTunes library. This was going to be hard enough without her falling apart every five minutes. Between her fear of flying and her tears over the silly electronics, Leland must be wondering what the hell he'd gotten himself into.

She clicked through some artists and settled on one, mildly surprised that Leland had Ludovico Einaudi in his playlists. He was still holding her hand as the others discussed who was meeting them at their destination. Everyone's voice sounded muffled. She eased back in her seat. Curiously, the constant roar of the engine mixed with the conversation and music became a kind of soothing white noise.

From her vantage point she took stock of Leland. He was certainly proving himself in a crisis. She was depending on him, whether it was a good idea or not. There were no other viable options.

Zach's illness had taught her that she had reserves of mental fortitude she wasn't aware of, but within the past twenty-four hours she'd fallen to pieces. She leaned further back in her seat, still mystified but grateful that the noises of the plane were tranquilizing at this point and not sending her into a hot panic. She drifted, catching only small details of their planning as she closed her eyes and tried to relax.

She was trusting these people with her son's life—not because she wanted to, but because she had to. The men were easier to hear than Risa over the engine's cacophony of sound. Nick had a contact who was meeting them with transportation so they could drive on their own to drop the money in Baxtla.

Leland leaned into her ear and her eyes flew open. She was disoriented for a moment. Apparently she'd fallen asleep.

His breath was warm on her cheek. "We're close. Jalapa has an airport, but Nick knows a private strip about twenty-five miles from Baxtla. That's where we're landing."

"It'll be a winding drive up Cofre De Perote to the town," said Marissa. "Most of that area is jungle. The foliage is lush, but the roads are more like beaten paths."

Anna sat up to clear the cobwebs and listen.

"It's also big cartel territory," added Leland.

"Risa and I have studied the topo maps." Nick adjusted some of the controls in front of him. "It's probably an hour or so from the airstrip when it's not raining."

Leland nodded. "I'm concerned about a possible ambush in the area we have to drive through before we get to Baxtla. The vegetation is so thick, it'll be hard to see lookout gunmen in the jungle."

Anna's tension ratcheted up as she listened. The panic was returning.

Unaware of her rising anxiety, Leland kept talking. "Ernesto Vega's entire operation is based in the Veracruz District, as well as Tomas Rivera's. It's crazy they don't work together, but good for us. Several men working for Vega would like nothing more than to get their hands on me or someone important to me. They've made sure I know it, too."

That statement sent a chilly finger of fear skittering down Anna's spine. Who was Ernesto Vega? She tried not to think about what it would mean to have a drug cartel gunning for you or those you loved. While the fear took her mind off how uncomfortable she was flying, the knowledge did nothing to ease her worry over Zach.

What did all these people have to do with the kidnapping? She would ask once they were on the ground, but at present keeping her fear of flying and her nausea at bay were paramount.

"The airport" consisted of a flattened-out place in the soil with mountains rising on either side. A pitiful-looking windsock hung from a pole. In the opposite direction was a tree line. A hard-packed trail led from the airstrip to a desolate main road running north and south.

A pickup was parked at what she assumed was the back end of the runway. A man wearing a baseball cap leaned against the hood of the truck as they landed. Yellow-tinged dust billowed up all around the plane, partially obscuring her view. The mountains rising around them made it seem like a small desert in the midst of a jungle. They were in the big Middle of Nowhere.

"Is this a private airstrip?" Anna asked while they waited for the dust to settle before opening the doors.

Marissa shrugged. "We're not sure who it belongs to officially, most likely one of the cartels. We're rolling the dice and using it because we know we're only staying for a few hours."

Nick spoke up, his voice sounding overly loud now that the engines were winding down. "As long as the cartels don't have flights scheduled, we're golden. But since drug dealers don't file flight plans, we're kind of guessti-mating when the airstrip will be open."

The gravity of his words hit Anna. "You mean they could show up at any time?"

"Pretty much. That's why I stay in close contact with Paulo." Nick unsnapped his safety harness and nodded to the guy jogging toward the plane. "I need current info on cartel shipping to use this strip."

Nick opened the door and Leland began unloading gear with Marissa. Baseball Cap arrived. There wasn't much luggage—a duffel bag containing the cash, Leland's backpack along with another pack Marissa had loaned Anna.

Baseball Cap immediately started chattering with Nick in Spanish, using big hand gestures and pointing to his watch.

Anna felt more like an albatross than an equal at this point but she was passable at Spanish. Living with Max had been good for something.

She tried to understand what Baseball Cap was saying, but he was talking too fast to get an exact translation. She picked out certain words though: immediate, delivery, guns, airplane, and *vamos*.

That didn't sound good.

Chapter Seventeen

Leland grabbed the duffel of cash as Nick's contact wound down. Something was wrong. The man was agitated.

Jumpy. Nervous. That wasn't unusual. Contacts in this line of work had cause to be edgy.

It was the look on Nick's face that had Leland worried. Whatever Paulo was telling him wasn't happy news.

Anna stood to the side and out of the way, but he had a feeling she knew exactly what Paulo was saying. Made sense, since her husband was Hispanic, that she'd understand the language. But for the first time since they'd met, her expression was unreadable.

Paulo finished his conversation and handed Nick a set of keys before heading out on foot toward the tree line and jungle, going in the opposite direction from the truck.

"What's going on?" asked Leland.

Nick handed him the keychain. "There's a Vega cartel drop expected any time now. Paulo's brother is a Vega lieutenant, so that's how he knows about it. He doesn't know exactly what is being delivered or who's coming to get it. Could be drugs, could be guns. But we can't leave the plane here as planned, not even for a half hour."

"What do you want to do?"

"I'll take off as soon as you've got everything unloaded. Risa will go on with you from here," said Nick.

Leland didn't hesitate, "No, she won't."

"Excuse me?" Marissa arched an eyebrow.

"You need to go with Nick. The plan we discussed was based on the two of you coming in behind us."

"Plans can be rearranged. They often are in the field. You need some kind of backup," she argued.

"In this particular case, one person isn't backup. They're a liability." *And I won't be responsible for taking any more people into this mess.*

"I can hold my own."

"I'm sure that's true. But you don't send people in alone out here, and that's all there is to it." Leland had learned that his first year of working for the DEA in Mexico.

"That's ridiculous. You're going in alone," Risa said.

"No, I'm going in with Anna—two people, two sets of eyes and ears. And before you get all cranked up, you have to know this has nothing to do with your being a woman."

"Of course it does." Marissa crossed her arms in front of her chest, obviously ready to dig in for an argument.

So diplomacy wasn't working, and they were running

out of time. Nick was observing the discussion with a be-mused expression. He'd obviously dealt with Marissa's tenacity before.

"Hell no! This is about putting as few people as possible in harm's way." Leland took a deep breath before he said something he regretted.

Ah, screw it. He was saying it anyway. "Did you see the news last month? What they did to that journalist down here? The man simply wrote about the cartel violence taking place in this area, and they gutted him and his wife before hanging them from a freakin' bridge."

Anna's sharp intake of breath had him turning to look at her. *Crap.* Her unreadable demeanor had vanished.

She blanched at his words. *Terrific.* He hated that he'd just given her something else to imagine happening to Zach.

But Marissa, like a terrier with a bone, wasn't fazed. "That wasn't in this same area," she said.

"But it was the same cartel, and I guarantee you they raped the woman before they killed her." He didn't look at Anna, knowing she had to be horrified by everything coming out of his mouth.

He wished Marissa would be more realistic about what going in without backup really meant. Her expression never changed, but he kept talking, hoping he was getting through to her on some level. There was no way in hell he was letting someone go into this situation without backup.

"In the past the cartels have refrained from killing DEA agents or US citizens. The backlash put too much pressure on the Mexican government and caused the cartels all kinds of grief. But that restraint has gone out the window." Leland shrugged. "And a woman alone? US agent or private citizen, they wouldn't be able to resist."

Marissa stared at him, unflinching. "You know, I'm part owner in AEGIS. I can insist on accompanying you."

Normally he'd have admired her persistence, but right now Leland didn't have time. He'd been worried she'd pull that *I'm the boss* card.

Gavin and Marissa had combined funds to form AEGIS. She was the public face of the company, yet another reason for her not to be alone out here. What a coup for the cartel to get hold of the owner of AEGIS, Inc.

He nodded. "Of course you can insist on going, but I hope you'll see the wisdom of not doing that. These people are brutally violent in ways that are difficult to imagine. We have no strategy planned for one-person backup. No matter who's in charge, we can't put anyone—man or woman—in that kind of danger with a half-assed plan."

Been there, done that, and it was a disaster. The Colton bust had been so poorly planned as to be laughable. It would have been absurd, if they hadn't killed a kid and crippled his mother.

"But Anna—" started Marissa.

"Anna has to come with me. It's her son, and they've insisted she come or he dies. There's no choice for her. There is for you. I can't keep Anna and her boy safe if I'm worried about what's happening to an asset alone out here, someone who could and would be used against us. "

Marissa looked as if she wanted to debate the issue

further, but Leland rolled right over her. "At this point, you'll be more of a liability than a help," he said.

"I don't like it."

"I understand that. But you know I'm right. Besides, we don't know what Nick will be up against when he comes to get us. I want to make sure his six is covered so we can all catch a ride back home when this mess is over."

Leland didn't have time to worry if he'd overstepped. Marissa wasn't his boss yet, and there was no way he wanted someone else here that he felt responsible for.

Nick, obviously the smarter man, had stayed silent through the entire exchange. Finally he spoke up. "As much as I hate to admit it, Risa, Leland's right. The plan's not effective with just one person being dropped at the bridge. I'd rather have you backing me up when we come to get them out."

Leland closed the last bag. "We're out of time to argue. You said Vega's shipment could be here at any minute. Anna and I need to get on the road if we're going to make it up to Baxtla by seven.

Marissa stared hard at both men before replying. "Alright, but I'm on the record not liking this."

"Understood," said Nick. "Give him your GPS locater. That's the best we can do."

Marissa looked at Nick reluctantly, obviously feeling like he'd turned on her. She pulled a small device from her cargo shorts pocket and handed it over to Leland.

"Just press here and it sends a GPS signal," she explained. "We'll be able to pinpoint your location to within five yards."

Leland examined the small device that looked like something from a spy movie. "That's very James Bondish."

"Yeah, well. Working with us has its perks."

She stooped to reopen Leland's backpack. "I'm going to need a gun or two from this arsenal we were planning to share."

"By all means," said Leland. "Take what you need, then please get the hell out of here." He smiled as he said it.

Marissa laughed and the tension eased. "Screw you. I've been kicked out of nicer countries than this." She pulled two Sig Sauer P226 9mms and several clips of ammunition from the bag.

Nick chuckled under his breath and they both climbed back into the plane.

Leland leaned in before they shut the door. "I'll call you on the sat phone when I have an extraction point."

"Or just use the chip. And be careful," said Nick. "Gavin'll be pissed if you get yourself killed before you can come to work for him."

"Gavin doesn't scare me." *At least not much.* Leland picked up the packs. "We gotta go," he told Anna, heading for the pickup.

Her eyes were full of questions, but she said nothing. There wasn't anything to say. They both knew she was a liability, but one he'd knowingly taken on.

He'd admit now that, yes, he was here because he felt responsible for Zach's disappearance. But there were no other options for Anna. No choice of whether she could stay or go.

They'd kill her boy if she didn't show with the money by the designated drop time. That was the only certainty they had about anything today.

Ignoring the pain in his ankle, Leland hustled into the ancient pickup truck, grateful it wasn't a stick shift and that the boot was on his left leg. They were headed toward the mountains before the plane took off.

He'd just made the turn from the hard-packed earthen trail around the airstrip onto the asphalt when a vehicle shot out of the trees and barreled down the main road. The airstrip got smaller in his rear-view mirror as the black SUV grew larger on the horizon. He hoped these weren't Vega's men making the drop, but they seemed the most likely to be in this desolate place.

On the present course, the two vehicles would pass each other. Would the men assume Leland was coming from the airstrip or from further away? He prayed the latter. There was no place to hide, so he would have to brazenly drive past them.

This truck of Paulo's was serviceable for getting where they needed to go, but it would be no match in a road race with a late-model SUV if Vega's men decided to follow. The road was horrific with potholes that seemed the size of the Grand Canyon. The only way to do this was to bluff with confidence. No one was supposed to know that anything was going down at the airstrip, so why would the occupants of the SUV be suspicious?

Because they knew about Zach and the money? A kidnapping with a large ransom demand wasn't something that would stay secret very long in this area. An American woman travelling with that amount of cash wouldn't stay secret at all.

Leland donned a spare ball cap lying on the seat between them and hunched down in front of the wheel. "Anna, I need you to get on the floor board. I don't want anyone to see you when we pass these guys."

Without a word she slid off the bench seat onto the rubberized car mat. "How's this?" She knelt beside him and looked up, her hands beside his right knee, her face level with his lap.

He looked into her eyes. The position she was in had so many carnal connotations. He gave himself a mental shake to clear the vision of what he'd like to see her doing if the circumstances were different.

"You're fine," he muttered.

She stared at him with such absolute faith, his hands tightened on the steering wheel. She shouldn't trust him. He wasn't invincible. He'd proven that in the past. Just ask Ellis Colton or his wife.

"Keep your head down, no matter what." *And don't look at me like I can slay dragons.*

FROM HER VANTAGE point on the floorboards, Anna watched Leland steer the truck and pull a gun from his shoulder holster. He checked the revolver before placing it on the seat beside her hands.

"Look in the pack on the floor beside you," he said. "There are two Glocks. They're loaded. Set the larger one of them next to this one."

Anna was normally scared of guns and felt her eyes grow wider as she dug into the bag. How many weapons did he have? Flashlight, first aid kit, thermal survival blanket, packets of what looked like freeze-dried food, and a water filter, along with two handguns plus ammunition.

Her fingers brushed against the hard surface of the guns. One was definitely smaller than the other. The sensation brought her up short. This wasn't just an "emergency kit."

"Are you really going to shoot those people?" she asked.

"I hope not." He nodded to the revolver on the seat beside his leg. "This is insurance."

She gingerly placed the larger of the two guns on the seat. Leland picked it up and checked the magazine without slowing down.

"Hopefully we're going to blow right past these folks, and they'll just be regular citizens out for a drive," he said.

She drew a harsh breath. "Alright, even I'm not that naïve."

He smiled coolly. "Never hurts to think positive."

They hit a particularly wicked pothole and she bumped her head on the glove box, seeing stars.

"Jesus. You okay?" He reached out to touch her shoulder.

She nodded. A mistake. The movement made her head spin more.

"It's this road. There must be holes the size of bathtubs in the asphalt. It's rattling the teeth out of my head," she said.

He squeezed her shoulder before putting his hand back on the steering wheel. He drove at a steady but sedate pace. "This truck is topping out at 50 mph." She appreciated he didn't say what they were both thinking. It would get ugly if the SUV tried to follow them.

She studied Leland's profile. With the cap on she couldn't see his features clearly. He'd shoved on a pair of aviator glasses from his pocket. With his dark hair and perpetually tanned skin she supposed he could pass for a local from a distance. She would have no such advantage with her blonde hair and blue eyes.

She couldn't see the SUV herself but knew it had to be getting closer from watching Leland's jaw tighten.

"Hang on," he said. "Here they come."

Chapter Eighteen

THE BLACK SUV blew past them, doing at least eighty miles per hour. Leland watched in the rear-view mirror as the vehicle's brake lights flashed. He pressed on his own accelerator, but it was useless. This truck wasn't budging above fifty-four miles per hour, and he was keenly aware that it wasn't armored like some DEA vehicles in Mexico. He focused on the SUV as it slowed to a complete stop in the middle of the roadway.

Then . . . nothing.

"Well, hell," he murmured.

"What is it?" asked Anna.

"They've stopped, and they're just sitting in the center of the road."

"What does that mean?"

"Don't know. Maybe they're waiting on orders from someone else. If they're meeting a plane, they've got to decide what's more important—us or the shipment they're picking up."

"I hope the shipment's winning," said Anna.

"From your lips to God's ears." The brake lights blinked off in his rear-view mirror and the SUV did a three-point turn on the country lane. "No such luck, they're turning around."

"Oh my God. Can we outrun them?"

He shrugged, not wanting to alarm her but needing to prepare her for what was coming. "Not in this heap." He pressed down on the accelerator anyway and watched as the SUV appeared closer and closer in his side mirror.

An arm holding an AK-47 popped out of the passenger's side window.

"Stay down!" He hunkered down himself and grabbed his Ruger from the seat as they rattled over the massive potholes and broken pieces of asphalt. Their best hope was that the gunman wouldn't be an accurate marksman on the rough road.

Seconds later shots rang out. Three in a row. One hit the rear window. Glass shattered. Anna screamed. The other two shots went wide.

Leland swerved to avoid a particularly large pothole and another bullet hit his side-view mirror. The glass disappeared. He glanced in the rear-view again. So much for the gunman not being accurate.

The SUV was within twenty yards.

He swerved again, going purely on instinct and hoping

to throw off the shooter's aim. The sound of bullets striking metal resonated through the cab. Anna squealed.

He glanced down to check on her. Her eyes were wide and her face pale, but she wasn't hit. He exhaled the breath he'd been holding and checked out the passenger-side window.

The shooter's arm had disappeared back inside the SUV. Was he reloading or giving up? Leland felt like he was pressing his foot through the partially rusted-out floorboard.

In the rear-view mirror he saw the SUV abruptly stop once again in the middle of the road. In ten seconds the vehicle had turned and was headed in the opposite direction, back toward the airstrip.

Why? He had no idea. But he wasn't going to complain. They'd survived. He didn't want to stop or even slow down. More than anything he wanted Anna on the floor until he was sure they were safe.

But that wasn't happening. She popped onto the ratty bench seat without asking and stared out the back broken window. The mountains were closer now.

"Where's the SUV?" she asked.

"They turned around."

"Why?" "No idea.

"What was that?"

He shrugged, a little irritated at her naiveté but trying to be patient. She truly had no idea what they were about to get into.

"It wasn't the welcome wagon, that's for damn sure," he explained, tamping down his frustration. "My best guess is drug dealers meeting their suppliers. They must have decided the shipment was more important than us, or maybe they just wanted to scare us off from hanging around while they met the incoming flight."

"Well, it worked. I certainly don't want to hang around."

"Me either." He caught her eye as she pushed the Glock away from her hip and closer to him.

Color was gradually returning to her face. She studied him a moment and when he would have kept staring, they hit a pothole and abruptly broke eye contact.

"How much time do we have before the deadline?" she asked. "I don't have a watch."

Leland checked his. "It's 5:45. Gives us a little over an hour to get to Baxtla.

"Will we make it?" Her anxiety level seemed higher now than when the bad guys were shooting moments ago.

"We'll be cutting it close, but we should get there by seven, barring any more complications."

She perched on the edge of her seat, practically vibrating with nerves. "You're sure?"

"Yeah, I'm sure. Trust me."

ANNA SMIRKED AT him. "You keep asking me to trust you. That's not easy for me."

He took his eyes off the road again to give her one of those piercing stares. "I know, but you have to trust someone. Why not trust me?"

For some reason the words took her by surprise.

Wasn't she trusting him already?

Or was it that she had no other option? She didn't have a good answer, so she said nothing.

They drove up the mountain without further incident. He asked her to put the Glock away. The landscape changed abruptly and vegetation thickened while the road conditions disintegrated. Massive vines cascaded down from huge trees on either side of the narrow track that was now more gravel and dirt than asphalt.

Branches draped across the road, almost touching the roof of the truck. The pickup's windows were down to combat the heat, and the sound of the jungle could occasionally be heard over the gasping engine. Birds sang and other animals chattered. The sky was barely visible overhead.

It was like being in a tunnel surrounded by more shades of green than she could count. They rolled over a tiny bridge above a gurgling stream. It would have been a gorgeous drive if the circumstances were different.

Sweat puddled at the base of her spine. Her heart beat so fast she had difficulty catching her breath. Anna was slowly unhinging as they wound their way up the mountain. Focused on driving, Leland seemed unaware of her distress.

She closed her eyes and concentrated on breathing without hyperventilating. She was grateful he wasn't speaking to her. Carrying on a conversation at this point would have been beyond her capabilities.

Fifteen minutes later he stopped the vehicle. She was surprised to see that the vegetation had cleared slightly, making the road appear a bit wider. She turned to face him with a question in her eyes.

"We're almost there," he explained. "And I need to talk to you. This is going to be hard. Promise me you'll do whatever I ask up here—no arguments, no hesitation."

Part of her bristled at his words, but the nervous, nauseous side of her was grateful he would be calling the shots.

"This is all about getting you and Zach out of here unharmed. Remember that, no matter what. I may ask you to do something that seems the complete opposite of what you think you should do, but don't hesitate and don't think. Do what I say. Everything from here on is about getting us out of this alive."

She nodded, unable to speak; her tongue was instantly dry and thick. Her mouth tasted of metallic fear. She couldn't suppress the shudder that ran through her.

He studied her, staring into her eyes. She didn't know what he was searching for but he seemed satisfied with what he read there in her face and put the truck back in gear.

Beyond that little clearing of vegetation there was no indication that a town was ahead. Baxtla sprang up seemingly out of nowhere, a dusty wide spot in what could scarcely be called a road.

Two donkeys grazed in a ditch beside the main drag. Several chickens scratched about in the middle of the dirt and gravel track, cackling and flapping as Leland drew closer. A handful of storefronts lined the dirt street, including a grocery and a tiny motel. At the far end stood a picturesque church.

The cantina beside the motel appeared to be the only one in town. A faded flamingo with feathers more brown than pink was painted on a large piece of warped plywood beside the entrance. Besides the donkeys and chickens, no life was apparent.

"It's almost seven o'clock. Maybe everyone is in the bar?" he suggested. Seemingly unfazed, Leland parked in front of the cantina. "Are you ready for this?"

"Does it matter if I am or not?"

His smile was grim. "Not really, but I need you to hold it together."

"I'll be fine."

He laughed but there was no humor in the sound. "I know what *fine* means when a woman says it."

He shook his head and reached past her to pull the extra weapons from his pack on the floor. He shoved the larger gun into his waistband and checked the magazine on a smaller one before sticking it into the top of his orthopedic boot along with the GPS locater.

"It's five till. Let's do this."

"Are we taking the money inside?" she asked.

"Yeah, our backpacks, too. This truck would be the first place someone would look."

He was right. The dilapidated vehicle would be an easy mark for anyone interested in the strangers.

"So we're just going to walk in there with the money?" she asked.

"I can't think of a better way to do it. To get Zach back we've got to play exactly by the rules laid out for us." He was closer to her on the bench seat than he'd been the entire drive, and he was staring at her again. His eyes seemed cooler than she remembered.

"I'm scared," she admitted.

His gaze warmed. "It's okay. I'm going to be with you the entire time."

He reached out to brush her cheek with his knuckles, and she felt a white-hot sensation race down her face and neck. The jolt she got when he touched her was reflected in the expression on his face. He'd felt it, too.

His hand dropped as if he'd been burned. He swallowed visibly. "Don't worry. It's going to be *fine*." He grinned at her, obviously trying to lighten the moment, but she was too scared to be cheered.

They got out and hurried toward the sad-looking Cantina El Flamenco. Swinging through the traditional half doors, they entered a darkened room. Anna's eyes gradually adjusted from the bright sunlight outside.

Ceiling fans spun lazily overhead, and an old-fashioned bar ran along the back wall with a large mirror behind and several barstools in front. The floor was concrete. Tables and chairs were scattered about. One table was covered with the remains of a domino game and another held a deck of cards and four half-finished drinks.

Curiously, a pool table that looked brand new was to the side of the bar. A door between the billiards table and bar was halfway open. Several glasses, partially filled with liquor, were on the sturdy oak counter, but the place was deserted.

"Where is everyone?" she asked, gripping the strap of her borrowed pack.

Leland straightened beside her. "Seems customers left in a hurry," he said.

"What would cause patrons to leave unfinished drinks at their places?"

"Baxtla's a cartel town. The law-abiding citizens know when it's best to get out of harm's way."

His words sounded ominous. She tried to swallow and couldn't, her mouth was too dry.

Now that he'd said so, she could see it was obvious these folks knew trouble was coming.

"Hello?" Leland called. "Anyone here?"

Anna's heart rate ratcheted up and she forced herself to breath as he pulled his revolver from the shoulder holster. He wound around scattered tables toward the door beside the bar and was about to knock when it slowly swung open.

Chapter Nineteen

LELAND TIGHTENED HIS grip on the Ruger, every instinct inside him screaming *setup*. Behind the door an older gray-haired man was seated at a scarred captain's desk. At the sight of Leland's gun, the man raised his hands from the workspace to the back of his head.

"I am unarmed," he said in precise but slightly accented English. "I have a message for the woman." He nodded toward a manila envelope at the corner of the desk.

Leland surveyed the windowless room, empty but for the man and the large piece of furniture that seemed strangely out of place. There was no way in or out unless one walked through the bar, still he didn't relax. "Where is everyone?" he asked.

"People in this town have a strong sense of self preservation. They know when to leave people alone to discuss *business*."

Great. The old man confirmed what he'd told Anna moments earlier. Everyone knew what they were doing here.

"Anna, pick up the packet and bring it back before you open it."

He didn't lower the gun even when she stood beside him once more. She eyed him before ripping the envelope open and turning it upside down. A braided, multi-colored strand of leather fell into her palm along with a folded sheet of paper.

Leland recognized the item before Anna murmured, "Zach's bracelet." He took the note while she turned the leather over and over in her hands.

The letter was written in block letters again, but the handwriting was different from yesterday's ransom note.

Leave the cash here. Go next door to the motel and wait for instructions. A message will be sent explaining where to pick up the boy.

"You can't believe we'll do this." Leland glared at the man as Anna studied the note. "Just leave the money and trust you to return the boy? We require more than a bracelet as proof of life before turning over the entire ransom."

Beside him Anna made a noise of protest, but Leland put his hand on her arm to keep her silent.

The old man gazed at her with something akin to sympathy in his eyes. "As I said, I am only a messenger. The men who have the boy wish him no harm. They realize he is ill. Currently he is being cared for in the appropriate environment with proper medication. It will take several hours to transport him here safely. They would like you to be their guests while you wait next door."

Guests? Right.

Leland felt a flash of anger but tamped it down. "We'd prefer to keep the money with us until the boy is here."

The man shook his head. "That is impossible. There will be no exchange unless you leave the money with me now."

Anna made another small keening sound in her throat. Leland glanced her way. If possible, her face had grown more pale, and she was biting that lower lip that always caused a serious tightening in his gut.

The man continued. "Do as you're instructed and the boy will be fine."

Anna touched his arm and he felt that shock of contact he'd noticed earlier in the truck. "Leland, please. We have to do as he says. If they have Zach—"

"Oh, they have him," said Leland. "The bracelet proves it." He moved closer to the desk. "Who do you work for?"

"Does it matter?" asked the old man. "You just need to follow the instructions."

"Whose instructions? Does Tomas Rivera have her son?"

"I'm not at liberty to say, but every man in this town knows you have cash. News like that spreads quickly. Keeping it safe until the exchange tomorrow could prove daunting. Even for you, Mr. Hollis."

Jesus, they knew who he was. Leland had almost convinced himself that this situation had nothing to do with him and the cartel wouldn't figure out he was in the area till they were gone.

He refused to allow the shock to show, but the old man had him. This was Rivera territory. If the cartel chose to come after Anna, the ransom, or him, Leland would be hard-pressed to stop them. If that happened, his argument was pointless. The money wouldn't be around tomorrow for the exchange anyway.

"Follow the instructions and you only have yourselves to keep safe. Won't that be challenge enough?" asked the old man.

"Without the cash we have no bargaining power, nothing to ensure her boy will be returned."

The man directed his words to Anna. "The people who have your son will keep their word. I can assure you."

"The people who took him in the first place?" Leland's voice was harsh, but subtlety wasn't working. No huge surprise. "They kidnapped an extremely ill boy. We have no way of knowing what *the people* will or won't do."

"Leland, please—" Anna reached out to grab his hand.

He ignored her. "We'll leave half the money here with you tonight. You can have the other half when the boy is delivered."

"That is not what I was instructed to do." The man's eyes flared.

"You don't have a choice. We leave you with half or we leave you with none."

STILL ON AUTOPILOT, Anna followed Leland out of the cantina toward the small motel next door. She was furious at what he'd done, the chance he'd just taken with

Zach's life. Yet she was willing to wait until she got him alone to hash it out.

The air was cooler and smelled like rain. The bright sun from earlier might never have been. The time felt later in the evening than it really was. Only thirty minutes had gone by while they were inside. Slow, fat raindrops began pelting her head as they hurried along the dirt sidewalk. They stepped through the motel's doorway as a huge clap of thunder rumbled, warning of more stormy weather to come.

Anna shook the water out of her hair and gazed around the lobby. It was a tired-looking establishment but clean. They waited as the desk clerk, a teenage girl wearing a Nine Inch Nails t-shirt, fussed at someone on the phone in barely accented English about the hotel's low butane supply. She ended the call with a rude Spanish expletive and checked them into a room that was already reserved in Leland's name.

The people who had Zach had known this was a forgone conclusion. They'd even known Leland was bringing her. What else had already been decided that Anna had no control over?

By the time they got to the room she was shivering, but not from the drop in temperature. Her shaking had started when Leland emptied half the ransom onto the old man's desk. Their contact had insisted they leave without the empty duffel bag. Leland had transferred the other half of the money to his and Anna's backpacks.

"For your safety," the man had said. "So no one will believe you still have the cash. I could keep you safer if you left it all."

Leland didn't believe showing themselves on the street without a duffel bag would make a difference, but he'd been willing to be cooperative on that point and she was grateful.

He closed their motel room door, and Anna heard the thumb latch click. There was no chain. Despite her anger, she was relieved they only had the one room. She didn't want to be left alone anywhere in this town.

Leland toured the accommodation, still carrying his backpack, but didn't explain what he was looking for. Their scantly furnished room was on the front of the building with an open window facing Baxtla's main thoroughfare. Scuffed dark wood paneling made it feel like they were in a cave.

Rain poured from the sky and lightning flashed close by. A double bed and rickety dresser were the only pieces of furniture. On the plus side, they had a private bath.

Leland pushed aside the threadbare curtain billowing in the storm's breeze and peered through the window's dilapidated screen before speaking. "I don't like being where everyone knows we are."

"Me, either." She put her backpack on the bed. "But shouldn't we be safe? Anyone watching would think we no longer have the cash, right?"

"That was the idea, yes. But I'm not confident our little ruse worked."

Anna sank onto the multi-colored spread, shuddering as the mattress gave an ominous squeak.

"Why did you do that?" She heard the anger in her tone, but at this point she didn't care what he thought.

Leland didn't look surprised at her question. He knew what she was talking about. "It was the only way to keep any bargaining power."

"How can you be sure the kidnappers won't take our not-following-instructions out on Zach? It would be so easy to hurt him."

He scrutinized her a moment before answering. "I can't be sure of anything, but one thing I do know. If we'd given that man all the ransom money, we would never see Zach alive again."

Her face blanched and for a moment she couldn't speak. She feared Leland was right, but his bluntness frightened her. Tears burned at the corner of her eyelids. She felt light-headed, dizzy, and definitely not up for a repeat of fainting at his feet like yesterday.

"I need to eat something," she muttered to herself.

"When was the last time you had a real meal?" His Southern cadence was more pronounced now than it had been earlier.

"Coffee this morning."

"Coffee doesn't count." He strode toward her from the window.

"The last time I had a meal was the night before last when I was with Max." *When I had too much to drink and not enough to eat.*

Leland studied her face for a moment before swinging his backpack onto the bed beside hers and digging into one of the pockets. "That I can fix. Let's eat." He slid his shoulder holster off and put it beside their packs along with the gun from his waistband.

She thought he would have only freeze-dried fare, but he came up with an energy bar, some granola, and chocolate candy. He ran water from the bathroom tap into a sport bottle with a special built-in filtration system.

"Don't want to add *turista* to this experience," he said, handing her the water bottle.

Uncomfortable sitting on the bed, she stood and sipped before biting into the energy bar, surprised at how famished she was. He took the filtered water and poured some into one of the freeze-dried packets, using the old dresser as a counter.

"Will that work without heating it up?" asked Anna, coming closer to watch him mix the liquid in.

He shrugged. "Heat doesn't make a whole lot of difference. This stuff tastes awful hot or cold."

"I could eat anything right now."

"Well, that's good. When you're starving, it's about the only time this crap is palatable."

She huffed a laugh and smiled for the first time in what felt like days. Breaking off half the energy bar, she handed it to him. "Let's split this."

He shook his head. "No need. I've got another."

He rearranged their packs, putting the other half of the ransom money and ammunition in his before combining his bag's remaining contents with hers. Ten minutes later he was stirring meatloaf and handing her a spoon. As predicted, it did taste a bit like cardboard, but she didn't mind. She was starving.

She ate half before handing him the spoon and packet back. Her fingers brushed his, setting off a new sizzle of awareness that shot up her arm. She froze and looked up to see the frank sexual heat in his gaze.

Lightning flashed at the window and thunder shattered the clouds as the rain continued beating down in earnest. Still shaken by the sexual zing, she started at the thunder. Her throat went dry.

"You okay?" he asked, reaching out to touch her shoulder.

She shook her head. *Why was this happening?* They'd been together all afternoon and she'd felt nothing.

Now suddenly she was aware of everything about him: the warmth coming off his body, even through his clothes; the deep jade color of his eyes; his broad hand on her shoulder; the scent of him. Heat, spice and man.

She wet her lips and his eyes flared a darker green. She had no idea what to say, but she knew what she wanted.

"We can't do this," she said.

"I know. It's insanity." His eyes pierced hers and she couldn't look away.

She wasn't sure who leaned forward first, but when her lips touched his, it didn't matter anymore. He angled his mouth into hers and slid his tongue along the seam of her lips. She deepened the kiss and was instantly adrift in a sea of sensation.

Her arms went around his neck. His hands moved to her hips, pulling her closer to the heat and hardness of him. She arched into his chest, holding on as he slipped a hand under her tank top and moved his fingers up to the side of her breast. His lips were at her temple.

They pulled and tugged at each other's clothing. She

helped him yank his shirt over his head. If she stopped to think, she'd realize this was crazy and made no sense. But she wasn't going to stop and think. All she could focus on was what she was feeling.

He lifted the hem of her top to raise it up and off then stood back to study her. The fire in his gaze took away any doubts she might have had about this interlude being some kind of misplaced pity. He was watching her face, his eyes focused so intently she forgot everything.

"Breathe, Anna." He touched her cheek and kissed his way from her jawline to her chest.

When he reached her bra, he undid the front clasp with one hand. Pushing the lacy garment out of the way, he bent down to pull her nipple into his mouth. She gasped as her skin pebbled and peaked then closed her eyes when his hand skimmed under her gauzy skirt. His hand skated up her thigh and she shivered when his fingers slid higher still.

She was awash in awareness. The exquisite feel of his sculpted chest was hot against her bare skin. The sound of the rain beating against the tin roof of the motel blocked out the world.

Her back bumped the paneling next to the dresser and she froze, but only for a moment. She smiled, opening her eyes to meet his intense stare. The expression on his face took her breath away.

"You are so damn beautiful," he murmured, pressing her to the wall.

He lifted her up and wrapped her legs around his hips, moving to cover her with his body. Her skirt was bunched around her waist and she felt the hard length of him touching her core. His hands caressed her bottom before his palms slipped past the edge of her panties.

She gasped when he pushed two fingers inside her, taking her to the brink. Higher and higher she spun before closing her eyes and pressing her face into his neck, unable to stand the passion of his gaze any longer. With a deep sigh, she shattered.

He held her against the wall as the waves of the orgasm crashed over her. After she could breathe again without gasping, she tilted her head up to meet his eyes. They were still dark and laser-focused on hers as she slid down his body.

Without hesitation she reached for him, unzipping his jeans. He hissed in a breath when she slipped her fingers beneath his underwear's elastic waistband to stroke her hand along the hard length of him.

He groaned and pulled her fingers away, lightly holding her wrists and pressing himself against her.

Touching his forehead to hers, he took a gulp of air. "I want this, Anna. I want you. Smart or stupid, I want to make love to you. But I don't have a condom, and . . ."

"I'm not on the pill," she finished for him. *And I've just slept with my ex, who has the morals of an alley cat.* She felt her face flush with the reminder of their illuminating visit to the ER last night.

He smiled faintly, but something in his eyes changed. That hadn't been what he was going to say.

There was a long pause as he searched her face before

he said, "We're going to stop now before we do something crazy."

Her cheeks burned, and she didn't need a mirror to know she was blushing a furious red. He was right. She knew he was right, regardless of his reasons for stopping.

She didn't know what to say, but she had to say something. This man was risking so much for her and for Zach. He was obviously attracted to her or giving a remarkable imitation of it. She didn't want him to think she was pouting because they weren't having sex.

She took a deep breath, determined to clear the air somehow. Before she could speak he abruptly released her hands, kissed her temple, and stepped back, his eyes no longer searching hers.

She'd missed the moment and longed to pull him back to her, to explain. Anything. Instead, she crossed her arms across her bare breasts, embarrassed now by her partial nudity. Her shirt was just behind him on the floor.

"Could you hand me my top, please?"

LELAND BENT DOWN to retrieve Anna's shirt and turned away, staring at the floor in front of him to give her privacy. What the hell was he doing? At least he'd given the room a cursory inspection to rule out cameras or bugs before he'd practically screwed her against the bedroom wall.

What he'd really wanted to tell her, before they'd gotten sidetracked with the birth control issue, was the same thing he'd wanted to tell her last night. She didn't have to do him to get Zach back. Whether or not they had sex had no bearing on whether he'd help find her son.

Not that he didn't want her. He did. So much so that his teeth ached.

He hadn't known her long but what he knew fascinated him. To have dealt with everything she had in the past year and to still be so strong. That inner strength captivated him.

It was important she not think he expected sex in exchange for his help. Sex wasn't some kind of payoff. He needed to clarify that right away.

Besides, neither of them was going to be able to sleep now. He sighed, zipped his cargo shorts and pulled on his t-shirt and shoulder holster with the Ruger. He shoved the larger Glock into his backpack. This was going to be a long evening.

The night breeze had shifted the shabby curtain to the side, leaving an unobscured view into the room. He turned to face her, wondering if anyone on the street had just gotten an eyeful.

A red laser dot reflected off the wide shoulder strap of her tank top. Recognizing the threat, he dove for her, shouting, "Down. Get down!"

Chapter Twenty

LELAND TACKLED ANNA around the waist and pulled her to the floor. A bullet hit the wall with a *sphlift*, right where she'd been standing a half second earlier.

He climbed on top of her, his heart rate skyrocketing, and covered her completely with his body. His boot was awkward. His knee came down between her legs, trapping her in the skirt. More shots slapped the stucco, but they were all hitting above his head.

The gunman must be using a silencer. A loud car engine revved in the street. Voices shouted and bullets flew through the window, no longer silenced.

How many shooters were there?

A flaming bottle whooshed through the window. Breaking on impact, the fire spread rapidly across the dry plywood floor. The pop of more bullets against the wall sounded deceptively benign.

"What's happening?" Anna's lips were at his ear.

Her warm breath would have felt seductive if not for the shots flying overhead and fire licking at his ass. He was crushing her with his body weight but it was the only way to protect her from the onslaught.

"Why are they shooting at us?" Her voice was thin, like she was having trouble breathing.

He raised up on his elbows to take his weight off of her chest but kept his head down next to hers. "They want the money."

"How do they know about the ransom?" she asked.

"Everyone within a hundred miles knows about it." He raised his head cautiously.

They were nose to nose, but he ignored the intimacy of the position. They had to get out of the smoke-filled room. In here, even with just half the money, they were sitting ducks.

He needed his bag. It held all his ammunition and the Glock 17. And they couldn't leave the cash, not now anyway. Having the money might be the only thing to keep them alive when they got out of here.

"Come on." He rolled to the side and tugged Anna's hand to pull her along with him. "But don't raise your head."

Another bullet hit the wall where she had been moments earlier. God, how many men were there? Knowing that could make a difference in getting out of this alive.

"The old man was right. We should have left all the ransom money with him." She wriggled along beside him as Leland reached onto the bed for his backpack and pulled extra speed loaders from the side pocket for his Ruger.

He tapped the bag. "This is our only leverage to getting Zach back, but we have to hang on to it until the exchange."

"So that whole charade of leaving the duffel and taking half the cash was worthless?"

"No, we had to try. This was just too big of a secret to keep." He zipped the pack and put it on both shoulders before pulling her bag off the bed as well.

She shuddered. "Or someone doesn't want us to get Zach back?"

He shrugged. "I don't know the answer to that, but we're not going to figure it out in here."

He helped her put her pack on. Anna gamely gripped her skirt in one hand as they belly-crawled across the floor to the door. He reached to unlock the thumb latch. After he peered around the doorframe, they clambered into the hallway and stood to run.

Leland didn't head toward the lobby. Instead, he pulled Anna down the hall along with him to the back of the building. Gritting his teeth against the pain in his ankle, he stumped along to the exit.

A screen door that had seen better days led out to a large stretch of gravel serving as a parking lot for the El Flamenco and the motel. Two cars were parked there. About twenty yards out in the middle of the lot was the butane tank he'd heard the clerk complaining about on the phone. The tank that was almost empty, or so she'd claimed.

Beyond the parking lot and butane tank was dense jungle, comprised of tall trees and vines. Leland had no idea how many trigger-happy fortune hunters were out here. At least two, more likely three to four. So far the shots had all been coming from the north end of the motel on the cantina side.

Thunder rumbled in the distance and the rain continued to beat down. He pressed his back to the wall, pulling Anna beside him. The desk clerk ran toward them from the lobby. Leland drew his gun and blocked her path before pushing the girl against the scuffed paneling, his arm across her neck.

"What do you want?" he demanded.

"I'm here to get you out," she said.

"What did you have in mind?"

She shrugged. "I had several ideas before the shooting started. "I'm supposed to take care of you."

"Who hired you?" She squirmed but he wasn't letting up on her throat.

Her eyes bulged in fear and her voice squeaked. "For this job? Rivera. He owns everything in this town. Money came in an envelope with instructions to look after you. At the time the request seemed easy. Just make sure you two have everything you need."

She stopped and took a labored breath before continuing. "I didn't ask questions. But I don't want his men coming after me tomorrow because two crazy Americans burned up in this fire trap of a motel."

Leland studied her a moment longer before letting up the pressure on her airway. "Do you know where we can hide?"

She nodded and rubbed her throat but didn't break eye contact.

"Where?"

"First, let's get out of the building."

"We're going to have to run for it," he said. "See the tree line there? That's where we're headed."

"Into the jungle?" Anna's voice broke on *jungle*.

"For now," said Leland. "Like she said, we've got to get out of this building. We can decide what we're going to do once we are away from here."

"But the shooters?" asked the girl.

"I'm going to distract them," said Leland.

Anna's eyes were as huge as the girl's had been earlier. "How?" she asked.

"Do you trust me?"

She nodded.

"Okay, that's all I need to know. I hope you were telling the truth about that tank being empty," he muttered to the girl.

She stared blankly at him for a beat until understanding dawned. "Yes, it's almost empty."

"Good." With the Ruger he took careful aim on the metal cylinder that was the size of a SMART car and pulled the trigger.

The explosion was instantaneous. The tank rocketed into the air, forming a mushroom cloud of flame. Fire spewed out from the cloud like water from a broken main.

He shielded Anna and the girl from the heat and pressure wave of the blast with his body, his back taking the brunt of the compression. They were on the ragged edge of being far enough away to be safe.

With the rain coming down in earnest, the fire couldn't catch hold of the dry underbrush, but acrid smoke formed a solid curtain. The north end of the parking lot was obscured. Shouts drifted down the hallway behind them. Some of the shooters were coming for them.

"It's time to go," he said.

Anna's face was chalk white as he grabbed her hand and the girl's. Together they headed for the trees. His boot slowed him down. He tripped on the uneven ground of the makeshift parking lot, almost taking everyone out. Still, they were shielded from any shots coming from the north by the flames and corrosive smoke.

To protect his lungs, Leland tried to hold his breath as he ran. The rain caused more smoke, and when they passed the flaming tank, the jungle in front of them and the motel behind them disappeared in the hazy gloom. He heard a couple more shots, but over the sounds of the hissing flames, he couldn't tell which side they were coming from.

They ran through a gray, caustic fog. Headed for the jungle, he wasn't entirely sure they were running in a straight line anymore. With every step, pain radiated up his ankle to his leg and back.

When was the last time he'd had a Vicodin? Putting any weight on the boot was agony. He must have done something to it in the dash from the motel.

They burst into the underbrush and vines of the jungle. Branches ripped at their clothes and a large limb with hand-sized leaves slapped him in the face. Twenty yards into the morass, the noise of the fire and chaos dissolved.

The grass was tall and the foliage thickened. Rain fell in a steady drizzle through primeval-sized leaves. Leland heard a couple of muffled shouts but beyond that, nothing. The girl abruptly dropped his hand, sinking down to a tree stump.

He pulled Anna closer. Her hair was on its way to being soaked. Her shirt was torn and her cheek scratched. Without a word she sank to the ground also, seemingly uncaring about the rain and mud. At least her face was no longer marble white.

Smoke drifted into the vines, but there was no worry that flames would spread to the jungle. The hard rain would see to that. Anna pulled on Leland's hand, and he sat beside her, relieved to be off his feet.

"Okay," Anna wheezed. "We're out of the motel, and we still have the money. What do we do now?"

ANNA SAT BESIDE Leland in the mud as rain beat down around her. She didn't care that she was dirty, wet and getting wetter by the minute. She was just grateful for the time being to be seated in the relative safety of a tropical palm and not worrying about someone putting a bullet in her back.

If she stopped to think about everything that had happened to her in the past two days, she might run screaming into the wet, gloomy night. Max had attacked her, she'd gone by ambulance to the ER, Zach had been kidnapped, men had shot at her, she'd flown to Mexico to deliver a ransom, almost had sex with a relative stranger, been fire-bombed in a motel room, then had more gunmen shoot at her. If she'd read all this in a book, she wouldn't have believed it.

The young girl was staring at her from a perch beside the tree trunk. Anna could feel her dark-eyed scrutiny across the rain-soaked space. "Any ideas?" Anna asked, no longer caring if Leland or the girl answered.

"We need to get out of here. They'll find us if we don't move," he said, leaning against the tree with his booted leg out in front of him.

He'd propped it on a fallen log at their feet. Anna wondered if he had hurt it when they ran just now. She certainly couldn't tell from his stoic expression.

"Are you sure we won't be safer waiting it out here?" she asked.

The girl didn't speak.

"We left a clear path," Leland replied, pointing toward their footprints in the muddy sand. "Once they figure out we aren't in the motel, they're sure to start looking outside."

Anna glanced at the broken foliage behind her. Yep, she'd left a trail through the underbrush a blind elephant could follow. "Who were those shooters?" she asked.

Leland shrugged. "Could have been people who heard about the ransom and wanted the money for themselves, or someone in this area who has it in for me and found out I'm here. Or it could be the folks who have Zach."

The thing that had been niggling at the back of her head all along coalesced into a coherent question. At last, what she should have asked eighteen hours earlier was occurring to her. "Would someone who wants to hurt you come after Zach to get at you?"

She didn't think he was going to answer at first. He stared at the toe of his boot cast, finally lifting his face to study hers.

"Would someone with a vendetta against you take it to that extreme?" repeated Anna. It was vitally important she have an answer to this question.

"I'm a DEA agent. I've made some enemies in the cartels."

He wasn't answering her question, but she didn't want to believe what that could mean. Had he been lying to her since Zach was taken? Her breath felt heavy in her chest, like she couldn't take in enough air.

"Do you think drug dealers could have Zach? Did you think that last night when he was first taken and not tell me?" Her stomach hurt from the implications of the question.

His green eyes never wavered as he answered. "I'd hoped it wasn't true, but yes, I considered the possibility that the cartel could have taken him last night. I was staying at the hotel because of threats I received due to a trial I was testifying in."

"Why didn't you tell me Zach's disappearance could be connected? You lied. Why did you deliberately keep that from me?"

"Because you had enough to deal with, and I wasn't

sure what the hell was going on. Telling you then would have run you off, and you needed help. Even if this whole mess doesn't have anything to do with me—and I'm still not convinced it does—you need my help to get Zach."

"But last night you said the shooting at the hotel was because of you," she argued, heedless of keeping her voice down.

"That's right, and I still believe it. The shooting incident at the hotel in Dallas *was* because of me. I don't think those were the same people who took Zach. I think we're dealing with two separate issues. You said it yourself. Why would the kidnappers come after you before you had time to pay the ransom? They had nothing to gain and everything to lose."

She shook her head in disgust. That last statement might be true, but it wasn't the real reason he hadn't told her. Exhaustion and fear were overridden by the fury washing through her. There was something else going on in his answer, but she didn't know what it was.

The girl was watching their argument with unabashed interest. Anna ignored her.

Why had Leland not said anything last night about his work possibly being the cause of Zach's kidnapping? She felt betrayed, just as she'd felt betrayed yesterday when she'd overheard Max in that hotel suite. She never would have let Leland help her if she'd suspected he was in any way responsible for Zach's disappearance.

As angry as she was, a part of her knew he was right to have kept the information from her. But she wasn't sure which was worse. That he'd lied to her to protect her, or that he was treating her like a child who couldn't handle the truth.

She abhorred lies. Lying had destroyed her marriage, long before she'd heard Max's phone conversation in Cancun. But there was certainly nothing to be done about it now.

Arguing was useless. It would be insanity to try and sort out the implications of Leland's lying to her while they were trying to keep ahead of the gunmen. They had to find something more than the temporary cover of the jungle.

She couldn't afford to let her anger overrun her common sense. Like it or not, he was right. She needed him at the moment. And that meant she was stuck with him.

It didn't mean she had to like it. But she could put those feelings aside until the appropriate time. Like Scarlett O'Hara, she'd think about that tomorrow.

"So, I repeat. What do we do now?" she asked.

The shocked look on his face told Anna that he was more than mildly surprised she'd dropped the subject.

"I know a place we'll be safe," the girl offered.

Leland glanced back and forth between Anna and the young motel clerk. "How far away is this 'safe place'?" he asked.

"It's at the edge of town. No one lives there but me and my grandmother."

"Can we stay hidden in the undergrowth getting there?" he asked.

The girl nodded.

"Sounds like a plan," said Anna.

"Let's do it." He stood slowly, giving deference to his booted foot in a way he hadn't since she first met him.

Anna suspected it had something to do with their mad race across the uneven graveled lot. The three of them headed through the vines and otherworldly-sized leaves. Anna slogged through the untamed vegetation behind the girl with Leland bringing up the rear.

The going was difficult. Mud sucked at their shoes and the brush was thick, particularly without a machete to hack a path. Anna was grateful for the flats Marissa had loaned her at the AEGIS office to wear, instead of her beach flip-flops, but they weren't holding up well. Everyone was soaked when they reached their destination.

The cottage was built of cement blocks painted the same green as the foliage around it. Almost like a hunting blind of sorts, the building blended perfectly into the inhospitable terrain. The shutters were tightly closed against the rainy night, but tiny strips of light leaked out around the edges of the windows.

The girl rapped insistently at the front door. That seemed strange to Anna. Leland tensed behind her.

Why would you knock at your own home?

A lock clicked and the door swung open. Light poured into the steamy darkness. Standing in the threshold was a shirtless man holding a massive handgun. Even without the weapon in his hand, he'd never be mistaken for a harmless individual.

A black tribal tattoo spilled across his chest, over a shoulder to his arm and down his side, disappearing under the loose waistband of his jeans. Leland cursed under his breath, and Anna knew they were in trouble.

"Agent Hollis," the man spoke with a heavy accent. "I've been waiting for you."

"Hello, Cesar. It's been a while."

Chapter Twenty-One

Leland knew this man?

Anna studied Cesar's face as the girl wound herself around him like a cat. He had the body of a thirty-five-year-old, but was at least ten years older. Yet the girl didn't seem the least deterred. She kissed his neck and ran her hands across his chest, her fingers dipping dangerously low across his crotch.

"Get in," Cesar ordered, waving them all inside with his gun. "Drop your packs on the floor."

Anna glanced at Leland. His face was unreadable, but she could see the tension in his stance and clenching jaw. She moved forward with him. It wasn't like there was a choice. Together they stepped over the threshold and the door closed behind them.

They took their packs off. Anna was careful to let hers slide to the floor.

"What took so long?" Cesar demanded in Spanish.

His voice wasn't as gruff as it had been earlier. And no wonder, given that the girl had now slipped her hand beneath his waistband and was murmuring in his ear as she stroked him.

Shocked, Anna looked away, focusing on the man's face instead as the whispered conversation continued. There was a cruel look around his eyes and mouth that made her uncomfortable, not to mention that ugly-looking gun he was holding.

Despite her roving hands, Cesar interrupted the girl impatiently. "How many were there?" he demanded in Spanish.

The teenager shook her head and shrugged. "I heard all the shooting and ran to the back of the motel."

Cesar cursed and muttered something under his breath. "Search them," he said.

The girl went to Leland first, running her hands across his body much as she had Cesar's. Anna got the distinct impression the girl would have been much more thorough if her boyfriend wasn't watching.

She removed Leland's revolver, the gun from his boot, the extra ammunition in his pocket, his sat phone, and what looked like a prescription bottle, handing them all over to Cesar, who wasted no time in smashing the phone and putting the two guns in his own waistband.

Cesar examined the pill bottle and stared at the boot cast with a smug smile before handing the medication to the girl to give back to Leland. "I see no reason for you to be in pain while you're with me, but we can't have someone tracking us with your sat phone, now can we, Agent Hollis?"

Still Leland said nothing.

Where was the GPS locater Marissa had given him?

The girl searched Anna and found only the Children's Transplant Center pager. She started to remove it from her skirt pocket and Anna went wild.

"No!" Anna cried. "Please. It's not a phone, there's no GPS. It's my son's transplant pager from the hospital. They'll use it to notify us when a donor is found. Please, I don't—"

Leland put his hand on her shoulder in an attempt to calm her and she turned toward him, babbling now. "I didn't tell you about it. I . . . God, I don't even take a shower without leaving it on the bathroom counter."

She felt herself tearing up as the girl dispassionately handed the pager to Cesar. The drug dealer examined it thoroughly before studying Anna.

"There's no GPS," she repeated. "Please. Don't destroy it. You can hang on to it yourself. Just let me know if it . . . if it goes off."

Even in her messy emotional state, she realized how pathetic that sounded. Cesar scrutinized the device once more and shook his head before handing it back to the young girl who in turn gave it to Anna.

The pager was warm from everyone holding it. An inordinate sense of relief swept over her as Anna squeezed the black plastic between her own palms. This was crazy. She knew that. The thing was most likely out of range, here in the middle of absolute nowhere, but the device had become a talisman for her over the past twelve months.

The pager would go off one day. She knew it. It had to.

The girl searched their packs as she spoke with Cesar in muted tones. She showed him Leland's stash of ammunition, the other gun, and the money. Cesar shoved the weapon back into the pack. They lingered over the cash for a long moment with the girl still murmuring to him, but Anna couldn't make out what she was saying.

"Go," he finally ordered in Spanish. "Your grandmother is in the back room."

She hurried through the door beside the fireplace and closed it behind her.

"There were at least two shooters, possibly more," said Leland.

Anna looked at Leland like he'd lost his mind. Cesar eyed him suspiciously.

"Why would I lie?" asked Leland, directing the question to both of them.

"Why would you help?" asked Anna.

Leland answered without taking his eyes off of Cesar's. "If he doesn't know the details, it's doubtful he is on their side. Which means he most likely is our only way out of here. Besides, if he'd been planning to shoot us, he'd have done it by now. Cesar doesn't hesitate to do what's necessary."

Anna didn't like what Leland was saying, but it made some sense—if any of this did. Cesar watched them throughout the exchange without speaking.

"So what do we do?" she asked.

Leland sighed. "I think it depends on our host here. What is your plan, Cesar? We're a long way from your brother's house."

Cesar smiled and tilted his head toward them. "Not that far. I'm trying to decide whether I should shoot you now and avoid the hassle or try to figure out what the hell you're doing in Mexico when you were specifically told not to come back unless you wanted to leave in a body bag."

"What can I say? Sometimes you just feel like visiting the Mayan Riviera." Leland sounded like he was shooting the breeze while waiting in line for a latte at Starbucks instead of being held at gunpoint.

Cesar's laugh was harsh. "I believe you're slightly off course. At this moment we're a hundred miles from the ocean."

"I'm a spontaneous kind of guy. We got to the beach and decided to do some exploring in the interior." The words were light, but the tone was growing darker.

Cesar shook his head. "After your recent testimony, I would have expected you to lie low for a bit."

"I felt the need to get away, change of scenery and all that. Besides, I thought you and your brother were grateful for my testimony this past week, or at least Ernesto was."

Cesar's eyes went arctic cold, and the impatience rolled off him in waves. "Ernesto might be grateful, but I'm not. You're still on my—How do you say it?—my shit list. So enough of the bull. What does Tomas Rivera want with you?"

Anna listened with an increasing sense of dread. Obviously this was one of the men in the area who had it in for Leland.

"I've no idea. Was it Rivera's people shooting at us just now? I would have thought it was your guys." Leland glanced at Anna before turning back to Cesar.

There was something in his eyes. Did he finally have clarification on who had Zach?

Leland stared at the man as he spoke. "Cesar is Ernesto Vega's top lieutenant and brother. The Vegas and the Riveras don't get on too well."

Cesar laughed. "You have a gift for understatement."

"I thought the girl was working for Rivera," said Anna.

"She does, sometimes. Tomas may own this town, but the girl is mine. She does what I tell her."

Anna nodded her understanding.

"Does Ernesto know what's going on here?" Leland asked.

Cesar shrugged, but his eyes went cooler if possible. "That's none of your concern. Don't fuck with me, Agent Hollis. You won't like what happens to your lady."

Anna inhaled sharply and pulled at Leland's shirt. He didn't look down at her before speaking. "Her son was kidnapped. We're pretty sure Tomas Rivera is behind it and is holding the boy for ransom. We've already given them half the cash. We were to hand over the remainder when they brought the boy back to us."

"I heard about this today." Cesar inclined his head toward the back room, indicating the girl. "She told me. Rivera's men told her to take care of the *gringos* who

came to the motel tonight. That would have been you."
Cesar looked skeptical. "Why did Rivera take the boy? Is
this woman rich?"

Anna finally spoke up. "Not particularly. I don't know
why they took him. He's very ill. He—" she glanced at
Leland and at the pager still clutched in her hand. "He
needs a heart transplant. Constant monitoring."

Cesar studied her, his dead shark eyes sending a cold
shudder through her body. "It makes no sense. Why
would Tomas kidnap someone so difficult to care for
unless . . ." His words trailed off.

"Unless what?" Anna asked.

Cesar didn't answer her.

"What?" She looked from one man to the other.

Leland put a hand on her arm to steady her. "Unless
he never intended for Zach to survive."

Chapter Twenty-Two

LELAND WATCHED THE color drain from her face as the words sank in.

"But why? Why would he want my son to die?" Her voice broke on the question as she looked to both men for answers.

"He's not just your son. He's Max Mercado's, too," said Leland.

Her eyes widened. "Oh God. You think Max is responsible for this?"

"Nothing else makes much sense." Leland didn't acknowledge the relief washing over him, knowing Zach's abduction most likely had not been his own fault.

Leland should feel like a shit for that to matter to him now when she was in such a crisis, but he couldn't help himself. It did matter. Not being responsible for the boy's disappearance mattered a lot.

"Businessmen in Mexico of your husband's stature

must have contacts and interactions with the cartels to keep their product moving. It's how their business runs smoothly," said Cesar.

Leland considered the man's words. This made sense. In all his tequila growing and production, it was quite plausible that Max Mercado had run afoul of Mexico's largest exporters.

Anna sank into the chair beside the door. "I don't want to believe this of Max, but after yesterday, I can't be that surprised."

They could hear shouts from outside getting closer. Whoever had been doing the shooting earlier was regrouping, and most likely intensifying the search for them.

"What do you want with us, Cesar?"

"That's an intriguing question, Agent Hollis. I'm still figuring out what I want. The prospect of jacking with Rivera's plans is always appealing."

"I don't understand," said Anna. The shouting voices grew closer.

"When my girl told me Rivera wanted you unharmed, I knew you were valuable. That's why I came. This afternoon word started circulating that *gringos* with a lot of American dollars were coming to town. Many in the area have more fear of poverty than of Rivera. That's why you've caused such a stir with your ransom money and attracted the attention of those unsavory characters outside. It only takes a few bad apples after all."

Cesar looked down at his revolver and checked the safety before continuing. "Those men outside want you.

They don't work for Rivera. They're only after the money they've heard you're carrying. But Rivera wants you, so that makes you a lucrative commodity to me, albeit one with a limited shelf life."

"Cut to the chase, Cesar. Are you going to turn us over to those people out there?" asked Leland.

Cesar stared at him, his eyes unreadable. A big smile broke out over his face. His gold front tooth glimmered in the light. "Not now."

"Why wouldn't you?" asked Leland.

"Maybe I'm feeling generous, or maybe I just hate Tomas Rivera more than I hate DEA agents. Do you really care? I can get you out of here." He continued to study Leland with his frosty gaze.

Cesar's being generous made Leland more nervous than anything that had happened so far.

"It's your lucky day, Agent Hollis. I'm going to help you. I have a Jeep. We can leave now."

Leland didn't believe in Cesar's kind of generosity and suspected he might have even been the one to help circulate word about the ransom money, drawing those "unsavory characters" to the area like chumming sharks in the ocean. But there weren't many options. The men outside were after the cash in his backpack. They didn't care what happened to Leland or Anna, and Cesar had no control over them.

He might be after the cash, too, but Cesar wasn't wielding a knife yet. Or he might turn them over to Rivera anyway. They heard a commotion coming from the other room.

Were the shooters here already?

An old woman using a cane shuffled into the room with towels and a blanket under her arm. She hobbled directly to Anna, ignoring Cesar. "It will be cold outside," she announced.

"We don't have time for this," said Cesar.

"Nonsense," argued the old woman. "You will make time. You have a long drive. In that open Jeep she will catch her death."

Strangely, Cesar deferred to his girlfriend's grandmother as the woman took one of the towels and scrubbed at Anna's hair like she was a toddler right out of the bath. Anna never looked up as the woman draped a blanket over her shoulders. Leland wondered if she was going into shock.

Raised voices drifted in from the small yard in front of the house. It was time to make a choice that on the surface seemed counterintuitive. He was going to trust a man who'd vowed to kill him if he ever set foot in Mexico again.

"Let's go," Leland said.

Cesar was watching him. He had to know what Leland was thinking. The smirk on his face was proof.

The voices outside grew to a small roar. Cesar's reasons didn't matter as much as getting away from the present situation.

"So are we going or what?" asked Leland.

Cesar nodded and picked up the backpack containing the cash and Leland's weapons, leaving the other behind on the floor. "Let's go."

Leland reached for Anna's hand and they hustled out through the back door, his ankle protesting every step. The GPS locater Marissa had given him at the airstrip had slipped all the way down to his ankle on their trek through the jungle to the cottage, but he didn't dare try to adjust it now. He was just relieved that Cesar's girl hadn't found it in her extremely thorough search earlier.

The rain was still coming down hard as they climbed into an open-air Jeep. Smoke from the motel explosion was drifting through the trees: thick, black and suffocating. Anna and Leland were both coughing by the time they reached the vehicle.

He couldn't see the shouting men, but he could hear them around the front of the house. They were closer, making their way toward the back of the building. He felt Anna's terror in the grip of her hand as he helped her onto the bench seat.

Cesar started the Jeep and the raised voices changed direction. There wasn't a road per se. It was more of a dirt track into the lush overgrowth of jungle.

Cesar stepped on the accelerator and the vehicle surged forward. Fronds of the massive tropical plants brushed the sides of the vehicle as they sped past. The men's voices faded, soon the air cleared and the rain slacked off.

The lights on the Jeep weren't particularly intense, but in the deep murkiness of the jungle they shone like a beacon on the dirt road. They were committed to Cesar for now.

They road in silence with Anna still huddled under

the blanket, trying to stay warm. Leland suspected that wasn't possible. It wasn't raining anymore, but the seats were soaked and the blanket was wet. He tried to focus on anything but the pain in his ankle.

Cesar stopped after they crossed a rickety wooden bridge. He got out of the Jeep without a word and pulled down the back tailgate, fumbling in the dark for a few moments before he located what he was after. Leland didn't trust the man, so he gingerly climbed out and joined him in the back. He was promptly handed a flashlight.

"Hold this," instructed Cesar. "I need to see what I'm doing."

The strong beam of the Maglite shone on a small block of what Leland realized was C-4. "Why are you doing this? They were on foot."

"We don't want anyone following, right?" Cesar was inserting a long fuse into the block of explosive as he spoke.

Damn. The man's going to start a war. On the other hand, they wouldn't be safe with any part of this mob on their ass.

"Then we are blowing this bridge now. We're not leaving it booby-trapped for some villager to ride over and set off," said Leland.

"Of course, I'm not a monster."

Leland knew better than that. He'd seen the monster in action.

The cartel lieutenant strode toward the bridge and stopped when Leland didn't immediately follow. "I need some help."

Leland sighed and clumped toward him.

The trestle bridge was old, and on closer inspection with the flashlight Leland realized he might not have wanted to cross it on foot, much less in the Jeep they'd just used. The pilings on the bottom looked sturdy enough, but long tree-trunk posts interspersed with two-by-fours made up the deck. If you veered too far to the right or left when crossing, your tires could get stuck or slide off the bridge completely.

Cesar walked halfway out to the middle. "Shine your light below the deck."

Leland leaned over as Cesar shimmied over the side of the bridge to stand on the massive wooden beam below. He climbed over the trestle, stopped for a couple of minutes with his back to Leland then came back up topside. He held the fuse in one hand and a cigarette lighter in the other.

"Get ready to move," Cesar advised. "I don't usually take care of these things myself anymore. I may have cut it a little close on time." His gold tooth winked at Leland again in the beam of the flashlight.

"How much time do you think you gave it?"

"Thirty seconds, give or take." Cesar smiled, lit the fuse, and took off like a track star.

Shit. His freaking boot felt like lead.

He started hobbling back to the Jeep as quickly as possible. Falling would be a disaster, so he shuffled fast rather than running the risk of stumbling to the ground. He got to the Jeep just as the explosive detonated.

Anna screamed.

Massive timbers flew into the air and tumbled back to the ground like lethal confetti. Flaming debris landed across the front of the Jeep's hood, way too close for comfort. But the bridge was effectively destroyed. No one would be coming this way for a while.

Leland hauled his butt into the front seat again, his ankle screaming in protest. Anna still had the blanket wrapped around her in the back, retreating further under it to shield herself from falling embers. Cesar was typing into his phone as if he were sitting in a coffee shop.

Had Cesar just tried to kill him?

Leland watched him for a moment, wondering what he was up to, then realized he didn't care he was hurting so badly. He undid the boot cast and readjusted the wide Velcro straps, moving the hidden GPS locater up higher around his calf.

Still, he needed something to take the edge off the agony, even if it dulled his senses. He fumbled in his pocket for the bottle of Vicodin and dry-swallowed three tablets.

He was hurting so much he couldn't concentrate. A slower reaction time was preferable to being blinded with pain.

Cesar looked up from his smart phone and stared at him. For a moment the drug dealer looked confused, but when he smiled, Leland knew. Knew that Cesar would soon figure out he had an "issue".

He wanted to close his eyes, but he had no choice. Keep staring or he'd be lost. Cesar would love knowing that Leland was becoming hooked on pain pills. The risk his growing dependence caused terrified him, and there was no hiding from himself any longer that it was a dependence.

He had to get a handle on this or he'd be putting himself and anyone he was trying to help in jeopardy because of it. Hell, he'd already done that. Despite what Gavin had said about Leland's not being able to predict it, he never should have let Zach go up to that hotel room by himself.

He fingered the bottle in his pocket as Cesar shifted the Jeep into drive, heading down the dirt track that passed for a road. He despised the weakness of being at the mercy of meds as much as he hated being at Cesar's mercy. The question was, did he abhor being weak more or less than he feared the extreme discomfort? He'd better figure that out, and soon, or he was going to get himself beyond the point of no return.

Anna sat beside him in complete silence as the Jeep sped through the night. He could feel her staring at him as the meds kicked in and the pain eased. He inhaled deeply and held onto the bottle in his pocket, gazing into the darkness as jungle foliage sped by.

Could he do this?

Could he toss the pills?

It would be a mistake to do it cold turkey, right now. Even the slight withdrawal symptoms he'd experience would put them at too great a risk. But the temptation was great. When he got out of this, the first thing he was going to do was stop. Get rid of this junk. Check into some kind of treatment place if he had to.

He let go of the bottle in his pocket, wishing he was strong enough to sling it from the Jeep. Instead he pulled his empty hand from his pocket, cursing under his breath.

"Are you okay?" she asked.

Not really, he thought, but nodded an affirmative.

"What's next?" she asked. The bridge explosion had taken her completely by surprise but effectively shaken her out of the shock she'd been in since they'd had to escape the burning motel.

"Cesar here is going to take us God knows where."

Cesar smiled. "God knows but few others. Perhaps it is time I told you. I'm taking you to Rivera's compound."

"What?" Anna choked the words out. "Why would you do that?"

"Because Tomas Rivera just agreed to give me a great deal of cash if I deliver you safely. He wants you badly, *chica.*"

Leland struggled against the numbing effect caused by the pain meds. Rivera was offering money for Anna? That didn't make sense. The ransom for Zach was what Rivera was about, or so Leland had thought.

"So you're going to sell me to him?" Anna was shouting now, completely back in the game while he slipped into the lethargy caused by the Vicodin. Leland could feel her adrenaline kick in.

"*Sell* is such a crass term. I prefer *bargain,*" said Cesar.

"Why does Rivera want her?" Leland asked.

"I don't care," replied Cesar. "I just know he does." He held up his phone. "He offered me two million dollars if I bring her to him. That tells me he's desperate and he'll go higher if I have what he wants."

"But why are you doing this?" asked Anna.

"I thought you were all about helping your brother defeat Rivera and taking back what was once Vega territory," said Leland. He didn't ask if this had anything to do with Tomas's wife, who was also Cesar's sister. Something told him sharing that bit of knowledge here would be unwise.

Cesar cut his eyes toward Leland then stared back at the dark path in front of them. "Who says I won't get some of Rivera's territory with this bargain?" Cesar laughed, and it wasn't a pretty sound. "Besides, for what he's offering to pay, I'd give Tomas Rivera my own grandmother."

Chapter Twenty-Three

"I STILL DON'T understand," said Anna. "Why did Rivera take my son?"

"Because he wanted you here," Leland stared at Cesar, the truth dawning at last. Rivera took Zach because he knew Anna would come to Mexico to get him.

"So it would seem," said Cesar.

"But why?" asked Anna, unable or unwilling to catch up.

Leland shook his head, struggling to clear his fuzzy thinking. He understood Cesar's motivation, or thought he did. Cash was easy to understand. But why did Rivera want Anna? He still had no idea.

"I don't know and I don't care," said Cesar. "But two million will set me up, so I won't work for anyone but myself. The only stipulation is that you, Ms. Mercado, must be healthy and whole, not harmed in any way."

"When did you strike this bargain?" asked Leland.

Cesar held up his phone. "A few moments ago."

"You mean to tell me you negotiated all that since we left the house and blew the bridge?" asked Anna.

Cesar gave a sly smile. "I've known since yesterday you were coming."

"How? We didn't find out until last night," said Anna.

Cesar shrugged. "One hears things."

Of course. Once Rivera had contacted Cesar's girl-friend *du jour* at the motel, Cesar had known.

"That's a lot of money," said Leland, stalling for time as he processed this new revelation. Now he understood Cesar's motivation. But he still didn't understand Rivera's.

"Yes, it is." Cesar pressed down on the accelerator. "I'm going to collect, too."

"Won't your brother have something to say about this?"

Cesar shook his head. "You needn't worry, Agent Hollis. Ernesto will never know. I have everything taken care of."

Cesar held up his phone again and kept talking. "Modern technology is a wonder, is it not?"

He slowed the Jeep, stopping in the middle of the road. The night lit up with five sets of headlights all around them. Leland could feel the guns trained on them. He and Anna had never had a chance.

Cesar lifted his hand to the lights then turned to look at Leland. "Currently, you're safer with me than out here on your own. Everyone in the area has heard about the money you are carrying and won't care whether you are dead or alive when they take it. I, on the other hand, won't let anything happen to you. I have my people here to keep you safe. You're my—how you say it?—ace in the hole."

The irony of the situation wasn't lost on Leland: telling them they were safe with at least half a dozen guns pointed their way. To punctuate the moment, the sky opened up once more and rain began to beat down on them in the open-air Jeep.

Cesar's grin was anything but reassuring. What he'd just said was so obviously a lie. The reward was for Anna to be delivered safe and sound. It didn't include a DEA agent.

Leland slowly reached into the top of his boot as several men approached the Jeep. Acting as if he were adjusting the straps to a more comfortable position, this time he activated the GPS locater.

Anna seemed to still be puzzling everything out, but Leland was up to speed, despite the buzz from the pain meds. He would have to view this as a glass-half-full situation. Otherwise, he'd howl.

This was the way he and Anna could get to Tomas Rivera's compound and find Zach. Cesar was going to take them directly where they most wanted to be. Fighting Cesar would be pointless now.

Leland just needed someone on the outside to know where the hell they were. The GPS locater better work as well as Marissa said it would. It would take a few hours for her and Nick to get into place, but they'd be there. He didn't respond when half a dozen men stood beside the vehicle and didn't resist when he was none-too-gently pulled from the Jeep and cuffed with plastic tie wraps in front of his body.

The rain continued down in earnest, and Cesar moved them to an SUV with a driver. He didn't separate them and gallantly handed Anna another dry blanket before climbing into the front passenger seat. Leland sat beside her in the back, wishing he could put his arm around her. She was obviously exhausted, shivering, and probably wondering what the hell he'd gotten them into.

"Relax," Cesar's low laugh sounded mean. "In this weather, we're hours from Rivera's compound."

No, this wasn't the ideal way to get to the boy. But given their choices, in the pouring rain and with no idea where Rivera's base was, this could work. How Leland would get Zach out was still a question, but he was working on it. And AEGIS resources were on the way.

THE SUN WAS just peeking over the horizon when they drove out of the jungle and onto what most people would consider a real road. Leland guessed it was somewhere between 6:30 and 7:30 AM. He braced himself as they sped across the combination of rock and dirt with potholes reaching down to China. His teeth were practically rattling in his head, but this road was smoother than what they'd driven over during the night.

Anna bounced into him on the seat once, then twice, before gripping the door. She seemed anxious to stay as far from him as possible. He hadn't had a chance to explain about the GPS device in his boot, or how being escorted into Rivera's compound was really a good thing. She could be furious with him or scared spitless. Given the circumstances, either state of mind made sense.

After a few miles they passed another gravel turnoff with signage indicating Mandinga and Antón Lizardo. That meant they were near Boca del Río and Veracruz. The ocean was to their left as they headed down the coastline.

Thirty minutes later they turned off the broken highway onto an actual asphalt road that led back into the jungle for about three miles. The road smoothed out considerably. No more bone-jarring bumps and swerves. Leland studied her, trying to communicate his confidence in the situation with his gaze, but she wouldn't even make eye contact.

Okay, so fury was probably her current inclination.

A gate barred the driveway and thick vegetation hung over the guardhouse that wouldn't have looked out of place in an upscale subdivision in the US. There was a speaker at the gate and what Leland knew had to be bulletproof glass in the large windows.

Cesar's driver leaned out of the car and spoke into the metal mouthpiece. "Cesar Vega to see Tomas Rivera."

No one answered and they never saw a live person, still the gates opened. Manicured trees lined the patterned concrete drive up to the front stone steps. The imposing Mediterranean-style villa was situated on a hill with beautiful tropical plants and flowers all around.

The surrounding grounds had been carved out of the jungle with a reserved hand. Wild palm trees and foliage blended with the manicured landscaping, making it seem that the house had always been there. A red tile roof topped the massive stucco and stone structure with arches, columns and an open floor plan that put the lie to the idea that most drug dealers lived in deep seclusion surrounded by guards. The rounded arch making up the front door looked Moroccan, sporting a massive decorative iron knocker crafted in an intricate design along with oversized iron hardware.

Anna still hadn't said a word, but she moved infinitesimally closer to him on the bench seat.

The SUV stopped as two massive men filed out of the door dressed in designer suits with AK-47s slung over their shoulders. Cesar got out of the passenger side and spoke with them. Leland couldn't understand much of the conversation, but there was lots of pointing and gesturing. The guards were antsy.

"What are they saying?" asked Anna.

"Explaining who we are. I think?" said Leland.

One bodyguard left the group and jogged back inside, returning moments later with a middle-aged man dressed informally in jeans. From the way the group deferred to him, Leland assumed this was Tomas Rivera himself or some senior lieutenant in the organization.

"Do you think that's Rivera?" she asked.

"Not sure."

"You don't recognize him? I thought you knew all these people."

Leland's laugh sounded bleak, even to his own ears. But at least she was talking to him. He just wished he had better answers. "The only picture the DEA has of Rivera is a blurry photo from over twenty years ago. An old Mexican Military ID when he was supposedly working to clean out the Vega cartel along the eastern coast of Mexico."

"I don't understand," she said.

"It's all about money." He didn't want to go into the details here and now. Tomas Rivera's men were the most brutal of all the cartels in Mexico. The DEA considered them more like terrorists than drug dealers.

They'd been trained in all kinds of covert tactics courtesy of Uncle Sam before they started working for the other side. And Rivera wasn't afraid to use that vicious knowledge against anyone who got in their way. Enemies, law enforcement, women, children. Yes, that information was probably best kept from Anna until they were safely through this.

Instead Leland said, "No one in the DEA has met Rivera face to face since he crossed over to work for the cartels, at least not that I know of, and that's been twenty years ago."

She nodded. The casually dressed man glanced at the SUV's tinted backseat windows like he knew they were discussing him before he turned back to talk with Cesar. Another guard jogged back inside and returned moments later with a black briefcase.

Cesar nodded to his driver standing by the vehicle and he opened Anna's door. The man he assumed was Tomas stared at her for at least thirty seconds but said nothing. Finally he motioned to the bodyguard holding the briefcase and it was handed over to Cesar. Vega popped the top, glanced inside, and nodded once to his driver, who moved to open the back SUV passenger door.

"Deal's done," Cesar said. "Get out."

Leland looked at him but didn't move. Instead he reached for Anna's hand with his cuffed ones, holding her beside him when she would have exited the car. "Seems to be done from where you sit but not for us," he said.

Leland was prepared to stay in the SUV while things got sorted out, but Anna was moving, trying to slide out of the vehicle.

"What's going on? Is Zach here? Will they let me see him?" she asked, letting go of Leland's hand and sliding across the seat at the same time.

"That's up to your new host," said Cesar, tipping his head in deference to the middle-aged man.

So this was Tomas Rivera. He didn't look like Leland had imagined, and Cesar wasn't planning to stick around. That much was obvious.

"They're trading us," Leland clarified and gave up trying to keep her in the SUV.

Instead, he slid over to get out with her. Cesar's man held up his hand to stop his exit from the vehicle. Realizing she was standing alone in a group of armed men, Anna reached back for him. The bodyguards all looked to Rivera. After a beat, he nodded and they let Leland climb out of the back seat with her.

"Told you I'd get you here safe and sound." Cesar took a large knife from his pocket and cut off Leland's zip-tie cuffs. Without another word he slipped into his vehicle.

Rivera headed back inside once his armed men surrounded Anna and Leland. She reached for Leland's hand and held on to him with a death grip as he rubbed his aching wrists. This was what he had wanted—to get to Rivera's compound and find Zach. Even so, circumstances weren't playing out quite the way he'd imagined.

When Cesar's car disappeared down the drive, the itch at Leland's neck began to feel like hives.

Chapter Twenty-Four

GRIPPING LELAND'S HAND and breathing through her nose, Anna stood in the drive attempting to calm her skyrocketing heart rate. Zach was here, or close by. He had to be.

She needed to see him—to know he was okay, to tell him she was here, to tell him they were going home and that everything was going to work out.

Trying to stay calm wasn't working. She could feel herself start to hyperventilate. The only thing keeping her grounded was Leland, clasping her hand firmly in his.

"It's gonna be okay," he murmured. "Stay close to me."

She watched him watch Cesar's car drive away. She wouldn't want him looking at her like that. The drug dealer would be a pile of ash if Leland had his wish.

The guards led them inside. Two in front and two behind. Rivera was nowhere to be seen.

Two guards peeled off while the other two men stayed

with Leland and Anna, leading them through the entryway into an open-air living area that contained a massive
sectional sofa and coffee table. Floor-to-ceiling sliding
glass panels were open, separating the living room from
a manmade tropical pool outside. Anna was stunned at
the grandeur of the home. It was like something out of
Architectural Digest. The "pool area" looked more like a
rain forest. Massive rocks formed a waterfall surrounded
by lush plant life.

Pink bougainvillea climbed the stucco walls surrounding the deep blue water. A steady breeze blew in.
The house had obviously been built with the mountain
breezes in mind. While the one blowing in now was
warm, her still-damp clothes from last night were multi-
plying the wind chill.

A large oil painting depicting a three-masted galleon
battling a stormy sea hung over the fireplace, taking up
the entire wall opposite the glass panels. A spiral staircase took up another corner of the room. The older man
stood at the fireplace, a guard on either side, looking like
the captain of the ship in the picture above his head.

"Welcome to my home."

"Are you Tomas Rivera?" she asked, already knowing
the answer.

"Yes, I am. Sit down."

Leland was still holding her hand. They sat on the
huge sofa side by side. Was she finally going to see Zach?
She could feel her anxiety ratcheting up.

"Please, where is my son? I'll do whatever you ask but
I need to see him."

"Indeed? That's very good to hear. All in good time," said Rivera. "First, we have business to discuss."

"Business? What kind of—" Leland squeezed her hand in a warning to be quiet and spoke over her.

"Cesar took the rest of our cash, but I'm assuming you don't really need it based on the reward you gave him. What other *business* do we have to talk about?" he asked.

Rivera smiled and settled his gaze on Anna. "You'll see. It concerns Mrs. Mercado and her son. I'll take you to see him soon. I'd prefer we talked first, and I'm sure you'd like to get cleaned up."

He stared pointedly at her dirty tank top and damp skirt. She didn't give a damn about freshening up, she only wanted to see Zach. It was on the tip of her tongue to say so, and there was a long moment of silence as she contemplated the ramifications of saying exactly what she thought.

Leland squeezed her hand again, reminding her that these men were extraordinarily dangerous. Antagonizing them would be foolish. Reluctantly, she nodded and clamped her mouth shut over the angry words.

"He's sleeping. You don't want to disturb him now, do you?"

Well, of course not. But she knew how to check on her son while he was sleeping and not wake him. She'd only been doing it for fourteen years, but arguing wouldn't get her any closer to seeing him.

"Is he alright?" She asked instead, biting her bottom lip.

Leland gave her hand another comforting squeeze.

Rivera nodded. "He's fine. He's had excellent care. We have a doctor who lives here."

He studied Leland for a moment before turning back to Anna. "Did you know Mexico is a destination for people who want to have expensive surgeries done at a fraction of the cost?"

"No, I didn't," she said.

"How much does it cost to have an organ transplant in the United States?" Rivera asked.

"I'm not sure. I believe it's somewhere between $200,000 and $400,000 depending on the type of transplant. I'm just grateful for our health insurance," said Anna.

"Yes. In Mexico a transplant costs considerably less than it does in the US. A $400,000 surgery in the US can cost $40,000 here. That cost difference has sparked a whole new industry called "transplant tourism." It's becoming quite popular in South America and Asia."

Anna had no idea where he was going with this, but she was fairly certain that she wasn't going to like it. Max had tried to talk her into having Zach's surgeries done here in Mexico, but she'd steadfastly refused. Perhaps it made her biased, but she didn't want to trust her son's care to anyone outside the doctors they knew in Dallas.

Rivera was still talking, touting the benefits of transplant surgery in Mexico and extoling the cutting edge research being done in Mexico City's hospitals and research centers. The conversation was like listening to Max.

"The problem in any country is finding the organs, particularly for rarer blood types. It's difficult to find the proper tissue matches, much more difficult than it is in the US. I know all this because my wife needs a bilateral lung transplant."

Anna exhaled. "I'm sorry. I realize it's very difficult to wait."

Despite what the man had done to her and Zach, having someone you loved that ill was cause for sympathy.

"Yes, Mrs. Mercado. Yes, it is. Carlita has been on the list for almost fourteen months. Her blood type is AB negative."

Anna had been focused on the floor, determined not to make eye contact no matter how tragic his story, but at those words she turned her head sharply to stare at Rivera. The chill she'd felt earlier on entering the breezy room deepened.

"Yes, I know," he said. "That's Zach's blood type also."

Anna continued to stare, feeling the blood drain from her face as understanding dawned and her world imploded.

"It's your blood type as well." Rivera spoke matter-of-factly, gazing a moment longer at her, then shook his head impatiently.

"I thought you would have figured this out by now," he said. "You're not a stupid woman, but I suppose it is unorthodox."

Anna could say nothing. Beside her Leland was silent. He probably hadn't figured out the implications of the conversation yet, but she had. She knew what Rivera was about to propose. It had crossed her mind as an impossible option, early on in Zach's diagnosis.

"Last year your son was admitted to Mexico City's Hope Medica for a series of tests," continued Rivera.

The chill inside her grew. She was surprised her teeth weren't chattering when she spoke. "Yes, his father wanted to consult doctors here in Mexico to see if there was anything that could be done as we waited for a donor."

"I know."

"How?" she asked, stricken by what she assumed was coming.

"I know Max."

She shook her head. Given her discussion with Cesar and Leland earlier, this shouldn't have been such unexpected news. Still, it was.

"How do you know my husband?"

"We had business together. Not very interesting business at that. What I did find fascinating was that your son also had AB negative blood and was seeking a transplant. Naturally, I was intrigued."

"Naturally," she echoed. Beside her, Leland was still silent.

"I'm a generous donor at Hope Medica. When I heard that young Zach was a match with my wife, the clinic 'agreed' to run extra tests before you left."

"What?" Leland finally spoke up. "How could you dictate what kind of tests were run on another patient?"

"Surely you know that there's very little money cannot buy, particularly here in Mexico. Max Mercado made some unfortunate investments and accumulated substantial debt. It was an easy thing to get his permission."

Oh God, Max. What were you thinking?

Anna took a deep breath, but it didn't help. Her head was spinning. She felt as if she were watching this conversation take place with someone else.

"Alas, your son's organs have been 'taxed' greatly by his heart disease. His lungs are of no use to my wife. But I continued to follow his case. AB negative is so very rare. Just in case you found a donor, I wanted to know about it. Your husband kept me in the loop."

Anna maintained a neutral face, even though inside she was screaming. Rivera was talking as if Zach were a possible organ donor for his wife and confirming that Max had been involved in all of this.

"But we didn't find a donor. We've been on the list for over a year as well," she said.

"Yes. However, you yourself are AB negative. Max let me know about that, too."

Max, you fool. What did you do?

Inside she grew colder and colder. "Yes, yes I am." That idea had been in the back of her mind, ever since they'd started this whole nightmarish ordeal a year ago with waiting for a donor. She knew what Rivera was going to say before he said it.

"Well, the solution is simple. In fact, it was Max's idea. Still, I suspect he had some ulterior motives. You've said you'd do anything for your son. I'm going to let you prove it."

Oh, sweet Jesus.

The chill inside her turned arctic. Ever since the doctors had told her about the rarity of her and Zach's blood types, she'd known there was an option that was theoretically possible but not feasible—at least not in the United States.

She'd lied to Rivera. She knew all about transplant tourism. In the darker hours of the past year she'd done quite a bit of online research as she considered looking for a doctor somewhere, anywhere who'd do what Rivera was about to suggest. Obviously, she hadn't been looking in the right place.

"You can give your heart to Zach," Rivera said.

Chapter Twenty-Five

LELAND WASN'T SURE he'd heard the man correctly. The idea was so beyond bizarre, he couldn't wrap his head around the idea that Anna would consider giving up her life for her son's heart transplant. Anna, on the other hand, looked as if this was what she'd been expecting.

"Why would you care about my son receiving a heart?" she asked.

Ignoring Leland, Rivera gave her a look of mild impatience. "Oh, come now. Surely you aren't that slow. Your lungs won't be necessary after you donate your heart."

"Of course," she whispered at the same time Leland exploded, "Hell, no! You can't ask her to do this."

Anna'd dropped his hand during the discussion earlier, but now he reached out and grasped it again. Part of him wanted to believe that if he held on tightly enough, nothing could happen to her. The conversation was so surreal, so horrifying, he expected to hear the theme from the *Twilight Zone* at any moment.

"*Ask* her to do this?" Rivera snarled contemptuously. "Agent Hollis, I could just as easily kill you both right here in my living room. I might as well let her life count for something. Hell, I just bought her from Vega. I think it's rather generous of me to give her this opportunity."

"Generous?" Leland echoed, not even trying to contain his incredulity. "This is obscene."

"I have no choice," insisted Rivera.

Anna was frozen in place like a marble statue. Gripping her cold fingers, he knew he needed to calm down or Rivera would simply separate them. Angry as he was, Leland couldn't give the man any reason to do that. He had to get her and Zach the hell out of here.

Rivera stared at Anna and shook his head as his eyes took on a faraway look. "No, I've seen obscenity. I've committed it against others. This is not it."

Leland had a fair idea of the obscenities Rivera was referring to. The man's propensity for gruesome violence had long ago sealed his place as the most vicious of cartel leaders.

A guard appeared in the living room doorway. "Antonio will take you both back to your room," continued Rivera.

"No!" Anna shouted, at last showing some emotion. "I need to see Zach first. I'll do what you want, but let me see him before . . . before we do this," she stammered. "I must talk to him."

"Of course," interrupted Rivera. "It will be a few hours

before the doctor has everything finalized and ready for the procedure tonight. I'll send for you when the boy wakes up."

"Please" Anna pleaded. "I have to see Zach now. I'll do whatever you want, but I insist on seeing my boy now." Her voice broke on the last word.

She was talking like she was going to be telling Zach goodbye. As if she'd already made her choice and this was going to happen.

"Rivera, there has to be another way," Leland argued.

"Trust me. I've been looking for another way for over a year. Don't make this any harder for Mrs. Mercado than it has to be."

Right, like Leland was making this difficult. He ground his teeth in frustration, stamping out the horror to focus on the problem.

"Mrs. Mercado, your son is sleeping at present. Truly. I am not lying to you."

He picked up a tablet computer from the hearth beside him and turned the screen to face her. Somewhere a camera was pointed toward a hospital bed. The whole room was decorated like an upscale hotel room.

Zach was in the bed, a heart monitor beside him. His eyes were closed but his hands were open, palms facing upward on either side of his pale face.

Anna made a keening sound as she drank in the sight of him. Leland's gut clenched at her agony.

Seemingly oblivious to her pain, Rivera continued. "I assure you, you will see the boy as soon as he wakes. I understand you'd like to spend as much time as possible together before the procedure."

Rivera spoke as if this was a tonsillectomy, and she'd be serving Zach ice cream when it was over.

Leland bit his lip to remain silent beside her. Anna stared at the screen, her eyes filled to overflowing before she took an audible breath and blinked away the tears.

"Alright. I'll trust you because I have no other option. But you will give me the respect you would to anyone doing what I'm about to for your wife. You allow me to spend my last hours with my child."

It wasn't a threat and it wasn't a request. It was a declaration. A reminder to Rivera that honor should be accorded in this most unique situation.

She'd have had better luck if they were dealing with the Vegas. Ernesto Vega was rabid about honor. From what Leland knew of Rivera, the man was not as attached to the concept.

Rivera raised an eyebrow at her tone but didn't argue. "I will make sure you see him as soon as he wakes up. It should be in the next hour or so. I'll have Antonio escort you back now. You can shower and change. Someone will bring you breakfast."

"I'll see him when he wakes up." She sighed the words as if to convince herself. Her face was pale but her voice was quiet, resigned.

Belatedly, it occurred to Leland that she'd probably considered this possibility of giving herself up for Zach before. Before she'd ever come to Mexico. Before she'd ever met Leland. Months ago, before they'd even scheduled Zach for the LVAD. A mother like Anna would do that.

"It will be okay," She leaned into him and whispered. "I need you with me to make it through this. Please don't give him a reason to take you away."

He studied her chalk white face, noting the tension in her jaw as she voiced his thoughts almost word for word. She was holding it together by the slimmest of threads.

"Listen to her, Agent Hollis. She's the only one of you thinking clearly."

Leland started to speak again, but Anna wove her fingers through his once more and squeezed gently. His lashing out would only punish her, so he tamped down the frustration rolling off him in waves.

"Please," she said. "Let's go."

Leland didn't reply. He simply stood, pulling her to her feet beside him.

He concentrated on not crushing her hand in his as they followed Antonio up the spiral staircase, climbing to a hallway lined with mirrors and several doors. Halfway down the passage Antonio stopped in front of an ornate door that opened into an opulent suite.

The fantastic incongruity continued as the armed guarded showed them into the room like a bellhop at The Savoy. A king size iron bed with a canopied top and luxurious tapestried duvet dominated the space. A leather loveseat and overstuffed chair were arranged in front of a completely outfitted mahogany entertainment center. The bathroom was larger than his Dallas apartment with a separate jetted tub large enough for multiple bathers, and a glass shower with more spray nozzles than a car wash.

The tour wasn't finished until the guard showed them the closet off the bathroom. The massive walk-in space held two fluffy robes and a dress with a tag still attached. He'd bet a month's salary it was Anna's size. A pair of jeans and a collared linen shirt for him hung beside the dress. Shoes for each of them were still in the boxes on the floor.

After informing them that breakfast would be brought up in about an hour, the bellhop guard left and closed the door firmly behind him. An audible click from the outside indicated they were now locked inside a luxury prison.

ONCE THE GUARD left, Leland let go of her hand. Anna immediately missed the warmth of his palm against hers. She was so cold now that she felt numb.

Icy fingers of fear seemed to have reached inside her body, causing her temperature to drop from the inside out. Tears that had threatened all night now burned the corners of her eyes. She turned away so Leland wouldn't see her weep.

"I'm going to get cleaned up. The faster I do this, the faster I can see Zach." Her voice broke again on his name.

Would they really let her see him before the procedure? How was she ever going to tell him goodbye? Who was going to take care of him when this was all over and she was gone?

Struggling to keep the tears at bay, she sniffed once and headed for the bathroom.

Leland followed her. "Anna, you can't do this. There has to be another way."

"This could be Zach's only chance. I can't say no. And I can't fight you."

There were no other options, and arguing was pointless. The only thing she could do now was pretend it wasn't happening.

"I'll be quick so you can shower, too." She felt him standing behind her, his body heat like a small furnace, but she couldn't turn around.

She'd break if she looked at him. God, if she started crying now, she'd never stop. Instead, she reached inside the shower and turned the massive chrome tap all the way up to hot. The multi-nozzled shower gushed like a geyser as she walked to the sink.

Again, Leland was right behind her.

To avoid meeting his eyes in the mirror, she opened the top narrow drawer under the countertop.

The contents were rather startling. Rivera had stocked this suite with everything a guest could possibly need. Two toothbrushes still wrapped in plastic, toothpaste, a razor, a small collection of luxurious makeup, hairbrushes, combs, condoms, and tampons. She stared at the drawer's offerings, working to get a grip on her emotions and desperate to focus on something besides the despair welling up inside.

How was she going to get through the next few hours?

How was she going to say goodbye to her son?

How was Zach ever going to deal with the inevitable guilt and anger toward her when the transplant was over?

"Anna," Leland touched her shoulder, but she held up her hand without turning.

"Please don't be nice to me," she begged. "I'll come completely unglued."

He didn't argue or pull away. Instead he reached out and wrapped her in his arms, her back to his front. Rather than just feeling that warmth behind her, his body heat surrounded her.

"It's okay." His breath was warm against her ear. "Now would be a good time to do that."

It was the tenderness in his voice that undid her. She sobbed aloud and turned in his arms, grabbing hold of him like the lifeline he'd become in the past thirty-six hours. He held her tight, rubbing her back in tiny circles and breathing comforting words as she cried.

Steam from the shower surrounded them as she wept. Under normal circumstances Anna would be embarrassed at her outburst of emotion, but the situation was as far from normal as could be. She was grateful for the comfort of Leland kissing the top of her head and pulling her closer.

Everything else was a jumble of chaotic noise in her head. Still, the sound of water hitting the shower glass doors and tiled floor was unexpectedly soothing.

I can't think about what I'm going to do. I have to go through with it. It's the only way. She repeated the mantra in her mind.

She didn't know how long they stood there. Leland's heart beat steadily under her cheek and she slid her arms around his neck, burying her nose in his chest. He smelled like man and rain and heat.

She no longer felt the bone-deep chill that had over-whelmed her since the open-air Jeep ride last night. She tilted her head to look up and Leland's forest-colored gaze caught her. Despair changed to something earthier as she stood locked in his arms.

She stared at his mouth and he stared back. He was going to kiss her. She could tell from the expression in his eyes. She wanted him, too. Badly.

No ulterior motive. No bargaining for help. She just wanted . . . him and the oblivion he could offer.

He bent his head slowly, as if he didn't want to startle her. His mouth brushed hers—gently at first, almost cautiously.

She closed her eyes when his tongue swept past her lips and pressed her mouth more firmly to his. His hands slid lower on her waist, coaxing her toward him. He deepened the kiss and all the heartfelt anguish of the past twenty-four hours slid away. Not banished forever but buried for a while.

Her fingers were in his hair and she pulled his face closer to hers. The edge of the cool marble counter bumped against the back of her thighs. His hands were on her butt and moved to her hips. When he lifted her up to the countertop, he moved to stand between her knees, pressing himself against her center—hard and insistent.

The bathroom was rapidly filling with steam, and muggy condensation covered every surface. The atmosphere felt so surreal, she stopped kissing him.

Leland stepped back. "Tell me what you want. If you don't want to do this, we can st—"

She put a finger to his lips. "No, I want this. It's just—"

She looked around the misty bathroom, at Leland's face. His hair was curling on the ends in the steam.

She absolutely wanted this. She needed it. If she was going to go along with Rivera's plan, she was going to take this time. This moment. Now.

She shook her head, unable to explain it in words. If she attempted to, Leland would try to talk her out of giving her heart to Zach, and she couldn't face arguing with him, not here.

So she did the best thing she could think of to make sure he knew she had no doubts. She tugged the tank top over her head, unhooked her bra, slid it from her shoulders and reached for the belt buckle on his cargo shorts.

Chapter Twenty-Six

LELAND WATCHED ANNA take her shirt off—his mind fragmented from the chaos of processing Rivera's plan, figuring out how they were getting out of here and seeing all that beautiful bare skin. He knew that Nick and Risa had to be closing in on the compound's location now if the GPS in his boot was working. All they could do was wait, but Anna's hands at his belt made him want to howl with frustration.

He needed to convince her that this—sex—was a bad idea, even though he didn't want to stop her. No matter, that issue would be resolved soon enough when he told her about the possibility of the suite being bugged. He wished they were somewhere, anywhere else but here.

He leaned forward and her bare breasts pressed into his shirt. He kissed the shell of her ear. Tilting his lips toward her face, he whispered, "They may be watching us."

She stiffened in his arms, but didn't push him away or cover herself as he would have expected. Instead, she pulled him closer.

"Seriously? Why would they bug a bathroom?"

"Even among associates he might entertain as guests, Rivera has too many enemies who want him dead to not have the room wired. There's probably a camera as well." He brushed a strand of hair from her face, hating to bring that ugliness here, now.

Falling water from the space-aged showerhead echoed off the marble floor and walls with a thundering din. He forced himself to pull away and turn the tap on in the pool-sized tub as well. "I doubt they can pick up anything over the sound of the water. With the bath filling, we should be safe."

He watched her take in the foggy bathroom. The mirrors were completely obscured as steam rose from the tub and continued to roll over the top of the shower door.

"What could a camera possibly pick up in here right now?" she asked.

He smiled for the first time in what felt like days. "Good point."

He slipped his arms around her and moved to stand between her knees again. Telling himself she was in his arms so they could talk despite the cameras, he knew he was avoiding the truth.

This was more than his just wanting to hold her. He needed to hold her. He had to believe she wasn't going through with the transplant procedure and giving in without any argument or fight. There was no way, no way in hell.

No matter what she said, he couldn't let her even consider doing it. He wasn't going to allow her to give up that way. She had to see that there was another solution. Rivera believed the choice he was giving Anna was generous. To Leland it was twisted and monstrous.

Even if she went through with it, there was no guarantee Rivera would follow through with Zach's operation. The man betrayed even his most loyal followers time and time again. Why would he keep his promise to Anna?

Leland understood a mother's love was sacrificial, but this had nothing to do with love. Rivera was perverting the relationship. Leland had always known the man was a sadist, but blackmailing Anna into giving up her life for his wife was beyond obscene.

And Max, the fucker, had arranged it all. Leland had no doubt this was how Max was having his "debt" to Rivera forgiven. He and Anna hadn't even talked about that part of the obscenity. He couldn't imagine the betrayal she must be feeling.

Leland's jaw ached from clenching it so hard.

Anna slid her hands back to his waistband. "Stop thinking. I don't care about cameras. Do you?"

He shook his head. Cameras and bugs be damned. Of course he'd make love to her. That was no hardship.

He'd wanted her pretty much since he'd seen her in that Best Western hotel room. He just hadn't wanted to admit it. Now he'd do anything for her, except allow her to abandon hope and give up.

He studied her a moment longer before he kissed her. How could he convince her? How could he show her that life was the only choice? There was a way to save Zach without sacrificing Anna. She just had to give him more time to come up with the plan.

His lips were at her cheek again. "We've got to stall. Nick and the AEGIS team will be here. They won't just leave us."

She tilted her head to look in his eyes.

"How will they even know where we are? You don't have the GPS locater anymore, do you?"

He leaned in, kissing her to cover his answer. Let her think he was concerned about bugs. He kissed her now because he couldn't stand not to.

"The GPS was tucked in my boot. Cesar's girl didn't find it when she searched me. I activated it when his people met us in the jungle."

He kissed his way to her jaw and ear. "Nick and Marissa are on the way or may even already be here. We'll meet up and fly Zach immediately to Dallas."

He saw the protest growing in her eyes and heard himself talking faster. "You said the doctors were going to install temporary measures, a pump, to buy Zach more time. He can have that heart pump by tomorrow."

She shook her head, bumping his chin with her nose. "Even if we flew out of here in the next hour, Zach could end up in the same place health-wise after we install the LVAD."

He stepped back. "God, Anna, you have to at least try. You can't just give up. Sacrifice your life? Zach wouldn't want that. How will he live with that?"

He pulled her to him, unable to accept that she was considering such a final course of action.

She swallowed audibly. "He'll know that he was loved beyond measure. Please, try to see this from my point of view. What if you were in my place? Wouldn't you give your life for your child's?"

She had a point. He knew she did. What would he do if their positions were reversed? It was sobering to think about.

In his work with the DEA he'd put himself in danger for others many times—for the people he worked with, for witnesses. But that had always been a consequence of the situation—in the heat of a firefight, part of his job.

He'd never volunteered to walk into a room and calmly sacrifice himself for a witness or another agent. Was there someone he would give his life for? No questions asked?

"Please don't fight me, even if you don't understand my reasoning. I can't do this and battle you, too. I'm going to see my son and tell him goodbye. If you care about either of us, help me. Help me do this right." She stared at him unblinking, begging him with her eyes to stop fighting her.

He loosened his hold on her, unable to believe she was still willing to go through with the donation even with the possibility of rescue on the way. He couldn't stop her.

She tried to pull him closer. "Hold me. I'm scared. I need you to help me get through this."

But that was the thing. If this went as she planned, she wouldn't survive. She wanted him to keep her strong while she died.

He couldn't say what he was thinking. That if things went as she planned, she wasn't going to make it through. The truth was too cruel. Instead, he took a deep breath and drew her to him as she laid her head against his chest.

He wouldn't let her down. Still, this was what he'd feared most, especially since the Colton catastrophe: someone innocent needing him, someone counting on him, and his failing them, their dying anyway.

But Anna was choosing to die.

The thought made him furious and desolate at the same time. He'd stop fighting her for now, but he wasn't giving her up. He couldn't.

Even if she hated him for interfering later, he wouldn't allow her to sacrifice herself when there were other options. No matter how it looked to Anna, there were ways out of here.

"Make love to me," she whispered against his chest.

He nodded. Maybe it was a betrayal when he was planning to stop her from going through with the procedure, but he couldn't say no. Gliding his hand down her naked back, he pressed her closer to him on the counter. His heart was beating so fast, she could probably feel it against her cheek.

"I don't care about the cameras," she reassured him. "I need you."

She slid her hands under his shirt. Her fingers were cool against his skin and he winced.

"Sorry," she said, helping him tug the shirt over his head. "You have on too many clothes."

Amazing. She was able to tease him at a time like this, when her world was falling apart.

If she could do it, he would too.

"Too many clothes, huh?"

"Well, yeah."

"We can fix that." He reached for the fastener on her skirt as she reached for his belt buckle again. He moved her hands away from his waist and she leaned forward, pressing her lips to his shoulder. He sucked in a breath when all that soft bare skin hit his chest. A light, flowery fragrance clung to her despite the fire, smoke, and rain they'd endured over the past twelve hours.

He broke contact with her only to slide her skirt and panties down those long legs, then she was back in his arms. He wanted to taste her.

She trembled as he skimmed his fingers along the slope of her breast. He took one of her nipples in his mouth and felt it pebble against his tongue. He followed her when she leaned back toward the mirror.

Circling her waist with his hands, he inched his fingers along her spine. A drop of condensation rolled down the glass behind them. He saw the tanned skin on the back of his palms contrasted against her ivory back.

The fog became thicker and his breath grew heavy from the steam. The counter was the perfect height as he pressed himself to her core. She moaned and lifted her hands from the marble to unbutton his cargo shorts.

Her hand brushed against his erection and he hissed in a breath. When she moved her fingers inside the elastic waist of his underwear, her hands were no longer cold but warm, inquisitive, and boldly competent. He wanted to inhale her as he kissed the top of her collarbone.

He was hard. She pulled him from his underwear and slid the briefs and shorts down his legs while he gripped her hips, moving her to the edge of the counter.

He was about to slip into her when he stopped and stepped back, keeping one hand between her legs. Her eyes widened as he opened the well-stocked guest drawer to the side of her.

"You don't have to do th—"

He interrupted her with a kiss, not wanting her to say he didn't need a condom. No matter what she thought, this wasn't the last time they were making love. He wasn't going to let her die here in Rivera's makeshift clinic.

He tore open the wrapper and she helped him cover himself, then he was pressing into her wet heat. She made a primal sound, deep in her throat that almost undid him.

Holding her to his chest, he pulled back as she wrapped her legs around his waist and he was deep inside her again. Pushing harder, wanting to imprint himself on her. To show her that her life was vital to him. With every kiss, every touch, he wanted her to know how important she was, how strong she was. How she couldn't leave this life without fighting.

They were both sucking in ragged breaths of oxygen, like they were running a sprint. He could feel her spiraling out and tightening around him. She cried out her release as he poured himself into her.

A steamy fog continued to rise around them. He held her to his chest, not wanting to let go. Leaning into the counter with her in his arms, he breathed in the scent of her. She might despise him later for this, for what he would do to stop her. But for now, she was his.

A voice in his head warned that these kinds of feelings could make him defenseless. Caring was risky and vulnerability always led to pain. He didn't have to look any further than Gavin and Kat to see the emotional Armageddon love invited.

He buried his nose in Anna's hair and dismissed the worry. At the moment, what did it matter? Emotional risk paled in comparison to their current physical danger.

If this didn't go like he planned, they could both be dead before the end of the day.

Chapter Twenty-Seven

THE KNOCK ON the door came an hour and a half later. Startled despite knowing the summons was imminent, Anna was dressed and lying on the bed in Leland's arms. They hadn't talked anymore of Rivera's plan. Instead they'd showered together, making love on the bench seat in the high-tech spa in deference to Leland's ankle. He'd taken off the boot before getting in under the spray and she'd actually smiled when she saw the GPS tucked down inside the padding.

The stitches in her arm got wet, but she'd assumed it didn't matter at this point. Leland had made her forget the wretched circumstances, even if just for a little while. Steam and fog had completely filled the glass enclosure before they'd turned off the water and returned to what they assumed was a bugged suite.

While they'd been otherwise occupied, breakfast had

been delivered. Bountiful plates of eggs, sausage, and pastry under silver domes were waiting for them, like room service in a luxury hotel. Food held no appeal for Anna, but she'd tried a couple of bites of toast and managed an entire glass of orange juice.

Ever mindful of the cameras and recording devices, they'd eaten in relative silence before lying down together to wait on Rivera's summons. Anna knew Leland wasn't okay with what she was about to do, but he wasn't fighting her anymore. Instead, he'd held her tenderly as she'd closed her eyes and rehearsed in her mind how she would tell Zach goodbye.

It was time. Surprisingly, Anna felt a surreal calm as Antonio rolled the tray out of the room and she rose from their bed. Her vision was fuzzy around the edges, almost dreamlike. Holding Leland's hand, she followed the guard down the long hall and spiral staircase. In her new dress and kitten heels, she was dressed for a garden party instead of a painful goodbye.

They met Rivera in the same open-air living area they'd been in earlier. The sky had clouded over outside, and the wind blew a decidedly chilly breeze into the room. Anna idly wondered who took care of closing the glass-panel walls when the weather turned nasty.

Rivera wasted no time on preliminaries. "Are you ready to see your son?"

Leland squeezed her hand. "Yes," Anna nodded.

Rivera led them through the living room and across the grand entry to a set of utilitarian stairs. They travelled two flights down before arriving at a large pressurized door at the bottom of the staircase. Here the air was noticeably cooler.

"We have to seal our medical clinic and filter the air for the operating theatre." Rivera spoke as if he was giving a tour, not like he was taking Anna to see her son for the last time.

Downstairs the look of the décor changed from luxurious antique-filled mansion to sterile modern clinic. Everything about the architecture was like a real hospital, down to the bare walls and fire alarm at the stairwell's entrance.

A large desk with a raised counter was midway down the hall where two women in scrubs stood, speaking with an older man in a white lab coat. Two recessed doors were across the hall from this mini nurse's station with another door near the stairs. Rivera stopped at the desk.

"Dr. Morales. This is Zach's mother, your donor."

The older man glanced up from his records to make fleeting eye contact. He was speaking in Spanish to the nurses but changed to English when he addressed Anna.

"Do you have any questions about your son's procedure?

Anna had dozens of questions. They were all acting as if this were a typical situation with a living organ donation. But when it all came down to it, she only had one concern.

"Please don't tell Zach about my being the donor heart before the operation. I understand he'll find out afterward, but before the . . . procedure, please don't tell him it's mine."

The doctor nodded. "Yes, I agree that would be best. We'll put him to sleep before we bring you into the operating room. I have a couple of family history questionnaires for you—some information about Zach that we need. Would you rather answer them now or after you see your boy?"

Anna swallowed. That sense of surreal calm she'd felt earlier had fled. Already she could feel her heart rate increasing. She wasn't going to be in any coherent shape after she saw Zach.

"I'd rather take care of it before I see him."

Morales handed her a clipboard with two sheets of questions and indicated she could sit in the chair beside the desk. She sat and began to check off the answers.

This part seemed familiar. She'd filled out volumes of paperwork over the past twelve months and answered many of the same questions. Despite the insanity of the moment, this was normal. She felt herself calming again.

The nurse asked if she could go ahead and take her blood pressure. Anna nodded. Now would be better. Her heart rate was only going to go up as they proceeded. Her blood pressure was high, but no one commented. Rivera and Leland stood by without speaking as the nurse undid the blood pressure cuff.

Anna finished the questionnaire and the nurse took the rest of her vitals. Leland moved to stand beside her and put his hand on her shoulder. She couldn't look at him.

She knew he didn't understand, but she had to do this. It was Zach's only sure chance. She didn't want to argue with him anymore, yet she knew if they were left alone he'd have plenty to say.

"Please, can I see my son now?" she asked.

"Of course," Rivera said magnanimously. Nodding to the nurse who'd taken her blood pressure, he led her to the recessed door across from the nurse's desk.

"I want to see him alone," she said.

"Naturally, but only for a few moments. We have much to prepare for," said Rivera, apparently forgetting he'd promised her *as much time as possible* with her son a few hours ago. She didn't argue, recognizing it would do no good and only squander what time she did have.

She could tell Leland wanted to say something, but she gripped his hand and squeezed. He understood and remained silent. It was maddening, but she wouldn't put it beyond Rivera to vindictively refuse to allow her a goodbye if she or Leland made him angry.

"Go on, Mrs. Mercado," he instructed.

She only hesitated a moment before entering the high-tech hospital room that looked like a mini-hotel suite. Zach lay on the bed, just as she'd seen on the monitor earlier. His eyes were closed. His color was okay, not great. She stood in the doorway and watched him doze.

How many nights over the past year had she watched him sleeping, just to reassure herself he was alive and still with her?

She'd sat in the chair she'd rocked him in as an infant and watched him breathing—praying for an answer, for a donor. She'd never dreamed the answer would come in quite this way.

She took a deep breath. She was ready to do this, to give herself up for him. She wasn't scared for herself but apprehensive for him. She didn't want him to live with Max or with guilt. To grow up with his father would change Zach in ways that she didn't like to think about.

This was the part she was most worried about.

Who would listen to him, guide him, truly love him? Max was out of the question. God, she didn't have time to unravel her feelings about what her husband's involvement in this scheme meant. Obviously, the man was too selfish, too angry, too morally bankrupt to raise their son.

And Anna's family, well, Liz was the only real option. Zach's aunt would gladly take care of him, and he could be happy with her. That was something she'd have to ask Rivera about, if she could write a letter to Liz beforehand. Surely, he'd let her.

She just . . . she didn't want to leave Zach yet. She felt the tears on her face as she stood staring and quickly brushed them away.

She moved closer to the bed, intending to take his hand and wake him gently, but she bumped the tray table and jostled left over silverware. His eyes flew open.

"Mom." His voice cracked as only a teenage boy's could. "You're here. Are you okay?"

She nodded and reached for his hand—took it, held on, and told the biggest lie she ever had. "Yes, darling, everything is alright. I'm fine. We're both going to be okay."

When he'd been diagnosed with his heart condition he'd made her swear she would always tell him the truth, no matter what. And she'd sworn to do that, even if it took her skin off.

Today she couldn't bear to keep that promise. She couldn't tell him everything that was about to happen, that he was going to be fine but she wasn't going to be here with him. Afterward, he was going to hate that she hadn't told him the truth, but she couldn't see any upside. He'd freak out and insist she not do it. That would only upset him and possibly delay the surgery or make things more stressful.

And in the end, Rivera would get his way. Anna would be the donor for his wife and her son. So in her last moments with Zach, she was going to lie. She only hoped that later he could forgive her.

She smiled because this should be good news. "They've found a donor! You're going to get a heart."

Tears burned behind her eyelids, but she refused to let them fall. He'd know something was wrong and this was supposed to be what they'd been waiting over a year for.

Instead, he looked puzzled. "Here? Why here? Why did these people take me from Dallas?"

"It's confusing I know. Your dad arranged it all. When he got arrested things got complicated and mis- um . . . miscommunicated," she stammered.

"You never wanted me to have the surgery in Mexico," he said.

She nodded and swallowed before answering. "I know, but finding a donor changed my mind." She tried to smile again. This time it felt like she was grimacing.

Despite that, Zach seemed to accept her explanation.

He was a little out of it, but that didn't surprise her. His oxygen saturation levels were lower than normal, so his thinking wasn't as clear.

She sat on the edge of his bed and reached for his hand. "You know how much I love you, right?"

Her beautiful boy grinned. "Yeah, Mom. I know. I love you, too. For everything you've done. I know it's been really hard. Thank you. I can't wait to make it up to you. To take care of you for a change."

She bit the inside of her cheek to keep the tears at bay. Oh God, how could she do this? He was going to be so angry when he was told what had happened.

She studied him, trying to imagine what he would look like a year from now, five years from now, ten years from now. As a grown man.

She took another deep breath. "I'll look forward to that."

She sniffed and several tears ran down her cheek. But it was okay to cry now. He'd just think she was being sentimental.

"They're going to be in here soon to do all the preliminaries. I'd asked to see you alone first," she said.

He nodded. "It doesn't seem real. I've waited so long. Can you believe it?"

"No, I can't." She couldn't say anything else and was almost relived when there was a knock at the door. Dr. Morales and Leland came in.

"Hey!" Zach lit up when he saw Leland.

"Hey yourself, guy."

"Mom didn't say you were here, too." He looked at her with another puzzled expression.

"Yeah, I helped her get to Mexico," Leland explained.

"Cool, thanks." He squeezed Anna's hand. "I'm so glad she's here. This is amazing news about the donor. I wish Dad could be here, too, since he planned it all."

Anna struggled not to visibly cringe beside him at the words. Leland clenched his jaw and put his hand on her elbow. She could feel the tension in his fingers.

Zach was blissfully unaware of his verbal gaffe. "I guess he's still in Dallas. But I'll see him soon, right?"

Leland looked to Anna for direction on answering the question and she nodded.

"That's right," Leland said.

She didn't make any more eye contact with him. She couldn't. She had to get out before she broke down completely.

"Darling, the doctor's here to do that pre-op stuff. I'm going to have to leave."

"You can't stay?" Zach asked, a tiny bit of fear in his eyes.

Oh baby, I'm so sorry. Please don't be scared. It's going to be okay. You're going to be okay.

She shook her head, no longer trusting herself to speak. Morales spoke up. "The regulations are a little different here than in US hospitals."

Indeed. Anna found a sick gallows humor in the doctor's understatement. She was on a very thin edge and needed to get out of the room.

"But I'll see you after?" said Zach.

The doctor didn't answer and Anna nodded. "Of course."

Still holding Zach's hand, she leaned over the bed to kiss him. He surprised her and raised up to give her a tight hug.

"I love you, Mom. I'm glad this is almost over."

She swallowed and wiped her eyes. "I love you, too, baby. I'm so proud of you. There's nothing I wouldn't do for you. Remember that, okay?"

Forgive me for not telling you everything.

He squeezed her neck again, and she kissed him on the cheek before turning to leave. Grateful the door was only a few steps away, she was going to melt in a puddle when she got outside the room.

The doctor, finally seeming to clue in as to how difficult this was for her, moved to Zach's bedside and checked the IV. Anna escaped with Leland behind her. Antonio was waiting to escort them. Rivera was nowhere to be seen.

Once the door to Zach's room closed behind her, Anna's whole body began to shake, but she kept following the guard. He led them down the hall toward the stairs to another hospital room just like Zach's. She scarcely made it to the room's recliner and would have crumbled to the floor if Leland hadn't been there to catch her.

The door shut firmly behind them, but she didn't cry. At last, she was beyond tears.

SHE WAS COMPLETELY wrecked. At a total loss for where to start and what to say, Leland sat in the chair and pulled Anna to his lap.

"I'm not sad for me," she said. "I just can't stand the thought of leaving him alone."

She was shaking like she had palsy. Leland stared at the door while running his hand up and down her arm. At his touch, she burrowed into his chest.

The nurse who'd taken her vitals earlier knocked but didn't wait before stepping in. Mechanically holding out her arm for the blood pressure cuff when asked, Anna didn't raise her head or untangle herself from Leland.

"The doctor says we'll be getting underway with the procedure in the next hour. You'll need to change before we start."

She pointed to a gown on the bed. "They'll be here for you in about twenty-five minutes."

The nurse was trying to be professional, but watching her deliver the news, Leland could tell the woman was struggling. Anna didn't move her head from his chest. He wasn't sure she was even hearing the instructions.

The nurse addressed him. "I can give her something for the anxiety if you think it would help. It might make this easier."

At that Anna raised her head. "No, that won't be necessary. I . . . I need to write a letter," she stammered. "Could I have some paper, please?"

"Certainly." The nurse moved to the bedside table and pulled a tablet and pen from it. "Here you are. If you change your mind about the sedative, buzz for me."

The nurse left and Anna rested her head back on his shoulder. "I'm not sure I can do this," she said.

He started to speak, but she put a finger to his lips. "Don't say I don't have to. I do. There's no other way."

He swallowed his words and took a deep breath, wanting to give her some clue as to what he was planning before he took the decision completely out of her hands. "I won't let this happen. I can't let you give in."

"Don't you see? I'm not giving in. I'm giving my son a chance to start again."

"No, I can't accept that. I won't. Don't *you* see, Anna? He needs you, alive and in his life. He won't understand or be grateful for this sacrifice. It'll scar him for life. And who will raise him if you're gone? Max? He'll be in jail."

She shook her head as her eyes filled with tears and her face fell. "Please. I can't argue with you about this anymore. Not when there's so little time left."

He didn't speak. Everything he'd been running from in his life and in his work was here: his blossoming addiction, his failures, knowing his own worth, protecting the people who mattered, being enough. Was he good enough to overcome his fears and his failures?

Right now he wasn't sure, but Anna made him want to be. For the first time since he'd woken up after the Colton raid, he longed to be good enough and to know he made a difference.

Anna didn't understand what she was worth to those around her or how important her presence was in her son's life. With a shock, Leland realized they were dealing with some of the same insecurities but on completely different levels.

He hadn't wanted to be needed by or responsible to

anyone. But once he'd met her and Zach, he only wanted to protect them. Still, dammit, here he was—defeated, angry, and failing again.

Unaware of his struggle, she turned to him. "I know you've no reason to do this. But when it's over, when you're both home and safe, please look in on Zach."

Leland didn't want to go there, so he ignored the wave of despair that swept over him at her words. She wasn't going to change her mind. He had no gun and no way of contacting Nick or Marissa to know if they were indeed close by, but he wasn't giving up.

He wasn't giving Anna up.

She gazed into his eyes, begging him to look out for her son when she was gone. He nodded and let her think he was agreeing to let her do this, to die for Zach. But he wasn't. He wasn't letting her sacrifice herself. He wasn't losing her when he'd just found her.

Instead, he was getting her out of here. Zach, too. She might hate him later, but she wasn't going to die here today.

Her whole body was shaking so he leaned into her, kissing her softly on the cheek, working his way down her neck then back to her lips as she melted further into his chest. He'd give her anything she needed in this moment, except what she wanted most.

He felt her anguish and her passion when she slid her hands around his shoulders. He took the kiss deeper. Still, he held her gently, moving his hands up her arms to her neck until his fingers were at the vagus nerve below her ear.

At first she didn't realize what was happening. Reaching her hand up, she tried to pull his thumb away. "Leland, that kind of hurts—"

Then she was falling away, her eyes rolling back into her head, and she was out. For how long, he wasn't sure.

When she came to, she'd feel like hell for about twenty minutes. But he couldn't fight her while trying to get both her and Zach out of the compound. Besides, they were running out of time.

She'd be furious for what she'd see as his stealing this chance from Zach. But he wasn't having either of them on his conscience. He already carried enough guilt from the failures of his past. He carried her to the bed and gently laid her on the covers.

Since the door to the hall was recessed in a small alcove, he could open it without anyone seeing him, unless they were walking directly in front of the room. He slid outside and took a quick peek down the hall.

The nurse's desk was to the left and the staircase to the main house was on the right. Two women in scrubs stood at the nurse's station. Glancing back again toward the stairs, Leland saw what he was looking for.

Chapter Twenty-Eight

A RED FIRE alarm was mounted about ten feet away down the hall. The only problem was it was too far for him to reach and pull the alarm from the recessed doorway. He would have to time things perfectly.

He bent down and watched the nurses chatting. Ever aware of the clock ticking, his chance came when one of the women went into Zach's room and the other turned her back to him and hunched over the desktop computer.

Slowly he stood and rushed down the hallway to the stairwell, just close enough to reach the alarm. He pulled the white bar down in one smooth action and dashed back to the room as the klaxons began shrieking.

Anna was still out cold on the bed. The sounds of running feet and shouting voices passed the door. He didn't know how long it would take them to check on things or figure out that this was a false alarm, but he only needed a momentary distraction to get Anna and Zach out.

He cracked open the door as one of the nurses rushed past along with Antonio and Rivera. Dr. Morales and the other nurse were nowhere to be seen. This was the riskiest part. He was counting on Rivera and the doctor staying with the more important patient, Rivera's wife. Hopefully, the nurses weren't carrying guns. That was a big gamble, but there was no other way.

He slid outside once again and headed for the nurse's station. Ignoring the computer screen, he went for the desk drawers. The first held pencils, pens, office supplies. The second contained alcohol swabs, syringes, a bottle of pills, and the rubber strap used to tie a patient's arm when taking blood.

The bottle of medication rolled to the right, putting the label in full view. Zach Mercado was the patient listed. It was Atenolol, the white pills from the hotel. They would most likely need those for the trip home. *When* they got out of here. Leland pocketed the bottle.

He glanced up and down the hall, very conscious that time was slipping away and he wasn't finding what he needed. He opened the bottom drawer to a handbag that looked like it would qualify as a piece of carry-on luggage with the airlines. Maybe this was the jackpot.

He dumped the contents of the purse in the drawer. Breathing a sigh of relief, he fished a cellphone out of the mysterious jumble that was a woman's pocketbook. He gave the bag another upside down shake and realized there was something else in the large side pocket.

He recognized the shape before opening the zippered compartment and smiled darkly. This angel of mercy carried a Smith & Wesson snub nose .38 Special. Apparently her compassion was a tad selective.

The revolver was fully loaded. He checked to make sure there was a bullet in the chamber before he slid it to the waistband of his new jeans and turned on the phone.

Sin servicio glowed in white letters. *No service*. There were no bars indicating reception. Of course, they were underground.

He scanned the computer screen. It was open to a webcam in an operating theatre. White-coated individuals moved around the sterile room.

He considered the idea of sending an email to Gavin but dismissed it when he heard voices and looked up. Someone was about to come around the corner. He was completely out of time and ran across the hall as best he could with his boot to Zach's room.

Not knowing if anyone was with the boy, he quietly pushed the door open.

"Hey! What's going on?" Zach sat up in bed.

"Do you trust me?" asked Leland.

Zach studied him before answering, "Yeah, yeah I do."

Leland gave him a quick nod. "We're getting out of here. I know you have a lot of questions. I can't answer them until we're safe."

"Okay?" Anna's boy sat up straighter, the puzzlement obvious on his face and in his voice.

"Can you get around on your own?" Leland was concerned about the heart situation.

"I can't run a marathon, but I can get around."

"No worries. I won't be running any races here, either."
Leland ignored the vicious stab of pain in his ankle. He
didn't have time to worry about that.

Zach slid off the mattress. He wore gym shorts and a
t-shirt with a huge pocket on the front. Slipping his feet
into flip-flops under the bed, he removed the wireless
heart monitor from his oversized t-shirt pocket, along
with a finger monitor. The lines on the machine behind
him went flat and started beeping. The alert was loud, but
the fire alarm was louder.

Zach reached up and bumped a button to silence the
machine. "It'll go off again in about three minutes."

Okay. So they had a timeline laid out. Leland did some
quick mental calculations.

"Don't run yourself down following me. I can help
you. Let me know if your heart gets wonky."

Zach nodded and Leland slid his arm around the boy's
shoulders as he opened the door. The hall was still empty.

"We're going to the stairwell and I'm getting your
mom. Got it?"

Zach nodded again. His eyes grew round with worry,
but he didn't ask questions. They hurried down the hall.

Realistically, Leland was past being able to run with
his boot. He couldn't move so fast that Zach would get
into trouble. But once they were up the stairs, it would be
a different story.

The fire alarm was still screeching, hiding any noise
that they were making but also hampering Leland's ability to hear others approaching.

They dashed past Anna's room and into the stairwell. The stairs were like those in an office building with a large open area underneath the bottom set. The pressurized door was open on the landing above and they were halfway up when Leland heard steps coming from the top floor.

He stumped back down the stairs, pulling Zach with him. Together they slipped beneath the open area beneath the steps. A nurse, talking on her phone in Spanish, was on the landing just above them. The alarm reverberated off the walls.

Leland could make out her saying, "*Falsa alarma.*" That meant it was only a matter of seconds before they figured out which alarm had been set off and who had done it. She stood on the upper stairs, finishing her conversation, and walked partway down the steps they were hidden under.

Leland pulled the pilfered phone from his pocket, checking for service again. Grateful he'd memorized Nick's number, he typed a text explaining where they were.

Immediately the phone vibrated with a returning message. He squeezed the case tight, praying the noise wouldn't register with the woman above him over the wailing alarm.

He need not have worried. She was having some kind of argument and was oblivious to their hiding below the stairs.

A wave of relief washed over him as he read Nick's return text: "Already here. See you in a few."

Thank God. This half-assed plan of his might just work.

LELAND WAITED TILL the woman walked all the way down the stairs and through the pressurized door.

"Wait here," he whispered to Zach.

He counted to ten before slipping out from under the stairwell and hurrying to Anna's room as best he could. The boot was feeling heavier and heavier. She was still out. If he was lucky, the nurse would check on Zach first before coming here, then most likely she'd freak when she realized her patient was gone.

He bent to pick Anna up as someone knocked on the door.

Damn. So much for luck.

He slid behind the door as the nurse breezed inside. Her eyebrows were already raised in question at seeing Anna lying on the bed when he grabbed her from behind and put the .38 Special to her temple. The woman didn't fight him as he pushed her forward to the wall and moved a hand to her neck, using the same vagus nerve pressure point he had with Anna.

The nurse was out immediately. He laid her gently in the easy chair and gathered Anna in his arms to hustle down the hall. Anna'd been out for less than ten minutes. That was all the time he was going to need or this wasn't going to work at all. He hoped Nick would show up soon.

Zach poked his head around the corner as Leland

stumped into the stairwell. "What's wrong with her?" he demanded.

"She's alright. She'll wake up in a few minutes." Leland figured he'd get more cooperation if he didn't tell the boy that he'd knocked his mother out cold with a nerve compression move he'd learned in martial arts class.

"We've got to get upstairs. Can you make it on your own?" Leland asked.

"Yeah, I can do it."

They started the climb. Leland headed up slowly, partly because he was carrying Anna and partly because of his ankle. Zach travelled at a steady but sedate pace behind him.

"I've got your white pills if you need 'em," Leland said, glancing over his shoulder.

Zach looked relieved. "Great."

The alarm continued to reverberate in the stairwell. They were halfway up the stairs when the klaxons stopped clamoring. The quiet was ominous. Now everyone knew this had been a false alarm. They had only moments to get out of the compound.

A door on the landing above slammed open and footsteps sounded on the stairs. There was nowhere to go. They were too far up and too slow to race back down.

"Get behind me," Leland ordered, pulling the snub nose .38 from his waistband.

Then Nick was standing in front of him, his Sig Sauer drawn and an AK-47 slung around his shoulder as well. "Well, hell," said Nick. "What took you so long? I was about to get worried."

Leland laughed quietly. "It's only now you're worried? Wonderful. I thought maybe we were in trouble."

Nick grinned. "Seriously, man, I'm glad to see you. I just finished up."

"Finished up what?"

"Tell you in the car." Nick started to take Anna, but Leland shook his head.

"Help the boy," he said and kept moving up the stairs. At the top of the stairwell he peeked out into the entryway, hoping his new luck would hold.

He glanced back at Zach, trying to monitor how the boy was doing. His skin was pale, but he wasn't breathing heavily. His eyes were alert, all good signs.

Leland's ankle was screaming with pain, but their lives depended on his ignoring it for now. Anna was coming to in his arms, but he couldn't take the time to put her down. No one was in the entryway so he shifted her to his shoulder in a fireman's hold as he, Nick, and Zach headed for the front door.

Two empty SUVs were parked in the driveway. Where was everyone? He opened the driver's side of the first car, but there were no keys so he hobbled to the second vehicle hoping he was saving time.

Bingo. Keys swung from the ignition.

From further down the drive, he heard another vehicle approaching and felt his phone vibrate against his hip.

At the same time Anna spoke. "Where am I, dammit?" She punctuated her question with a sharp slap to his back.

She was mad. That was a good sign, and he felt a fleeting moment of relief. He slipped the phone from his pocket to read a text from Marissa.

"We r here."

He lowered Anna to the ground. Her eyes were glazed but slowly filling with rage as she stared up at him. "You . . . you," she stuttered, then she saw Zach and Nick beside him. Myriad emotions washed over her face—confusion, anger, love. She ignored Leland to gather Zach in her arms.

He settled inside. They'd sort this out later. For now, they'd move faster with her awake.

Shouts in the doorway behind him had him swinging around to see Rivera and two gunmen.

"Stop!" shouted Rivera.

A banana yellow Hummer was thundering up the drive, but Leland wasn't positive it was his ride. He couldn't believe AEGIS would be arriving in such a conspicuous vehicle. Either way the Hummer wasn't going to make it in time to stop Rivera's men from shooting him, Anna, Zach, and Nick.

The other empty SUV was between the gunmen and Leland's small group as he made a split-second decision. The thing he'd been thinking about since Rivera had said he wanted Anna's lungs. He pulled Zach from her arms and pushed Nick and the boy behind him.

Holding her in front of them all, he slid the revolver from his waistband and put the gun to Anna's temple.

Chapter Twenty-Nine

"JESUS, LELAND," HE heard Nick mutter behind him. "What the fuck you doing?"

"Mom! No!" shouted Zach at the same time.

Leland ignored them all, concentrating instead on the woman in his arms and the men pointing their assault rifles at him.

"*Alto!*" shouted Leland. *Stop.* In English he spoke directly to Rivera. "Shoot me, I'll kill your wife's donor."

He heard Anna's sharp intake of breath and felt her body stiffen in his arms.

"Do you trust me?" he whispered only to her.

"Leland? What are you doing?" Zach pulled at his waist.

"Stop it, kid!" Leland's voice was ice cold and his hands were rock steady, but his heart was quaking.

"You can't—" argued Zach.

"Shut up!" He couldn't fake this, not if the boy was fighting him.

"It's okay, baby," Anna said. "It's gonna be okay."

At first Leland thought she was talking to him, then he realized she was trying to soothe her son. He couldn't see her eyes. Did she really think he would pull the trigger?

"Trust me," he murmured into her hair.

His hand was around her waist and he pulled her tight up against him in a grim parody of a lover's embrace. He made a show of shoving the gun against her breast.

"No chance for harvesting lungs if I shoot her in the chest." Leland was betting that Rivera's men thought he would indeed kill her.

His only hope for saving them from a bloodbath lay in the men not shooting for fear of hitting Anna. Despite the coverage of the empty SUV, he, Nick and the boy were dead if he lowered his weapon.

"You'd kill that woman to shield yourself?" sneered Rivera.

"I have no choice," said Leland. Repeating Rivera's words from earlier, he squeezed her waist at the same time, desperately trying to communicate to Anna that this was all a ruse on his part.

He heard the Hummer pull up behind him. He was so screwed if this was another group of Rivera's men and not Marissa.

"Our ride's here, man," said Nick, the only person who didn't appear to be completely freaking out over the situation.

The door opened behind them. He didn't turn around, but he smiled when he heard Risa ask, "Are we late for the party?"

Leland didn't visibly acknowledge the relief he felt at recognizing her voice. He still had to stall till Zach and Anna were safely in the car.

"You'd have taken this woman's life to save your wife's," Leland called to Rivera. "You said her life was as precious to you as your own."

"Get in," he heard Nick tell Zach. Backing to the vehicle, Leland felt hands on his shoulder.

"I've got him in range," Nick spoke under his breath. "Almost there."

Leland eased backward, still taking care to keep Anna in front of them as Marissa pulled Zach into the back of the Hummer.

Rivera kept talking, obviously desperate to keep Anna there. "Of course, I would have taken her life. I see what you're doing, Agent Hollis. But it won't work. Even with your friends here, I will find you. You still have to get out of the city."

Nick moved to stand beside him with an AK-47 in his hands pointed at Rivera and his men. "Move. I've got you both covered."

Leland pulled back with Anna in front of him, glancing once over his shoulder. Zach was in the backseat, glaring at him with undisguised malevolence. Risa was hanging onto the boy's arm to keep him from coming after Leland.

"Okay, Anna. We're getting in."

He tugged her with him, his arm around her waist, her ass flush against his groin, and the underside of her breast brushing against his wrist. Even with Nick covering them Leland wasn't turning his back from Rivera. He guided Anna along with him until he felt the seat hit his own butt.

Only then did he lower the .38 from her chest. Ducking, he jerked her backward into his lap in the vehicle. Another man Leland had never seen before was driving.

He was glancing back toward Rivera when it happened. Someone blinked. Leland would never know who shot first, but it wasn't him and it wasn't Nick.

For a moment he was reminded of the night at the Coltons, except no babies were screaming. It was just the explosive *thump-thump-thump* of guns firing and the smell of gunpowder as all hell broke loose.

Nick was outside the vehicle when the barrage began. Leland pulled Anna over his own legs and boot to the seat beside him so he was shielding her body with his. The slap of a bullet by his head had Leland pushing Anna down hard into the floorboard. Marissa already had Zach down there and was back up on the seat returning fire. Nick seemed to be holding his own with the automatic weapon behind that other empty SUV, but he couldn't do it alone.

"Risa, whatever happens, y'all get the hell out of here," said Leland.

"Drive, Hollywood, go!" shouted Nick.

Marissa looked like she wanted to argue, but another bullet shattered the passenger glass and hit the headrest beside the driver. She nodded.

"Do not wait for us," Leland said. "You've got to get out of here before someone gets shot." He leaped from the car with the .38 Special. His feet hit the ground as Nick fell. Leland crouched and scrambled to get to the downed man.

Nick was already bleeding profusely. "What the hell?" he growled. "You were in the damn car and almost gone."

"Yeah, but you weren't." Leland looked at Nick's chest wound and took a deep breath. "I'm not leaving anyone behind."

Anna screamed his name at the same time Leland hollered at Marissa. "Go, go, go!"

Nick pushed his AK-47 into Leland's hands and pulled the Sig Sauer from his waistband as the Hummer sped off. The empty SUV was now their only cover.

"Jesus, this isn't good." Nick's lips were white with pain.

"It's gonna be okay," said Leland. "The keys to that SUV are in the ignition."

He used the assault rifle to lay down a blanket of bullets along the entryway. Most of Rivera's men had ducked for cover when the shooting started, but two hadn't been quick enough, their bodies sprawled on the steps. If Leland could get Nick into the SUV they might be able to get out of here.

It should have been easy, but Rivera would be calling in reinforcements from other parts of the compound at any time. Leland was surprised that they weren't here already.

He had to get Nick inside that vehicle and get away, or they were going to die in Tomas Rivera's driveway.

Leland pulled at Nick. "Can you get up?"

"Yeah, think so." But his face had gone gray and the 9mm went slack in his hand. Nick was hit twice that Leland could see.

Rivera called from the steps and the men stopped shooting. "Don't take this personally, Agent Hollis, but we're going to kill you now, you and your friend. And we'll find the woman. This city belongs to me. There's no place they can hide."

Leland ignored the taunt and opened the back door to shove Nick inside. He was slamming it shut when he felt a searing pain along the top of his left shoulder.

Shit.

He was saved from being knocked on his ass only because he was hanging onto the backseat door handle with his right hand.

Reaching for the driver's side door, he had moments before that adrenaline rush would be overridden by the agony of a gunshot wound. He pulled himself into the front seat and ducked as the glass shattered in the passenger-side window. Bullets slapped the upholstery beside him.

Cranking the engine, he thanked God when it caught on the first try and he floored it. "Which way do I turn at the drive?" He called over his shoulder to Nick.

"Left," came the mumbled reply.

Mashing the accelerator to the floor, he sped down the driveway.

"The airstrip's about three miles outside Boca del Río." Nick didn't sound good. Certainly not like he could fly them anywhere.

Leland would try and iron that particular wrinkle out after they were safely off Rivera's property. Speeding down the drive he followed the signs for Boca del Río and worried about the lack of sound coming from the back seat.

"What's going on back there?"

"Oh, just lying here bleeding. What the hell do you think I'm doing?"

"Jeez, I thought SEALS were tough."

"Screw you, Hollis."

Okay, so Nick sounded testy. If he felt good enough to be hostile, that was probably a good thing. Leland wanted to keep him talking, but he also needed to concentrate on speeding over the potholed road, putting as much distance between them and the Rivera compound as possible.

After a couple of minutes he tried again. "Nick, talk to me."

"Don't want to talk. I've been shot, dammit. This hurts like a bitch."

Leland glanced over his shoulder and nodded but was secretly shocked at the amount of blood streaming down the seat. "Okay, crybaby, give me your phone. I've got to call Risa."

He didn't get a response, but when he reached over the backseat Nick handed him a cell phone covered with blood. Leland wiped the screen on his pants leg before speaking. "We gotta get you to a doctor and find the others."

"I pulled up the number," whispered Nick.

Leland glanced down and touched the screen. Risa answered on the first ring.

"It's Leland. Got to find a doctor for Nick. He's bad."

She didn't hesitate. "Where are you?"

"Driving through Antón Lizardo, headed for Boca del Río."

"We're just a few minutes ahead of you. Gavin has a contact in Antón Lizardo. Give me a minute to get the address."

He heard Marissa speaking, then a deeper male voice, then Risa instructing Anna to hand a bag over the seat.

Anna. Would she ever trust him again? He'd taken Zach away from the compound and the transplant. He'd held a gun to her head.

A pedestrian stepped into the street and Leland swerved, the front wheels of the SUV skidded onto the dirt shoulder then bumped back up to the cobbled road. He couldn't think about his problems with Anna just now. He'd get himself or someone else killed.

"Okay. Bryan knows someone there, too. One of our old contacts." Marissa rattled off an address. "I'm shooting it to Nick's phone."

The phone in Leland's hand *dinged* with an incoming text. It was a map. "Got it. I'll meet you there."

Chapter Thirty

LELAND WOVE THROUGH the dirty streets of Antón Lizardo. The houses crowded each other in varying shades of faded gray. A few pieces of clothing hung on the occasional clothesline. Lonely flowerpots dotted the bleak faces of otherwise ramshackle buildings. Few people were on the streets despite the hour. It was as if residents knew they were safer indoors.

Leland found the building Risa had indicated and parked the non-descript but shiny SUV out front. Large sun-bleached doors that most likely led into a courtyard were shut tight. His shoulder throbbed now, and he was hyper aware of the blood running down his arm and dripping onto his seat.

He wondered briefly if Rivera's SUV was LoJacked and prayed it wasn't or they were SOL. Most drug dealers didn't use GPS-type preventatives in their cars because the technology could be used by authorities to track the criminals themselves instead. Glancing back at Nick confirmed that he didn't have time for hiding the car.

Besides, who in their right mind would steal a car from a cartel leader when it was obvious who it belonged to? He'd noticed the license plate in the drive, before all hell had broken loose. It was personalized as "Rivera3."

Leland got out and had his hand raised to knock on one of the faded doors when it opened. A surprisingly young man answered. Blond-haired and blue-eyed, he glanced over Leland's shoulder to the large SUV.

"Walters?" Leland asked.

"AEGIS?" The man studied Leland as he asked the single word question.

Leland nodded. "Got a man badly wounded."

"You don't exactly have a scratch." Walters stared pointedly at Leland's arm, which was now dripping large spots of blood onto the faded sidewalk. Still, it was nothing compared to the puddle Nick was lying in on the back seat.

"Let's get him inside." Walters opened the two doors, revealing a courtyard and several cages filled with barking dogs. *Pull your vehicle in here*, he urged. "No LoJack, right?"

Leland smiled grimly as the doctor's thoughts echoed his own. "For Rivera? Highly doubtful."

Walters nodded then stared when the unusually colored Hummer pulled up behind Leland's SUV. He waved both cars inside the courtyard. Leland was out of his vehicle immediately as Walters opened the back door to get Nick.

Anna and Zach scurried out of the backseat and closed the courtyard doors, hiding them from any passersby. He wanted to talk to Anna, but now wasn't the time. The driver who Nick had called "Hollywood" introduced himself as Bryan Fisher. He and Risa stood together on either side of Walters, ready to help slide Nick off the backseat.

With his shoulder injury, Leland wasn't able to really help much with the lifting. Fisher and Walters moved Nick carefully to a small surgery area. Blood-soaked and pale, he appeared unconscious. Under Walters's direction Marissa moved a small stainless-steel table in place for them to put Nick down.

Leland and Fisher moved out of the way, and Fisher picked up a huge wad of sterile gauze. "Let's do something about this till Walters can get to you."

"I'm fine to wait for the doctor—"

"Ah, come on, man. Don't be a pussy. Besides, he's gonna be a while." Fisher slipped on a pair of gloves.

Leland nodded, not terribly enthusiastic about the prospect.

"Don't worry, I've had some training. Let's find a place to sit you down." Fisher gathered more supplies, and they picked out a spot in the corner.

He'd obviously spent quite a bit of time here. Weighing in at 225 and built like a tank, the other AEGIS employee appeared to be ex-military, except for his longish dark blond hair and five o'clock shadow. Taller than Leland, he had a boyishly handsome face and didn't look over thirty until you saw his clear gray eyes.

The expression was vaguely familiar and disconcerting, like the eyes of an old man in a younger man's face. Fisher looked as if he'd seen too much ugliness in the world and was weary of it. The combination of those eyes and his build sent a big *don't mess with me vibe* to anyone who was paying attention. Leland figured most of Gavin's employees gave that kind of impression. It would be fairly useful in their line of work.

"How did you get involved in this?" Leland settled his hips against a stainless-steel counter along the wall as Fisher helped him slide his shirt off.

"Was on my way back from another job when Gavin asked me to meet Risa and Nick. Glad I was available. Looks like I'm going to be flying us home, as Nick's indisposed."

"Yeah. That being the case, I'm real happy you're here, even if you don't know what you're doing with my shoulder."

Fisher snorted a laugh and kept working, but his eyes didn't look quite so sad. "Glad I was in the area."

"Nick called you 'Hollywood.'"

Fisher shook his head. "Long story." One he obviously didn't care to discuss.

Hissing in a breath, Leland gritted his teeth as Fisher applied disinfectant to his shoulder wound then pressed down with gauze to staunch the bleeding.

Damn. It hurt.

He tried concentrating on what they were doing to Nick instead of what was happening to his own gunshot wound. The table Nick lay on was unnaturally short and looked as if it had been made for a child, particularly when Walters and Marissa arranged his body on the flat surface. Risa pulled another table over to support his lower legs.

"You do realize this is a vet clinic?" Walters asked.

Risa cracked-up. "That's more appropriate than you realize."

Leland smiled. Now the size of everything made sense.

A woman appeared at the door wearing a robe and nothing else.

"This is Angelina, my assistant," explained Walters.

Without bothering to step out of their line of sight, Angelina slid out of her robe and stepped into green scrubs. Leland was so surprised at her lack of modesty, he didn't even turn his head until she was almost dressed in the scrubs.

Fisher seemed equally frozen in place but only raised an eyebrow. "Don't mind us," he muttered, pressing down again on Leland's shoulder.

Leland sucked in another deep breath at the discomfort, and Angelina nodded to the two men. She proceeded to prove herself more than decorative as Walters called out orders like he was in a metropolitan ER. It didn't seem to bother him that his girlfriend-assistant had just performed an impromptu strip show for everyone.

Watching them work on Nick, Leland was impressed with the scope of the vet clinic's supplies. Angelina pulled IV bags and monitors around the table like this was an everyday occurrence. And it could have been for all they knew. For the right price, Walters might welcome anyone with a bullet wound that didn't want to go to a hospital.

Leland realized he was staring at the activity but no longer seeing anything when the doctor spoke. "Thanks, Bryan. We'll take care of your friend there properly in a bit. Angie, get a line in. Now."

"I'm fine." Leland settled more firmly against the counter as Walters and Angie worked to stabilize Nick.

"Right," said Walters.

"This may be a vet clinic, but the man sure as hell knows what he's doing," said Fisher.

"I see he does." Marissa had joined them and was clearly as impressed as Leland at the veterinarian's efficiency.

Anna and Zach were talking quietly nearby and doing their best to avoid seeing what was happening to Nick. Leland understood. They'd had enough of medical procedures over the past twelve months to last a lifetime.

"Do you need to sit, honey?"

"No, Mom, I'm fine. I'm just really confused."

"I know. We need to talk," she said.

Leland doubted Zach would get the real story in that conversation. But it wasn't really his business. Was it?

Fisher grabbed another wad of sterile surgical dressing and pressed it to the shoulder. "You're a lucky man. Looks like a very deep graze only. You may have nicked the subclavian artery, but I don't think so. It's definitely not perforated or you'd have bled out by now."

"Well hell, that's comforting."

"Considering the alternatives, it should be." Fisher

smiled and squirted something out of a large bottle into the wound.

Leland squeezed his eyes shut in a vain attempt to block out the pain. It didn't work.

"I'm irrigating this with saline for now, and I'm gonna pack it with gauze till Walters can take a look."

Leland nodded, grinding his teeth to avoid whimpering. Marissa's phone rang and she answered. He focused on her voice and could tell it was Gavin from her end of the conversation. Anna and Zach slipped away into the courtyard and Leland studied them from his vantage point on his makeshift bed.

Pale and looking a little shaky, the boy stared at the cages of dogs. Did he need his white pills? Leland reached into his jeans pocket and felt for the bottle. Instead, his fingers closed around his own prescription of pain medication. Zach's meds were in his other pocket.

So about his little Vicodin issue? It seemed a moot point at present. He'd gladly swallow as many pills as necessary to ease the excruciating discomfort of whatever the hell it was Fisher was doing. But he couldn't do that. He needed to stay sharp. Still, the painkillers rolling around in his pocket were incredibly tempting.

Once they were home and out of this mess, he was throwing the shit away. There were no other options. He wasn't addicted, but he was on his way if he didn't get a handle on the situation.

How long would it take to get completely clean? Could he do that? Would his shoulder slow the process down?

No. He could do it. This could be the first step to

changing all those things he so desperately wanted different in his life.

God, he hurt, all over.

"Where'd you learn all this?" Leland asked in an attempt to get his mind on something, anything else. The adrenaline was slowing down. The only good thing about being shot in the shoulder was that it took his mind off how much his ankle was screaming at him.

"Afghanistan."

Fisher didn't elaborate and Leland didn't need him to. He had firsthand knowledge of what that experience entailed, and his shoulder graze was insignificant compared to what Fisher had likely seen there.

He pulled up some medication in a syringe. "I'm sorry I can only give you a topical pain killer. It's not much, but if I give you a narcotic, you'll be woozy. We need you coherent."

Leland nodded.

"This should hold you till Walters can take a look." Fisher administered the shot around the edges of the wound and the site slowly numbed. As he fashioned a bandage, Leland focused on Anna through the remarkably clean windows.

She was smiling and petting a dog through the wire cage along with Zach when he noticed the smile disappear and she suddenly went still. He felt a frisson of concern.

Fisher finished taping him up and slipped off the bloody gloves. "Well, it's not completely done, but at least you aren't bleeding all over everyone now."

"Definitely a step in the right direction." Shirtless, Leland stood and moved to walk outside, feeling only slightly light-headed. He was anxious to check on Anna but stopped to shake Fisher's hand. "Thank you."

Fisher shrugged. "No problem."

When he got to the courtyard Anna was pale and gripping Zach's arm as she stared into the palm of her hand. Leland moved closer, slowly recognizing what she had cradled in her fingers.

The pager.

"Anna?"

She glanced up at him. The fear in her eyes from earlier was gone.

"Oh my god," she gushed. "It's CTC. They've got a heart for Zach." Her voice was wobbly. "I have to call them . . . right away."

She stared into his face, a look of shock and relief simultaneously colliding in her eyes. "I don't have a phone."

"Here," Leland tugged Nick's forgotten smartphone from his pocket and wiped at the blood still partially covering the screen before handing it over. She didn't look at him again as she walked away to the far side of the courtyard and made the call.

"I don't understand," said Zach. "I thought . . . I thought we had a heart back at that mansion. What's the deal?"

So Anna hadn't told him what was going on. That wasn't exactly a surprise, but it sure as hell wasn't Leland's place to enlighten the boy.

"You need to ask your mom about this."

"She won't tell me. She thinks she needs to protect me." Zach shook his head and crossed his arms with an air of teenage defiance. "As if she could protect me from my heart stopping. It pisses me off that she doesn't think I can handle the truth."

Leland considered the situation and wondered if he could possibly explain. The kid needed to know what his mother had been willing to sacrifice for him and what his dad had "arranged." But Leland wasn't the person to set the record straight.

He'd knocked Anna unconscious and threatened her life. Hadn't he done enough to her without butting his nose into this?

"I'm fourteen years old, dammit. I'm old enough to know the truth about my own health."

The boy had a valid point. Zach should know the truth. About everything—his heart, his mom, and his dad.

After the hell the man had put them through, Zach shouldn't go through life believing Max Mercado was some sort of hero. Max had been willing to kill his own wife, the boy's mother. Leland still wasn't sure Rivera would have followed through with Zach's transplant. There'd only been one surgical team in evidence at Rivera's clinic.

He sat down beside Zach on the low stone wall next to the dog cages. The scent of disinfectant and a stench no amount of bleach could ever cover wafted over them. Things weren't going to get more private any time soon.

He probably should just keep his mouth shut, but after another glance at Zach's intractable expression, Leland couldn't do it. He couldn't have the boy thinking his mom was in any way to blame.

"Your mom was going to give her heart for the transplant. Your dad arranged it all as payment for a debt he owed. That's why you were kidnapped from the hotel room. They wanted to force your mom to come to Mexico so they could do the surgery here."

Zach's quizzical air was frozen in place so Leland kept going.

"The man who owned that house, Tomas Rivera, wanted you and your mom because his wife has y'all's same rare blood type, and she needed a lung transplant. Your dad agreed to let Rivera have your mom's organs for Rivera's wife if they'd operate on you, too, and give you Anna's heart."

He stopped talking and took a deep breath. He'd explained. Zach's eyes widened and he gazed into the courtyard, speechless.

It had probably been a little too fast, but Leland figured the "ripping a bandage off" approach was best. He was pretty sure he'd done the right thing, but he was concerned about the boy's reaction, not to mention Anna's. He reached in his other pocket to feel for the bottle of Zach's heart pills and relaxed slightly.

The boy shook his head vehemently from side to side, a look of utter confusion on his face. "But Mom told me . . ." His voice trailed off as Leland assumed he was remembering exactly what Anna had and hadn't said in that hospital room at Rivera's compound.

Zach's eyes filled with tears. "She would have done that? For me? But . . ."

Leland nodded. "I couldn't talk her out of it. That's why . . ." Now it was his turn to trail off.

"That's why you knocked her out and why you knew she could be a shield in the driveway," finished Zach.

"She wouldn't have come out of there willingly. She wanted you to have a new heart that much, and Rivera needed her badly."

Zach stared at a fuzzy black dog in the cage in front of them. "I can't believe she would have—" His voice broke. "That she would have done that for me. She would have given up everything."

His eyes were wet, but when he looked up at Leland, his face was peaceful. "Thank you for telling me. She never would have."

"No, I don't believe she would have, either. Not sure it was my place, but you needed to know. If I were in your shoes, I'd want to know."

Zach nodded and they both glanced at Anna, still on the phone. "How's your shoulder?" The boy asked.

"Deep graze. Hurts like a bitch."

Zach smiled at his profanity as Leland had hoped he would. "Thank you for helping us. I don't know what to say. *Thank you* doesn't seem enough."

"You don't have to say anything." Leland reached out and shook the boy's hand. "You can always trust me. It's my job."

Leland realized he meant that. Taking care of people *was* his job. They sat in companionable silence for a moment, petting the dogs through the cage bars and watching as Anna ended the call and hurried over to speak with Marissa.

"It looks like you may have some good news."

Zach sighed. "Maybe."

Marissa seemed to listen then made a quick call herself before she motioned for Fisher to join them. They all talked before making their way to Zach and Leland. Anna didn't acknowledge his presence, but the uncertainty in her face from earlier had clearly turned to relief. She was completely focused on Zach.

"CTC has a heart," Anna reached out and took the boy's hands in hers as she spoke. "The donor is on a ventilator but will have to come off soon. We just have to tell them if we can get there. We have a little less than five hours."

"Can we make it in time?" The hope in Zach's voice was palpable.

Anna looked to Marissa for the answer. "Yes. Our plane is at an airstrip, about twenty minutes from here. We'll be in the air three hours. If we leave right now, we can get there. But we have to get on the plane immediately."

"What about Nick?" asked Leland.

"We're leaving him here till I can drop you all at the airport and come back. Bryan will fly you home." Marissa was typing a text as she spoke.

"Why don't I stay here with Nick?" suggested Leland.

"Because you don't work for AEGIS yet. And you'll be in more danger than me if you stay. Besides, you won't be much help riding shotgun with that shoulder. Rivera's gunning for you and he's got cause to want you dead."

"Well, I know he's angry, but no more so at me than Nick or anyone else here, right?"

Marissa shook her head. "Afraid so. I heard from Gavin. Rivera's compound was just leveled in an explosion. Early reports are it was a gas leak. It must have blown right after we got out of there, but the timing is a little too convenient. Gavin was asking if we had anything to do with it."

"Did you?" Leland's mind immediately went to his conversation with Nick in the stairwell of Rivera's house.

"No," said Marissa, irritation evident in her tone.

"Don't get pissy," replied Leland. "When Nick found us at Rivera's, he said he was just 'finishing up.' I assumed."

"Yeah," Fisher spoke up. "I can see how that would look suspicious to you. It would look bad to Rivera as well, if he knew." He focused on Marissa. "But Nick was setting surveillance equipment, that's all. No explosives. Rivera doesn't know about that. He just knows you, Anna, and Zach were running loose before the place blew up."

Risa jumped in. "We don't do wet work, ever. Not that people haven't tried to hire us for that before. Gavin refuses and I agree. But we needed some information for a case we've been working on for a while."

"What kind of case?" Leland asked, painfully aware that they really didn't have time for this.

Risa exchanged another long glance with Fisher. He nodded and she answered. "Kidnapping. The Elizabeth Yarborough case."

Leland blew out a breath in surprise. "The college student who was doing foreign aid work? I thought she got murdered by her American boyfriend when he came for a visit. Didn't they arrest the guy?"

"Yeah, but he didn't do it," Fisher explained. "And currently he's rotting in a Mexican prison because authorities don't want to look at what really happened. There's a lot of human trafficking down here. We've got reason to think Rivera's men may have had Elizabeth at one time. We were hoping we could get something from bugging the compound."

"How long have y'all been working this?"

"Too damn long," Fisher said.

"A while," answered Marissa at the same time.

It was time to change the subject. "So if Nick didn't set explosives, who did?" asked Leland.

"No idea, but the timing is just too coincidental to have been anything else, and . . ." Risa's voice trailed off.

"No one here believes in coincidences," added Leland.

"And the place was leveled," finished Fisher.

"Could have been the Vegas or another cartel," offered Marissa. "We're not sure if Rivera was there. He sent men to follow us out of the compound, but whether he was with them or not is anybody's guess. Early indications are that no one on the premises survived."

Anna and Zach had been listening quietly. "Oh no," she said. "All those doctors and—"

"His wife," said Leland, finally understanding the real issue.

"So you see why we need to get you all out of here ASAP?" asked Marissa. "If Rivera is alive, he will think you did this and take action."

"I sure as hell don't want to be coming back down here for you tomorrow," said Fisher.

"I understand," said Leland.

"I'll get the car." Fisher headed for the Hummer.

Marissa nodded. "I've got to talk to Walters about Nick." She headed for the doctor, leaving Anna, Leland and Zach together.

Leland waited a beat, thinking Anna might say something. But she didn't. He started to speak but didn't know how to begin. *I'm sorry* was insufficient and *I was only doing this for your own good* was patronizing.

So he said nothing. The anger simmered off her in waves and the moment was lost. She never even glanced at him as she pulled Zach with her toward the Hummer.

Chapter Thirty-One

THIS WAS HAPPENING too fast.

Anna was still processing everything that had transpired in the last hour as Leland and Bryan talked ammunition for their handguns and got the Hummer ready to leave the courtyard. They piled in with Marissa driving, and Bryan shut the gate behind them.

Shirtless, Leland was on the other side of Zach, who suddenly didn't seem nearly as mad at Leland as he'd been when they first arrived at the vet clinic. His shoulder was still bleeding despite the work Fisher had done on him.

She didn't know what to say or how she felt.

He'd held a gun to her head. He'd knocked her out. He'd endangered her son's life. She knew all the actions he'd taken since she met him two days ago had been about keeping her safe. Still, she couldn't reconcile her emotions.

While they'd been gearing up to go, Anna called her sister Liz, quickly explaining as much as she could and asking her to have an ambulance at the airport when they arrived. Zach was looking good. A little pale but there was a light in his eyes that she knew was reflected in her own.

After all this time, all this trouble, all this anguish, he was going to have a donor, not a stopgap pump but a real solution—*if* they could get out of Mexico.

She took a breath. One crisis at a time.

Leland and Bryan were divvying up weapons, passing magazines across the seat when Marissa rounded a hairpin corner at breathtaking speed and came on a line of cars blocking the road. When Anna saw the men standing beside their dusty SUVs with AK-47s, she immediately understood what was happening.

"No!" She slid to the floor without being told, pulling Zach along with her in the process.

"It's Rivera," said Fisher. Marissa threw the vehicle in reverse while Leland and Bryan hung out the windows and fired. Anna threw herself over Zach as they were slung around a corner and the Hummer started moving forward again.

"You got anything with more firepower than these handguns?" asked Leland.

"In the back," said Marissa, focusing on the road. "Big case. Grenade launcher."

"Jesus," Leland turned to look over his shoulder. "Not that I mind, but where'd you get this?"

"Long story," Bryan said.

Anna looked up from the floorboard and felt like she'd been here before. Leland wouldn't be able to crawl over that seat with his shoulder, so she raised her head and peeked into the cargo bay at the long flat case.

"Anna? Can you see the case Risa's talking about?" Bryan asked.

She lifted her whole body to the seat and reached for it. "Yeah, I've got it." For the second time in as many hours she heard a bullet shatter the passenger window and thump into the upholstery beside her. She fought not to scream out loud when Leland threw himself over her and pushed her to the floor again.

She looked up to thank him, but he was focused on the unopened case.

"How many shells are in here?" asked Leland.

"Four. Single shot." Bryan leaned out the window to thoroughly check the side mirror before looking back at them. "Can you handle that with your shoulder?" Leland nodded. "Here's what we've got to do. You're gonna drop me and the case and go on. I'll make sure they don't follow."

"What?!" Marissa's eyes never wavered from the road. "I seem to recall something about no one being left without backup."

Leland barked a laugh. "Hell, I knew that argument would come back to bite me in the butt. Risa, you know we don't have time to fight about this."

"Dammit, I don't want to leave you alone."

"I appreciate that, but you know this is the only way for y'all to get to the airstrip." He leaned forward over the back of the driver's seat and pointed. "Up here and around that corner. See the fountain? Slow down there."

"Got it." But Risa didn't sound happy.

Were they going to just leave him here? That didn't make Anna happy either.

"I need you to open the door when we stop and push the case out for me. Okay?" Leland was looking at her, waiting for her answer.

God, now it was *really* going too fast. She just needed a few more minutes. She had things to tell him. What, exactly, she wasn't sure, but she knew she wasn't ready to say *goodbye* yet.

"Alright," she murmured, not saying what she was really thinking. "Are you sure?" she finally asked.

God, there was so much more she wanted, needed to tell him, and they were down to only moments before it was too late. He looked down at her and smiled. Despite the dire circumstances, there was something in his eyes she hadn't seen before. "Yeah, I'm sure. Anna, back at the compound when I—"

They rounded the fountain and Marissa stood on the brakes, interrupting whatever he'd been about to say. They didn't even have a chance for *goodbye* before Leland was rolling out of the Hummer. Anna pushed the case out to him and he slammed the passenger door.

She looked through the broken glass to meet his piercing gaze. So much to say, and now they were completely out of time. He'd given her hope for the first time in so long. She desperately wanted to tell him.

His eyes were ablaze with unspoken emotion. With

startling clarity Anna realized he was feeling some of the same things she was.

No matter what happened, she couldn't be angry with him for getting her and Zach out of Rivera's. He'd done it because he cared for them. She just hadn't realized how much until now. He was willing to give his own life for hers. Nothing she could say would be adequate. She cared for him.

But it was more than that. Why was she just figuring this out now? When it was too late?

He nodded and Marissa stomped on the accelerator, the decision made. Everything would remain unsaid. Anna watched him through the shattered glass until Marissa rounded a corner and he disappeared from view.

"Thank you," she whispered. "I do trust you." And they were gone.

Chapter Thirty-Two

LELAND GAZED AT the Hummer barreling away for only a moment before he flung open the case and grabbed the M79 grenade launcher, a single-shot weapon resembling a pump-action shotgun.

This was what he'd dreaded and needed. What he'd been dealing with since the Colton debacle. Being here, being the only thing between innocent people and destruction. Wondering if he was good enough. But this was about more than standing between innocence and annihilation. This was about protecting someone he ... loved.

God, he was in love with Anna. He'd just realized it. Somewhere in the past two days, he'd fallen for her. The knowledge didn't scare him like he'd thought it would. He'd always assumed love made you defenseless and put you at risk. To the surprising contrary, that vulnerability made him feel whole. Made him stronger. He shook his head in disbelief, so stunned by the revelation he almost dropped the M79.

Too bad he was just realizing this now when it was too late to tell her, but he could do something about it. And he'd damn well do it right. He'd stop Rivera's men or die trying.

His vision wavered and the launcher felt slick beneath his clammy hands. The bandage was soaked through. His shoulder dripped blood on the dirt beside him. He'd done something else to it when he rolled from the Hummer.

Squeezing his eyes shut, he counted to five before opening them to stare into the case. There were four shells just as Fisher had said. Leland wiped his palms on his jeans, took a deep breath, and loaded the first one. Standing braced beside the fountain, he waited for Rivera's cars with the launcher aimed from his good shoulder.

Everything around him sharpened to a clear focus. Dust motes danced in the last rays of the late afternoon sun. Water splashed gently in the fountain behind him. Warm blood streamed down his arm from his less than graceful exit from the car.

With blinding clarity it came to him. This was what he was good at, being in the clinch. Regardless of his earlier doubts, he could do this. Anna and Zach were as good as on that plane and out of here.

The first SUV flew around the corner on two wheels. Leland didn't hesitate. He pulled the trigger and it looked like a movie stunt. The launcher kicked hard. Pain reverberated across his chest as the missile shot across the square and detonated on impact.

The car rose in the air, flipping backwards onto the vehicle following it. He reloaded as two more SUVs barreled through the flames. They were so close, he wasn't going to be able to get out of the way.

He was beyond running on his boot and woozy from the blood loss. Going forward was the only option. Despite the proximity, he steadied the launcher on his good shoulder again and pulled the trigger.

The third car disintegrated into a fireball, hurtling on to the sidewalk then through a building, while the fourth vehicle kept coming. He didn't have time to reload the launcher, so he dropped it and pulled out the snub nose .38 he'd liberated from the nurse's purse at Rivera's, grateful Fisher had given him ammo in the Hummer. He took a quick breath and aimed for the driver, emptying his magazine into the windshield as the car sped toward the fountain.

He dove into the water even as the SUV swerved once then relentlessly headed straight for him. He could hear the engine revving just before the water closed in over his head.

Searing pain speared his booted foot and raced up his entire left side with such intensity he opened his mouth in a gasp. Water entered his lungs and he was choking. He felt a dizzying pain in his head and everything went black.

Chapter Thirty-Three

LELAND WOKE SLOWLY to unfamiliar surroundings. The
bed was hard, but he felt no discomfort. His vision was
fuzzy as he floated on what he knew had to be a cloud
of heavy-duty painkillers. A fan swirled lazily overheard.
Nothing hurt anywhere, which surprised him, but his
mouth felt like cotton.

He licked his lips. They were dry and cracked, a minor
irritation in the grand scheme of things. His fingers
brushed against rough sheets and touched cool plaster at
his . . . thigh?

What the hell? His leg was in a cast? What had happened? Where was he? What about Anna and Zach? The
last thing he remembered was the SUV heading for him
in the square. Everything else was a blank.

He tried to sit up but could do no more than raise his
head off the pillow. Big mistake. That floating feeling disappeared in a howling screech of agony. All his questions

about what had happened and where he was were suddenly immaterial to the feeling of his brain sliding out of his skull.

He moaned and that small effort made his head ache even more. A persistent buzz of what sounded like a mosquito flying around his ears didn't help. He steeled himself to swat at the pest and turned his face to see Gavin sitting in the chair beside his bed.

God, that hurt. He squeezed his eyes closed then opened them again. His vision was still wavy.

Gavin stood over him.

What was going on?

His friend looked as bad as Leland felt—blood-shot eyes, three days' worth of stubble, and a bloody t-shirt.

"Don't try to talk." It sounded like Gavin was shouting at him.

Leland grimaced as the words bounced around between his ears. He pulled in a deep breath to control the pain. Gavin kept talking, oblivious to the discomfort he was causing.

"I know you have questions, but you need to rest for now. You're gonna be alright. We're going to get you home. Just sleep."

Leland tried to say "okay" or give an indication that he understood, but the words came out as another head-splitting moan.

Screw it, I can't do this right now. And that was his last coherent thought as he slid back into blessed oblivion.

When he woke again, his body was facing in the opposite direction. Was he in a different bed? There was no ceiling fan this time, but an AC unit was providing a wheezy white noise as it labored in the background.

His head still ached, but turning it on the pillow resulted in nothing like the howling agony he'd experienced earlier. Gavin was still there—now showered, shaved, and wearing a clean shirt. Leland raised an eyebrow despite the pain in his skull.

"I know I'm not dead 'cause you wouldn't be here if that were the case." His voice sounded rusty, like he hadn't used it in a while.

Gavin smiled, but the expression didn't reach his eyes.

"Could I have some water?"

Leland watched him pick up a covered cup with a straw from the bedside table. He held it for Leland to take a deep sip. His friend looked beyond exhausted. Damn, if Gavin was here that meant Kat was . . .

He closed his eyes against this new pain that went beyond a headache. An unfamiliar wave of nausea swept over him. He wasn't used to the act of thinking making his head hurt. Some of his former DEA colleagues and Army buddies would think that was a riot.

"Where am I?" he asked, unwilling to inquire about Kat yet.

"Private Mexican clinic. You've got a major concussion and your ankle is broken, again. But it's going to be fine." Gavin might be sad, but his voice was strong. "You've been unconscious for almost twenty-four hours."

"How did I get here?"

"Fisher called me after they dropped you in the square. Another team was already en route. They got to the fountain just as the ambulances arrived and helped fish you out of there. We had to move you from the original hospital in the area because we don't know what the situation is with Rivera. It didn't seem like a safe place to hang around, not knowing if he was alive or not."

"What are you doing here? Is Kat—" Leland didn't want to say dead. Instead, he said, "Gone?" And focused on Gavin's expression. His friend's eyes were so incredibly sad, and the lines bracketing his mouth were deeper than Leland recalled.

Gavin face was stoic as he nodded. "It was peaceful. She's not hurting anymore."

Leland started to shake his head, then stopped. His skull still couldn't handle that motion. "I'm sorry," he managed. "You didn't have to come."

How was Gavin standing it? Leland could see he was in pain.

"Don't like it when my people get dinged up. I had to come check on you. Besides, Kat would have wanted me to."

Gavin's eyes turned dark again. "The vet clinic was compromised. We were sure it was Rivera's men until Cesar Vega's body was reported found in the rubble."

"What happened?"

"Preliminary findings indicate chemicals in the clinic caught fire and exploded. I'm not sure that part was deliberate. It's a coincidence that doesn't feel like a coincidence. Nothing makes sense. We assume the attack was in retribution for Rivera's compound, but it's just a guess at this point."

"What about Nick and the clinic folks?"

If possible Gavin's eyes grew even more shadowed as he reached for a cardboard cup of coffee on the bedside table. "Not sure how they found out you'd all been there. Walters and his nurse have disappeared. We don't know if they're dead or alive, and we've no idea how Nick got out. I think some of the residents around the clinic must have pulled him out."

"Is he going to be okay?"

Gavin shrugged and put the cup back down. "It's touch-and-go. He was care-flighted to an ICU in Mexico City. Too unstable to move anywhere else at the moment. He hasn't woken up yet."

"Why are you here?" Leland's mouth still felt cottony and dry. His cracked lips hurt.

Gavin shook his head and offered him more water. "I can't leave you unprotected. Marissa has a team stationed around Nick, too, but you're the one Rivera would be after if he's still alive."

Leland had a sick feeling in the pit of his stomach. How had they found them? Had Rivera's SUV been Lo-Jacked after all?

"Anna and Zach?" he asked, finally getting to the question he'd been wanting the answer to since he first opened his eyes.

Gavin smiled slowly. "I have a protection team on them as well. They never would have made it out if you hadn't stayed behind. That much is clear. They flew straight to Dallas and got the transplant. Zach'll be in ICU for a few more days, but so far so good."

Leland had to clear his throat before he could speak. He was surprised but not dismayed at the emotion welling up inside. He'd known he was hooked on the boy and his mom. The rightness of that was a comfort.

"Max Mercado got out on bail three days ago and promptly disappeared. We're fairly certain he's back in Mexico by now."

"What do you think will happen?"

"It all depends on Tomas Rivera's status. The cartel is all about revenge. I sure as hell wouldn't want to be Max today. He screwed this whole deal for Rivera when he lost Anna in Cancun. But there were no other options for him once he got out on bail except running south, seeing as he's most likely going to face some type of conspiracy charges here."

"So, do you think Rivera survived?"

Gavin shrugged. "No idea. He's a hard man to kill. Officials haven't identified all the bodies from the scene at his compound yet. We do know his wife is dead." Gavin's eyes darkened at that last bit of information.

"When can I get out of here?"

"We'll talk to your doctor. He didn't want to move you again until you woke up, but I think he'll let you go soon. You're going to be on crutches again. Good thing your shoulder wound was only a grazing shot or you'd be stuck in a wheelchair for a while. As it is, getting around is going to be a pain in the ass, especially the first week or so. You're probably looking at a month in the cast then back in the boot."

Leland scowled. "Damn. Seriously?"

Gavin nodded.

More time in a cast and boot wasn't all bad. Leland was feeling whiny and he knew it. He had no right. Especially not here with his friend who'd just lost the love of his life. Leland was lucky to be alive. "There are worse things," he mumbled.

"Indeed," said Gavin, the sorrow of that truth reflecting in his eyes.

"I don't know how to thank you," said Leland.

"Come to work for me. You can figure it out."

"You sure you want me? You know what you're getting, right?"

Gavin tilted his head and stared at him, a question in his eyes.

"I'm burned out. I'm not addicted, but I take too much Vicodin. Hell, it's part of why I decided I couldn't work for the DEA anymore. So there's that, plus I don't work or play well with others. I prefer to work cases on my own."

Gavin smiled. "I knew . . . most of that. Truth be told, you were that way about working and playing with others when you came out of the army. But you're also the best agent I ever trained at the DEA. Hang in there. We'll sort this out."

Leland closed his eyes, surprised at how much working for Gavin appealed to him. How much someone believing in his ability mattered. How much starting over meant.

Chapter Thirty-Four

ANNA TOOK A sip of scalding coffee and grimaced. Ten days here and the brew hadn't improved one bit. She filled her cup anyway. Apparently, she was a slow learner and in desperate need of caffeine. It didn't matter. Zach was going to be okay. For that fantastically happy news, she'd drink horrifically bad coffee the rest of her life.

She smiled at her sister seated in the ICU waiting area. Liz had been here since the transplant itself, watching over both Anna and Zach like the mother hen she was. Liz scowled at the man in the corner before glancing at Anna.

"How many of them are there?" she asked, no longer bothering to whisper. "I still don't understand."

Anna sighed. She wasn't sure she did either, even with Bryan Fisher's explanation. Marissa insisted Zach and Anna have protection until they figured out the situation in Mexico with Rivera's men. Yesterday, Mexican officials had found what they thought was Tomas's body. Still, several different AEGIS guards had remained on a twelve-hour rotation with her and Zach since they'd arrived back in Dallas.

Anna had told Liz all this, but her sister couldn't seem to wrap her head around the situation. It was understandable. Zach kidnapped by a Mexican drug lord because the man wanted Anna's lungs for his own ailing wife? Anna wasn't sure she could have believed the story herself if she hadn't lived it.

"If the man, this Tomas Rivera and his wife are dead, why do you still need protection?" asked Liz.

Anna took a deep breath and decided to try once again. "It's complicated. They think he's dead, but Marissa is waiting for the official coroner's report to have positive confirmation. Even if he is dead, they want to know who's taking over for him. Will that new person try and make Zach or me pay for what happened down there?"

"Well, who are *they*? The police? It seems as if they should be in charge."

Anna laughed. It was the only thing she could do. It was that or beat her head against the paneled wall of the waiting room.

She'd gone to the police. Two days after Zach's surgery, she'd left the hospital with one of her AEGIS bodyguards and gone to Dallas police headquarters where officers had listened politely for a frustrating two hours but offered her no solutions. The next day two agents from the DEA had shown up in the waiting area right after one of the limited ICU visiting times. After hearing her story, they had agreed that AEGIS was most likely her best solution for now.

It wasn't that the local police and DEA didn't believe her, it was just there wasn't a lot that could be done at this point. The bad guys were dead or beyond the reach of the US government. AEGIS was better equipped and already in place, so she'd decided to table the issue with law enforcement until Zach was out of the hospital and home.

"I think we'll be fine with AEGIS folks, Liz. They seem to have everything under control. Besides what's wrong with having a lovely new guy to look at every twelve hours?"

Bryan and several very attractive men had been in the twelve-hour rotations. Did AEGIS have some kind of policy about only hiring handsome bodyguards? She hadn't heard a word from Leland, even though Bryan had told her he was out of the hospital and back from Mexico.

God, she wanted to see him. Wanted to tell him . . . so much, about how she felt. It wasn't just gratitude for what he'd done for her and Zach, although that had been huge. He'd saved her. He'd kept her from making the biggest mistake of her life.

But even that wasn't why she needed to talk to him. She'd only realized as she was leaving Leland in that fountain square what he'd come to mean to her. He'd given her courage and hope to face whatever life was bringing—what she'd been missing her entire life, something Max had never been able to give her, even before their marriage fell apart. Leland had been willing to give up everything, to sacrifice his life for hers.

Why hadn't he contacted her once he got home to the US? Had it all been just a job, an obligation for him with sex as a side benefit? She'd begged him to make love to her. Had he just been doing as she asked?

She felt churlish and ungrateful. She and Zach were getting a second chance. She really needed to get over this obsession with Leland.

Liz laughed, pulling Anna from that lost cause of a reverie. "Point taken. Have you heard from Max?"

Anna shuddered. Oh yeah, she'd heard. He'd sent a dozen roses the day after Zach's surgery with a note.

"Rejoicing in the health of our son. So glad this worked out."

It was creepy as hell, but there wasn't anything to be done. Max was in Mexico. Police had a record of his crossing the border the day he was released on bail. Anna didn't expect him back, although where he'd go south of the border was a mystery. Rivera or his replacement would likely have just as big a problem with Max as with her and Leland.

That was the only legitimate cloud on Anna's horizon and, granted, it was large. But even her fears about Max and Tomas Rivera couldn't dampen the joy she felt at knowing her son was safe and on his way to being well. She *felt* safe, for the first time in months.

She and Zach were starting over. She wasn't going to think about missing Leland, the one person who'd stood by her when she'd had no one else. Even though not having heard from him stung. That he hadn't been in touch to even check on Zach was painful. But she really had no right to expect that.

His "obligation" to her and Zach was over. She wasn't sure why he'd ever felt obligated in the first place. She was just grateful he'd been there. If he wanted to see them, he knew where they were or could certainly find them with relative ease.

The next visiting hour was coming up. Anna finished her hideously bad coffee and prepared to walk back to the ICU. The AEGIS bodyguard met her and Liz at the doorway that led back to the patient rooms.

"Ma'am, my replacement will get here while you're back with your boy. It's an agent you haven't met before. How would you like to handle that?"

"I can come out and meet him," offered Liz. "I know we need to know who's taking over for the evening."

The striking young agent nodded. "I'll let the nurse know when he arrives."

WEARING A BASEBALL cap and shorts to accommodate his fiberglass cast, Leland hauled himself up to the ICU at Baylor. Bryan had dropped him off and Leland was grateful that he hadn't had to park himself in the huge parking lot that showed the curvature of the earth.

He was sweating, but he wasn't sure if it was from the exertion of getting around with his cast and crutches or if he was nervous about seeing Anna. It had been ten days since he'd rolled out of the Hummer and not even said a hurried goodbye in that fountain square.

Would she even want to talk to him now?

He should've called from Gavin's cabin, but he didn't want to apologize for what had happened in Mexico over the phone. After Gavin had gotten him safely back to the US, Leland hadn't felt right leaving his friend to deal with Kat's funeral arrangements alone. Gavin had dropped everything just hours after his wife had died to come get him. So he'd gone back to Gavin's cabin and helped him pull all the preparations together.

At the same time Gavin had helped him without even realizing. His friend had kept Leland accountable as he went through those first days home from the hospital without prescription pain meds. Oh, he took big-ass doses of ibuprofen now, but there could be no more Vicodin . . . ever. Even with his injuries, he felt better and more clear-headed since before the Colton incident and his trauma there.

But it hurt to see Gavin so devastated. Standing by him now was the least Leland could do and the last, best way he could honor Kat. He'd finally mailed that resignation letter to his boss at the DEA with a copy to Ford Johnson. He was going to work for AEGIS. It was time for a new start.

Gavin's grief had showed Leland just how much loving people made you vulnerable. Friend, child, or lover— there was no escaping it. If you cared for people there was always a chance you could have your heart eviscerated, no matter how hard you tried to keep it safe.

Leland was ready to risk that vulnerability with Anna. In Mexico, he hadn't realized he was in love with her till it was too late. To not tell her now would only be compounding that mistake because he'd finally figured it out. With the right person, love is worth the risk.

They'd met under extraordinary circumstances—stressful, life-threatening circumstances. Not anything conducive to starting a relationship or life together. Still, he had to find out how she felt. Even if she didn't feel the same way, not knowing was worse than not telling her.

The L-shaped ICU waiting area was practically deserted with a sparsely decorated Christmas tree at one end and a guy hunched over on his cell phone with his back to the room in the opposite corner. Obviously someone who'd been camped out here for a while, multiple cardboard coffee cups littered the table beside him.

Leland wondered where the AEGIS guy was since Gavin had mentioned they had men on round-the-clock guard duty with Anna and Zach. The sign at the entryway to the waiting area indicated that he'd arrived at the tail end of visiting hours.

He grabbed his own cup of coffee, dumping enough powdered creamer in the tar-black liquid to turn it white and kill the hideous taste. Then began the interesting process of getting the not-so-freshly-brewed potion to a place where he could sit. He picked up an eight-week-old news magazine from the counter in front of him and, after a feat worthy of Cirque du Soleil, he got the coffee cup to an end table and sank into a deep leather couch.

One thing to be said for an ICU waiting area, they usually had comfortable sofas, if not the most current reading material or Starbucks-grade caffeine. Getting comfortable with his cast was a challenge. He finally ended up propping his leg on the coffee table in front of the couch.

He glanced at the large clock on the wall, and five seconds later Anna walked out of the air-locked doors talking over her shoulder to another woman who looked startlingly similar, most likely the sister she had mentioned. Anna was checking her ringing cell phone.

"I'll be right back. This is the insurance company. Can't dodge their call." She laughed as the doors closed between her and the woman who looked like her slightly older twin.

From under his baseball cap, Leland took a moment to study Anna before he said anything. She looked tired but peaceful for the first time since he'd met her. There was something different in her eyes.

She hadn't seen him yet and he was still trying to figure out how to start the conversation as she answered her call. "Hello. This is Anna Mercado."

She spoke quietly into her phone, but the man hunched behind her in the corner jerked his head up and turned to look straight at her back, pulling a Taurus .38 Special from under his jacket. Leland did a double take. It was Antonio, one of Rivera's guards. Leland had last seen the man on the steps of the mansion, shooting at them as he and Nick drove away.

Forcing his eyes back to the stale news on the page before him, Leland pulled the old magazine up to shield his own face further. He had a Sig Sauer 9mm, but it was tucked into an inside waistband holster, a bitch to get to from his current seating position. There was no way to reach it without leaning way forward with his heavy-as-lead cast and calling attention to himself.

Where the hell was the AEGIS guard?

Antonio still hadn't noticed him and stood with the Taurus, moving toward Anna from behind. He ignored Leland, most likely assuming he was a patient's family member and no real threat with his cast and crutches. Unaware of the danger, Anna was looking in the opposite direction from Rivera's man as she talked on the phone.

Her gaze lit on Leland and, despite his hat, recognition dawned in her eyes just as Antonio grabbed her arm and shoved his .38 Special in her face. She stopped talking, completely focused on the weapon. Her eyes grew wide with fear.

"Come with me," Antonio ordered in a barely audible undertone.

Frozen in place, Anna stared at Leland until Rivera's man pulled her to his side and pressed the barrel to her temple. "Move now."

Leland had a front row seat to his worst nightmare. He couldn't reach his weapon without alerting Antonio, so he sat dead still, studying his two-month old magazine as if he'd heard and noticed nothing.

"Move faster." Antonio roughly steered her forward by keeping the revolver pressed to the side of her face.

"What do you want with me?" she asked softly, her eyes never leaving Leland's. Fear was evident in her voice, but her eyes were calm.

Jesus. They'd been here before, only Leland had been the one holding a gun to her head. Three steps from the doorway she stumbled, pulling away from Rivera's man. Whether she was doing it on purpose or not, the timing was perfect.

Keeping his gaze lowered under the brim of the cap, Leland took the opportunity to lean forward. Pushing his nose practically to his knees, he slid his gun from its holster under cover of the news magazine.

"Don't move." Antonio saw the movement but not what Leland had done. Rivera's man pointed the Beretta but never made eye contact. Instead, he stared hard at Leland's cast before moving Anna closer to the emergency exit.

The door to the stairwell opened and Leland's sick sense of déjà vu was complete when Max and his bodyguard Emilio stepped into the ICU waiting area.

Anna stopped and stared from one man to another, obviously stunned by their appearance and the weapons in their hands. Emilio carried an AK-47 and Max had a Beretta 9mm.

Leland kept his head down, trying his best to become invisible with his magazine and cap. Still, he knew that Emilio had his assault rifle pointed directly at him.

"Just stay right there and you'll be fine," growled the huge bodyguard.

Leland nodded, knowing the man was lying. But he wasn't about to look up and give away his identity.

"What are you doing here?" Anna asked. Her voice sounded surprisingly strong considering the circumstances.

"Paying penance," said Max.

"Penance for what?"

Max's mouth twisted in a sarcastic smile. "For you, my darling wife. And the incredible fuck-up you caused in Mexico."

"You're blaming me?"

"Rivera's complex was blown to hell, deliberately. Rivera's wife is dead. No one's taken responsibility. The question is, who orchestrated it? Vega would be the obvious culprit, but he'd hardly target Tomas's wife—his own sister—no matter how deep their disagreements. So that leaves you and your DEA 'friend' as the objects of his wrath for now."

Rivera's alive? Leland kept his eyes lowered, forcing himself not to respond to that bombshell.

Anna faced Max, never giving a hint that she knew Leland was there. Perhaps she didn't think he could do anything given the circumstances. *Trust me, Anna. Just one more time.*

The Tequila King kept talking, never looking Leland's way since Emilio had him covered. Thankfully, Max wasn't recognizing him either, assuming Leland was a clueless bystander.

"Rivera's out for revenge. I screwed up, and he can't think of a better way to make me pay than to have me carry out the sentence."

"Sentence?" The quaver in her voice sounded like true apprehension, but Leland wasn't sure if she was acting, stalling or both.

"Rivera doesn't need your body anymore, but he absolutely wants your life."

"What good comes from killing me?"

"Rivera has his revenge, and I get my life back—my business, my sanity. Unless I kill you, my ass is on the line. So it's really not a difficult decision."

"But I'm the mother of your son." She didn't so much as flick her eyes toward Leland. Still, he knew what she was doing.

That's good, Anna. Keep him talking and focused on you while I figure this out.

"If I was willing to give you up to Rivera in Mexico, I'm certainly willing to give you up now. You don't get it, do you? I don't need you anymore. When he was sick, Zach needed you and you were an excellent caretaker. But my boy has a new heart. He no longer needs you as his nurse."

That the man was saying this as his son lay in ICU a few feet away seemed the height of ironic stupidity, but Leland had never thought Max could be accused of brilliance. He could, however, be accused of intense cruelty—as proven by his plan to force Anna into being a donor.

Rivera's home being targeted deliberately made no sense, but cartel violence rarely did. As to why Rivera would want Anna dead, that was perfectly clear.

Cartels were notoriously vindictive. Making Max do the deed was the most efficient way to make the Tequila King pay for his screw-up, while at the same time keeping him beholden to Tomas Rivera as long as the cartel leader deemed necessary. It also had the added benefit of sticking the knife into Leland without actually doing him physical violence.

Even without the bugs in their suite, Rivera had ascertained Leland's feelings for Anna. What better way to get his revenge than to have the woman Leland cared for killed? The torture would be particularly exquisite if Leland were to see a recording of the execution.

No doubt the ubiquitous security cameras in the hospital were documenting everything going on here. Max Mercado would never be able to legally set foot back on US soil again without being put under the jail. And Leland, being in law enforcement, would watch that tape over and over as he sought to avenge the woman he loved. Despite what Max was saying, this execution was more about Rivera making Max and Leland pay than Anna.

During Max's rant, Emilio had lowered his weapon slightly while Antonio loosened his hold on Anna.

Leland glanced down. The 9mm was invisible under the magazine pages but he wasn't going to be able to stand and shoot. He would have to aim from his seat on the sofa. Behind the news magazine he pointed the Sig at the guard as Max spoke.

"This is personal for Rivera—for me as well. For my family and my business it's all extraordinarily personal. You were never the right woman for me." Max gestured toward the exit with his gun. "We'll finish this in the stairwell, not here."

Antonio shoved Anna again, glanced down at Leland, and finally stared into his face. His eyes widened. Leland saw the exact moment the man recognized him.

Antonio tried to turn his revolver back to aim at him, but he was too late, and it cost him. Leland's blast was deafening as blood and brain matter spattered behind Anna.

Before Rivera's man had slumped to the carpeted floor, Leland was pointing his weapon at Emilio, dropping him with a second shot as the bodyguard pulled the automatic weapon up but fumbled with the trigger mechanism.

Leland turned to Max and found himself staring down the barrel of his Beretta. It was an intimidating gun, but The Tequila King was no cartel member and apparently had limited weapons training. Gone was the cool business executive.

Instead, Max's hands were shaking and his eyes darted back and forth between Leland and Anna. "Drop your weapon," he demanded.

Leland took a deep breath and calculated the risk. He'd been here too many times—a target in the crosshairs with innocent bystanders on the line. He came to a decision and ejected the 9mm magazine cartridge, keeping eye contact with Max as the ammunition hit the carpeted floor.

Leland started to lower the Sig. There was still one bullet in the chamber, but Max assumed he'd been disarmed completely when the magazine cartridge dropped.

Leland had been counting on that. He didn't hesitate. Max did.

The shot echoed around the room.

Max slid to the floor beside his dead bodyguard, a neat bullet hole in his forehead. Gunpowder and blood perfumed the air as Anna stood staring at Leland. This was not how he'd envisioned the scene when telling her his true feelings.

For a moment the waiting area was completely silent. Then chaos erupted. Two nurses and a man Leland assumed was the absent AEGIS bodyguard burst from the ICU. His gun was pointed directly at Leland's head.

The woman who'd been with Anna on the other side of the door was behind them, and she started screaming when she saw the three dead men on the floor. Security guards from the hospital were suddenly everywhere.

Leland was still sitting, but now his hands were in the air and empty. He'd dropped his Sig to the floor beside the crutches after shooting Max.

"He's with me!" Anna moved to block Leland from the guard's aim, shouting over the erupting pandemonium. Other than three drops of blood on the shoulder of her sweater, she'd escaped the carnage.

The guard dropped his arm, recognizing Leland wasn't a threat.

"You're here," she murmured, ignoring the uproar as she stared down at him.

"I couldn't stay away." He had a strange sense of having been here before, like the night they met in her Best Western hotel room surrounded by the police.

He reached for her hand and pulled her down beside him onto the sofa, where they both sank further into the buttery soft leather. He pulled back to stare into her blue eyes before burying his face in her hair and wrapping her in his arms—so damn grateful she was alive, he couldn't speak.

Her hair smelled the same way it had when he'd woken up with her that morning almost two weeks ago in the AEGIS office guest room.

"What was this about?" she asked.

"Rivera. Revenge."

"Is it over?" She pulled back from his embrace to scrutinize his face.

He wasn't going to lie to her. "Not completely. But for now, yes, it's over. This was about Max paying, not you. You're safe. I'm sure Rivera would still like a piece of me, but no one's going to hurt you or Zach." Not while he was around. He'd do his damnedest to make sure no one ever hurt her again. He kissed her as she slid her arms around his neck.

"What would I do without you?" she asked.

"You're never going to have to find that out." His voice was steady, but his heart was pounding.

She cocked her head to the side, studying him and continuing to ignore the cacophony around them. "I was joking," she said.

"I wasn't." He released his hold on her as she settled deeper into the sofa. He held his breath and hoped it was a good sign that she wasn't getting up and running away.

"So what are you saying exactly?" Anna asked, still oblivious to the chaos erupting around them.

He froze. "I'm not . . . I mean . . . I have no idea where this is going."

She nodded, giving no hint of what she was thinking.

"But I don't care. I know what I want." He kept talking. If he stopped, he'd never get through this.

"I'm not good at relationships. At risking my heart. But I care about you—you and Zach, both. I know I'm no picnic. I have baggage, but I want to be with you. Hell, I want to grow old with you and keep you safe. I don't want to let go of you just because we're back here and not in the midst of bullets and mayhem."

She didn't answer. Instead she stared down at his hands. Reaching for his palm, she threaded her fingers through his and finally met his searching gaze. "Who says you'd ever have to let me go?"

Daring to let himself hope, he sat in stunned silence watching her as the words sank in. She was saying *yes* to whatever this crazy thing was between them. The relief was so intense, he felt a little dizzy.

She leaned in to kiss him, her lips offering a promise of more to come. His thoughts were a jumble and he broke the kiss, pulling her toward him as best he could with the cast.

"You're sure you want to be with me?" He stared at her in wonder, determined to make sure he understood correctly. "After all this?" He couldn't keep the disbelief from his voice.

She leaned in to kiss him again, smiling at his look of surprise. "I guess you'll just have to trust me."

Acknowledgments

IT'S A BIT intimidating to sit down and try to thank everyone who has helped make a dream come true. I'm worried I'll inadvertently leave someone out, or I'll end up thanking everyone—including my kindergarten teacher. With *Hard Target* I'll have five books published, but this is the first time I've had the opportunity to include an acknowledgments page. With that thought in mind, here goes . . .

People have been so generous to me on my writing journey. No one creates or writes in a vacuum, and as I thought about what to say here, I realized just how many people have helped me along the way to take this story from the germ of an idea to the final words on the page (or e-reader). Any mistakes you may find in the story are mine, not theirs.

First, I want to thank Ellen Henderson—my critique partner and friend—who gave me the original concept for this book when she pointed me to a magazine article about children kidnapped in foreign countries by non-custodial parents. She said, "You need to write a story about this." And she kept telling me I could do it, even when I wasn't so sure myself.

Thanks to my friend Justin, who made such a difference in my own child's life and who was there at just the right time to spark ideas for this story.

Thank you to my agent—Helen Breitwieser of Cornerstone Literary—for her encouragement, her impeccable judgment, and for always believing in me and my work.

Many thanks to Lucia Macro at Avon Books, who believed in this story as well and took a chance on me. To my editor, Erika Tsang, who helped make Leland's story its very best while still making the process of revision surprisingly fun. And to her assistant, Chelsey Emmelhainz, who worked especially hard to make sure I was happy with the final result.

To all the folks at HarperCollins who have made this such a lovely experience and who have worked diligently on my behalf— Pam Spengler-Jaffee, Heidi Richter, cover artists, copyeditors, and others whose names I don't even know and who have labored behind the scenes. I appreciate all that you do.

Thank you to my friend Mike Simonds, Chief Deputy at Tarrant County Sheriff's Office, who always takes my calls and over the course of several books now has answered the most outrageous questions about criminals and law enforcement—without batting an eye or blushing.

Thank you also to Joyce Ann McLaughlin for taking the time to proofread and give such fantastic feedback.

To Lena Diaz for the lovely blurb and the information on "cordite." To James Rogers, Senior Forensic Investigator at Garland Police Department, for the technical details involved in how blood spatter works. And to Kat Baldwin—author and graphic designer extraordinaire— you've always made me look good. Thanks for continuing to do so.

Thanks especially to the "writer foxes"—Addison Fox, Lorraine Heath, Tracy Garrett, Jane Graves, J.D. Tyler, Suzanne Ferrell, Sandy Blair, Julie Benson, and Allie Burton. You ladies keep me sane and laughing.

Thank you to my friends and family for being so patient and understanding when I seemingly fall off the planet to write and don't return calls or emails. That you're still glad to hear from me and want to hang out when I do emerge from my writing cave is a huge blessing.

Thanks to my big brother Tim and to my parents— Gran and Te-Daddy—for always being interested in what I'm writing and saying you love it, even when it needs work. To my sister Libby for instilling my love of reading when we were growing up, even if we didn't do so great with sharing a bathroom. And to my brother Rabun, who encourages me to write even though he's not a reader.

Thank you to my daughter Michelle for being my beta reader and Spanish translator. To my son Russ for giving me the time and space to work . . . and for never complaining about eating frozen pizza.

And finally, to my husband Tom, none of this would be possible without you. Thank you for being the person who makes all the difference in my world.

Can't get enough Kay Thomas?
Keep reading for a sneak peek
at the next book in her heart-stopping Elite Ops series,

PERSONAL TARGET,

coming soon from Avon Impulse

An Excerpt from

PERSONAL TARGET

"NICK DONOVAN, YOU'RE going to die!"

Nick felt warm blood, the crushing impact, and a burst of agony as bullets tore into his shoulder. More shouts echoed from down the hall. He fought to catch his breath and think through the pain. He'd been sleeping after a back alley doctor patched him up, only to wake to this chaos.

A hulking shadow lumbering toward him in the room registered at the exact moment Nick realized there was something in his own hand. He looked down and clenched his fingers, a huge sense of relief washing over him as his palm closed around the familiar handle of a Sig Sauer P226 9mm.

Thank God. Someone had left him a gun.

He couldn't see well enough to aim with much accuracy, but at the rate the shadowy figure was headed toward him, aiming wouldn't be an issue for long. A deafening concussion rocked the room and a fireball whooshed in from the hallway. Nick rolled off his gurney to escape the conflagration, crashing to the terrazzo tile. Pain blossomed in his stomach and shoulder as an IV line gave way and medical tape ripped hairs from the back of his hand, spewing more blood everywhere.

Still, Nick hung on to the Sig—barely.

A smoky silhouette thrashed about on the floor a few feet to his left. Fire licked at the cool tiles under them both, and more shots blazed around Nick's head from the opposite direction. He crawled toward a massive stainless steel cabinet that had been toppled during the, Jesus . . . the explosion?

For a fleeting moment he wondered if this was some kind of hallucination brought on by the medication for his injuries sustained earlier at Rivera's compound, but the excruciating pain and the stench of smoke told him this was all too real and happening right now. Smoke continued filling the room. He couldn't figure out where the shots were coming from. The smoky silhouette on the floor near him quit moving.

Shit, shit, shit. What in hell was going on? His whole body still hurt from the wounds he'd suffered at Rivera's and now his shoulder. His right hand was going numb.

Where was everyone? Where was Marissa?

He had a vague memory of arriving at what looked like a veterinarian's clinic, complete with dog cages in the yard. Bryan Fisher and Leland Hollis had been there. Someone carried him inside. After that everything went hazy and gray till he woke up alone in this insanity.

How long had he been out? Hours? Days?

He wasn't going to be able to do anything to help himself much longer. Another man moved through the thickening smoke—head down, running low. The smoky apparition was fifteen feet away when Nick wrapped his left hand around his right and fired twice. His fingers kept sliding off the trigger, sticky with blood and no longer working correctly.

Even through the haze he could see that the shadow was Cesar Vega, the enforcer half of the most lethal drug cartel in Mexico. Nick knew he'd hit him at least once. No way he'd missed at this range, despite his impaired vision and dexterity. Cesar continued racing toward him like a freight train, promising certain death with a booming voice that sounded like a concrete mixer. Between the threats, Nick could hear Cesar cursing in Spanish as he thundered through the doorway, heedless of the crackling flames. The dealer must be coked up and operating on adrenaline, even as he was bleeding out.

Nick tried to check the clip on the Sig, but his right hand was now completely numb and he was never more grateful to be ambidextrous. Once he was finally able to switch hands with the gun and wrap his left index finger back around the trigger, he was out of ammo. *Perfect.*

Cesar's progress slowed, the freight train was finally running low on steam, but the dealer still had an AK-47 with plenty of bullets. He stumbled and tripped. The impact of his body hitting the tiled floor was like the collision of a mac truck hitting a concrete wall, and the room shook. Cesar's assault rifle skittered across the floor.

This was Nick's chance, but he couldn't move. The stitches across his stomach had torn when he rolled off the gurney. Blood seeped from new wounds at his shoulder. He and Cesar lay side-by-side, Nick's own blood mingling with the drug dealer's.

Cesar's lips were blood-stained as he whispered just loud enough for Nick to hear. "They're coming after yours now, and you can't stop them." The dying man laughed, his laughter changing to a cough as his damaged lungs filled with blood. Even so, he managed to rasp out one last threat. "It's personal now. Your family will be dead in six weeks."

The shocking words were meant to taunt, a final insult. Cesar never would have said it if he hadn't thought Nick was dying, too. Nick struggled to sit up, and Cesar's eyes widened in surprise. Obviously, he hadn't been expecting Nick to move.

Nick leaned close to the downed man's ear. "My family will be fine. I always see to it."

Cesar's eyes closed for the last time, and Nick heard another deep rumble starting further back in the building. *Damn.* He recognized that sound. He glanced at the door, seemingly a thousand miles away. He'd never make it.

He looked back at Cesar, dead now in a puddle of blood. The dealer's dying threat galvanized him to action. He rolled toward the wall, wrenching himself to his feet. His vision swam and blood seeped into his eyes, but he hung on and moved his ass. Whatever happened, he was getting out. There was no other option. Nick Donovan took care of his family.

JENNIFER GRAYSON BACKED into the driveway and turned off the ignition. Her day from hell was almost over. She'd always enjoyed the last week before Christmas break, but not this year. Newly divorced and alone in a town she hadn't lived in since high school, Christmas felt like something to be endured—not celebrated.

As a college professor, this week of final exams had been unmitigated insanity. Her graduate students were bug-nuts crazy—obsessing over their final course grades and how their test scores and papers would affect internship opportunities. Give her clueless college freshman partying their brains out any day.

Maybe part of her was just plain depressed. Her divorce papers had arrived in the mailbox earlier this week. Due to the financial strain dissolving a marriage induced, she'd had to cancel her sabbatical this spring for the Paleo-Niger Project. Withdrawing from the project had cut deeper than the divorce itself.

That a philandering husband was less disappointing than a cancelled archaeological dig certainly testified to the state of her marriage to begin with, even before Collin's affair with his grad student.

She slammed the car door a little harder than necessary. Bah, this was crazy. It was almost Christmas. She stood in the driveway waiting for the garage door to rise.

Light from the full moon reflected off her windshield and illuminated the driveway. Breathing in the cool night air, she looked up at the stars through the bare limbs of a massive red oak. Just because she was in a place where she hadn't lived for ten years was no reason to be maudlin. She was going to start thinking of things to be thankful for this instant.

For starters, she was grateful she was housesitting for her best friend and could get a change of scenery from her very small apartment with its the limited hot water supply. Angela Donovan and her family were on a Mediterranean cruise for the holiday, meeting up with her husband's brother Nick.

The lick of regret and lust hit Jennifer simultaneously. But since she was turning lemons into lemonade tonight, she focused on her thankfulness resolution and banished Nick Donovan, with his heart-stopping kisses and heartbreaking tendencies, from her thoughts. She would not dwell on things that could no longer be changed.

Right now she wanted a glass of wine, a good book, and a long soaking bath with an unlimited supply of hot water. That was something to look forward to.

She reached for the light switch on the wall. As the overhead bulb flashed on, an arm snaked out of nowhere and grabbed her around the waist, pulling her against a hard, pungent smelling body. A wickedly serrated knife flashed in front of her eyes.

"Don't move and don't scream. You won't get hurt." The voice held a heavy Hispanic accent.

Onions and body odor overwhelmed her senses. Her

knees wobbled and her stomach lurched. She nodded her head and the man's grip tightened.

"I said don't move!" The hand at her waist crept up her ribcage and his fingers brushed the underside of her breasts. She tried not to shudder.

What was happening? Her mind raced to catch up. *This couldn't be possible.*

Another voice from across the room hissed. "No, she's not to be touched. It's only for show. That was a condition."

"Who's to know?" The hand continued to skate along her ribs and rub the front of her shirt. Fingers brushed across her chest once more rather brusquely. "She'll not tell."

The lights went out, plunging the room into darkness.

"Vega would find out. We don't want to risk it."

Jennifer looked up, but the man speaking was cloaked in the darkness. Two silhouettes were outlined by a light from the microwave clock in the kitchen.

"Hosea, you take her. Tie her hands and feet then strip her from the waist up. Snap the picture and get her out of here. We don't know when the rest of the family will be home."

The man Jennifer assumed was Hosea grabbed her by the shoulders. He didn't smell as horrific as the other man, not that it meant anything. Criminals could shower like anyone else. She started to struggle before she remembered the knife. Hosea just held on tighter and steered her through the kitchen toward the living room and the fireplace.

She viewed the surreal scene and felt herself slip away.

The Christmas tree was lit. Angela's, Drew's, and the children's stockings were all hanging in front of the cheerily decorated mantel.

"Sit here, Mrs. Donovan."

The courtesy was so out of place with what was happening, it took Jennifer a moment to realize he was talking to her. They thought she was Angela? Hosea pushed her into a chair in front of the tree and began tying her feet as the other hygiene-challenged man who'd been touching her earlier stepped back to watch. Jennifer could feel his malevolent gaze on her in the dim light.

"Excuse me," Hosea bound her hands behind her back and stepped in front of her. Before she knew what he was doing, Hosea'd grabbed the sides of her blouse and ripped.

Pearl buttons bounced on the carpet and she heard one *ping* off the brick hearth behind her. She was so shocked she couldn't speak, not even to protest. She tried to suck in air as she sat with her silk shirt around her waist in her Victoria's Secret bra. It was the sexy red and black one she'd bought last spring in efforts to rekindle Collin's interest in sex, in her, and in their marriage—like that had turned out so well.

Full blown panic welled up inside and her detachment was gone. It was impossible to breathe. Tears gathered at the edges of Jennifer's eyes. She fought to keep them in check, knowing she'd be lost if she started to cry.

Oh, God. She wanted to cover herself, but with her hands tied there was nothing she could do. The men viewed her dispassionately.

"It's not enough," said the third voice from the shadows.

"I agree," said Hosea. "She needs marks."

"Just one though. No more," said the shadow voice.

"Yes." Hosea put his hand on Onion Man's chest to stop him from coming forward. "I'll do it," Hosea insisted, and without warning he lifted his hand and struck her with his open palm.

Her head flew back with the force of the blow and she bit her lip. Tears of shock and pain burst from their damn as she began to weep in earnest. She hung her head and felt blood run down the corner of her mouth. The man who'd copped a feel stepped forward, grabbed her chin, and tilted it up to study her face a moment. His foul breath wafted over her and bile rose in back of her throat. He nodded and smiled cruelly. "Good."

The other man hidden in the darkness said, "She's ready."

Hosea propped a newspaper in front of her stomach, balancing it just under her breasts. "Hold your head up and look into the camera." He never looked at her body, but stared only into her eyes. "It's not personal, Ms. Donovan."

The third man in the shadows began snapping pictures, the flash going off like a strobe light in the dimly lit room. But Jennifer knew Hosea was lying. Everything about this was as personal as it got.

About the Author

KAY THOMAS didn't grow up burning to be a writer. She wasn't even much of a reader until fourth grade. That's when her sister read *The Black Stallion* aloud to her. For hours Kay was enthralled—shipwrecked and riding an untamed horse across desert sand. Then tragedy struck. Her sister lost her voice. But Kay couldn't wait to hear what happened in the story, so she picked up that book, finished reading it herself, and went in search of more adventures at the local library.

Today Kay lives in Dallas with her husband, two children, and a shockingly spoiled Boston terrier. Her award-winning novels have been published internationally. Learn more about her online at www.KayThomas.net.

Visit www.AuthorTracker.com for exclusive information on your favorite HarperCollins authors.

Give in to your impulses . . .
Read on for a sneak peek at four brand-new
e-book original tales of romance
from Avon Books.
Available now wherever e-books are sold.

RESCUED BY A STRANGER

By Lizbeth Selvig

CHASING MORGAN

BOOK FOUR: THE HUNTED SERIES

By Jennifer Ryan

THROWING HEAT

A DIAMONDS AND DUGOUTS NOVEL

By Jennifer Seasons

PRIVATE RESEARCH

AN EROTIC NOVELLA

By Sabrina Darby

An Excerpt from

RESCUED BY A STRANGER

by Lizbeth Selvig

When a stranger arrives in town on a vintage
motorcycle, Jill Carpenter has no idea her life
is about to change forever. She never expected
that her own personal knight in shining armor
would be an incredibly charming and handsome
southern man—but one with a deep secret. When
Jill's dreams of becoming an Olympic equestrian
start coming true, Chase's past finally returns to
haunt him. Can they get beyond dreams to find the
love that will rescue their two hearts? Find out in
the follow-up to *The Rancher and the Rock Star.*

"Angel?" Jill called. "C'mon, girl. Let's go get you something to eat." She'd responded to her new name all evening. Jill frowned.

Chase gave a soft, staccato, dog-calling whistle. Angel stuck her head out from a stall a third of the way down the aisle. "There she is. C'mon, girl."

Angel disappeared into the stall.

"Weird," Jill said, heading down the aisle.

At the door to a freshly bedded empty stall, they found Angel curled beside a mound of sweet, fragrant hay, staring up as if expecting them.

"Silly girl," Jill said. "You don't have to stay here. We're taking you home. Come."

Angel didn't budge. She rested her head between her paws and gazed through raised doggy brows. Chase led the way into the stall. "Everything all right, pup?" He stroked her head.

Jill reached for the dog, too, and her hand landed on Chase's. They both froze. Slowly he rotated his palm and wove his fingers through hers. The few minor fireworks she'd felt in the car earlier were nothing compared to the explosion now detonating up her arm and down her back.

"I've been trying to avoid this since I got off that dang horse." His voice cracked into a low whisper.

"Why?"

He stood and pulled her to her feet. "Because I am not a guy someone as young and good as you are should let do this."

"You've saved my life and rescued a dog. Are you trying to tell me I should be *worried* about you?"

She touched his face, bold enough in the dark to do what light had made her too shy to try.

"Maybe."

The hard, smooth fingertips of his free hand slid inexorably up her forearm and covered the hand on his cheek. Drawing it down to his side, he pulled her whole body close, and the little twister of excitement in her stomach burst into a thousand quicksilver thrills. Her eyelids slipped closed, and his next question touched them in warm puffs of breath.

"If I were to kiss you right now, would it be too soon?"

Her eyes flew open, and she searched his shadowy gaze, incredulous. "You're asking permission? Who does that?"

"Seemed like the right thing."

"Well, permission granted. Now hush."

She freed her hands, placed them on his cheeks, roughened with beard stubble, and rose on tiptoe to meet his mouth while he gripped the back of her head.

The soft kiss nearly knocked her breathless. Chase dropped more hot kisses on each corner of her mouth and down her chin, feathered her nose and her cheeks, and finally returned to her mouth. Again and again he plied her bottom lip with his teeth, stunning her with his insistent exploration. The pressure of his lips and the clean, masculine scent of his skin took away her equilibrium. She could only follow the motions of his head and revel in the heat stoking the fire in her belly.

He pulled away at last and pressed parted lips to her forehead.

An Excerpt from

CHASING MORGAN
Book Four: The Hunted Series
by Jennifer Ryan

Morgan Standish can see things other people
can't. She can see the past and future. These
hidden gifts have prevented her from getting
close to anyone—except FBI agent Tyler Reed.
Morgan is connected to him in a way even she can't
explain. She's solved several cases for him in the
past, but will her gifts be enough to bring down
a serial killer whose ultimate goal is to kill her?
Find out in Book Four of The Hunted Series.

Morgan's fingers flew across the laptop keyboard propped on her knees. She took a deep breath, cleared her mind, and looked out past her pink-painted toes resting on the railing and across her yard to the densely wooded area at the edge of her property. Her mind's eye found her guest winding his way through the trees. She still had time before Jack stepped out of the woods separating her land from his. She couldn't wait to meet him.

Images, knowings, they just came to her. She'd accepted that part of herself a long time ago. As she got older, she'd learned to use her gift to seek out answers.

She finished her buy-and-sell orders and switched from her day trading page to check her psychic website and read the questions submitted by customers. She answered several quickly, letting the others settle in her mind until the answers came to her.

One stood out. The innocuous question about getting a job held an eerie vibe.

The familiar strange pulsation came over her. The world disappeared, as though a door had slammed on reality. The images came to her like hammer blows, one right after the other, and she took the onslaught, knowing something important needed to be seen and understood.

An older woman lying in a bed, hooked up to a machine feeding her medication. Frail and ill, she had translucent skin and dark circles marring her tortured eyes. Her pain washed over Morgan like a tsunami.

The woman yelled at someone, her face contorted into something mean and hateful. An unhappy woman—one who'd spent her whole life blaming others and trying to make them as miserable as she was.

A pristine white pillow floating down, inciting panic, amplified to terror when it covered the woman's face, her frail body swallowed by the sheets.

Morgan had an overwhelming feeling of suffocation.

The woman tried desperately to suck in a breath, but couldn't. Unable to move her lethargic limbs, she lay petrified and helpless under his unyielding hands. Lights flashed on her closed eyelids.

Death came calling.

A man stood next to the bed, holding the pillow like a shield. His mouth opened on a contorted, evil, hysterical laugh that rang in her ears and made her skin crawl. She squeezed her eyes closed to blot out his malevolent image and thoughts.

Murderer!

The word rang in her head as the terrifying emotions overtook her.

Morgan threw up a wall in her mind, blocking the cascade of disturbing pictures and feelings. She took several deep breaths and concentrated on the white roses growing in profusion just below the porch railing. Their sweet fragrance filled the air. With every breath, she centered herself and found her inner calm, pushing out the anger and rage left over from the vision. Her body felt like a lead weight, lightening as her energy came back. The drowsiness faded with each new breath. She'd be fine in a few minutes.

The man on horseback emerged from the trees, coming toward her home. Her guest had arrived.

Focused on the computer screen, she slowly and meticulously typed her answer to the man who had asked about a job and inadvertently opened himself up to telling her who he really was at heart.

She replied simply:

You'll get the job, but you can't hide from what you did.
You need help. Turn yourself in to the police.

An Excerpt from

THROWING HEAT
A Diamonds and Dugouts Novel
by Jennifer Seasons

Nightclub manager Leslie Cutter has never
been one to back down from a bet. So when
Peter Kowalskin, pitcher for the Denver
Rush baseball team, bets her that she can't
keep her hands off of him, she's not about
to let the arrogant, gorgeous playboy win.
But as things heat up, this combustible pair
will have to decide just how much they're
willing to wager on one another . . . and on
a future that just might last forever.

"Is there something you want?" he demanded with a raised eyebrow, amused at being able to throw her words right back at her.

"You wish," Leslie retorted and tossed him a dismissive glance. Only he caught the gleam of interest in her eyes and knew her for the liar that she was.

Peter took a step toward her, closing the gap by a good foot until only an arm's reach separated them. He leaned forward and caged her in by placing a hand on each armrest of her chair. Her eyes widened the tiniest bit, but she held her ground.

"I wish many, many things."

"Really?" she questioned and shifted slightly away from him in her chair. "Such as what?"

Peter couldn't help noticing that her breathing had gone

shallow. How about that? "I wish to win the World Series this season." It would be a hell of a way to go out.

Her gaze landed on his mouth and flicked away. "Boring."

Humor sparked inside him at that, and he chuckled. "You want exciting?"

She shrugged. "Why not? Amuse me."

That worked for him. Hell yeah. If she didn't watch herself, he was going to excite the pants right off of her.

Just excitement, arousal, and sexual pleasure. That was what he was looking for this time around. And it was going to be fun leading her up to it.

But if he wanted her there, then he had to start.

Pushing until he'd tipped her chair back and only the balls of her feet were on the desk, her painted toes curling for a grip, Peter lowered his head until his mouth was against her ear. She smelled like coconut again, and his gut went tight.

"I wish I had you bent over this desk right here with your hot bare ass in the air."

She made a small sound in her throat and replied, "Less boring."

Peter grinned. Christ, the woman was tough. "Do you remember what I did to you that night in Miami? The thing that made you come hard, twice—one on top of the other?" He sure as hell did. It had involved his tongue, his fingers, and Leslie on all fours with her face buried in a pillow, moaning his name like she was begging for deliverance.

She tried to cover it, but he heard her quick intake of breath. "It wasn't that memorable."

Bullshit.

He slid a hand from the armrest and squeezed the top of her right leg, his thumb rubbing lazily back and forth on the skin of her inner thigh. Her muscles tensed, but she didn't pull away.

"Need a reminder?"

An Excerpt from

PRIVATE RESEARCH
An Erotic Novella
by Sabrina Darby

The last person Mina Cavallari expects to
encounter in the depths of the National
Archives while doing research on a thesis is
Sebastian Graham, an outrageously sexy financial
whiz. Sebastian is conducting a little research of
his own into the history of what he thinks is just
another London underworld myth, the fabled
Harridan House. When he discovers that the
private sex club still exists, he convinces Mina
to join him on an odyssey into the intricacies of
desire, pleasure, and, most surprisingly of all, love.

It was the most innocuous of sentences: "A cappuccino, please." Three words—without a verb to ground them, even. Yet, at the sound, my hand stilled mid-motion, my own paper coffee cup paused halfway between table and mouth. I looked over to the counter of the cafe. It was mid-afternoon, quieter than it had been when I'd come in earlier for a quick lunch, and only three people were in line behind the tall, slim-hipped, blond-haired man whose curve of shoulder and loose-limbed stance struck a chord in me as clearly as his voice.

Of course it couldn't be. In two years, surely, I had forgotten the exact tenor of his voice, was now confusing some other deep, posh English accent with his. Yet I watched the man, waited for him to turn around, as if there were any significant chance that in a city of eight million people, during the middle of the business day, I'd run into the one English acquaintance I had. At the National Archives, no less.

SABRINA DARBY

At the first glimpse of his profile, I sucked in my breath sharply, nearly dropping my coffee. Then he turned fully, looking around, likely for the counter with napkins and sugar. I watched his gaze pass over me and then snap back in recognition. I was both pleased and terrified. I'd come to London to put the past behind me, not to face down my demons. I'd been doing rather well these last months, but maybe this was part of some cosmic plan. As my time in England wound down, in order to move forward with my life, I had to come face to face with Sebastian Graham again.

"Mina!" He had an impressive way of making his voice heard across a room without shouting, and as he walked toward me, I put my cup down and stood, all too aware that while he looked like a fashionable professional about town, I still looked like a grad student--no makeup, hair pulled back in a ponytail, wearing jeans, sneakers, and a sweater.

"This is a pleasant surprise. Research for your dissertation? Anne Gracechurch, right?"

I nodded, bemused that he remembered a detail from what had surely been a throwaway conversation two years earlier. But of course I really shouldn't have been. Seb was brilliant, and brilliance wasn't the sort of thing that just faded away.

Neither, apparently, was his ability to make my pulse beat a bit faster or to tie up my tongue for a few seconds before I found my stride. He wasn't traditionally handsome, at least not in an American way. Too lean, too angular, hair receding a bit at the temples, and I was fairly certain he was now just shy of thirty. But I'd found him attractive from the first moment I'd met him.

I still did.

"That's right. What are you doing here? I mean, at the Archives."

"Ah." He shifted and smiled at me, and there was something about that smile that felt wicked and secretive. "A small genealogical project. Mind if I join you?"

I shook my head and sat back down. He pulled out his chair and sat, too, folding his long legs one over the other. Why was that sexy to me?

I focused on his face. He was pale. Much paler than he'd been in New Jersey, like he now spent most of his time indoors. Which should have been a turn-off. Yet, despite everything, I sat there imagining him in the kitchen of my apartment wearing nothing but boxer shorts. Apparently my memory was as good as his.

And I still remembered the crushing humiliation and disappointment of that last time we'd talked.